# THE PRUDENTIAL LIGHT

*Cry Havoc Book Four*

## CRY HAVOC

## DONNA MAREE HANSON

ISBN ebook 978-1-922360-22-9

ISBN paperback 978-1-922360-23-6

ISBN Hardback 978-1-922360-25-0

ISBN Large print hardback 978-1-922360-26-7

Edited by Brianne Collins

Proofread by Jason Nahrung

Cover art Croco Designs

Internal artwork Donna Maree Hanson

Chinese Characters Haruki Yoshida

*To the older heroines who have stories to tell.*

# PROLOGUE

***F**robisher Manor, Kiddlington, Oxfordshire, 1864*

*A memoir by Prudence Wainwright*

The following revelations are for my close family and friends only.

I am foremost a lady, or consider myself so, no matter how others will judge me. Writing a memoir was never something I thought of doing before. However, as my family and friends have demonstrated an earnest curiosity about my life, I have acquiesced. Of course, I have had adventures, but some of them I never wanted to bring to mind again, let alone put to paper. People may judge my past deeds harshly. I did what I did in the time and the particular situations I found myself in—some of which were dire indeed.

A few of my actions might be considered shameful by polite society. I would hate to see them cast in that light because they are inextricably linked to precious memories that still, after all this time, bring tears to my eyes.

I am sure my friends will understand me better when they have read my story...

AFTER WRITING THE ABOVE, SOMETHING HAPPENED TO SET MY nerves aquiver. Should I even begin this process of documenting my past deeds? Surely to do so would potentially jeopardise my present and future happiness, and perhaps even the happiness of those dear to me. I am pacing up and down in my room and wringing my hands, unable to sit still and think rationally.

You would think at the age of forty-five, I would be able to deal with any situation.

I know it is a risk to write these things down. I do not even know how those revelations will seem when brought to the light of day. What if my family and friends reject and revile me for my past actions?

As I reflect on my life, particularly the last few years, I own that my friends have had to put up with a great deal from me. I have at times been hostile, odious and resentful. One of my worst failings has been overestimating my own worth and position. Sometimes my family and acquaintances humoured me; at worst they merely tolerated me.

Not that I want pity. Far from it. I would hate to be pitied. Sympathy? Yes, perhaps. Understanding? For certain.

I have experience.

I know things.

Being an older woman, I find I am often misjudged, dismissed, ignored. It is the plight of a female to be undervalued, overlooked, except if she is beautiful or useful in keeping house and breeding children. But in this society, once you are past a certain age, you do not even have that meagre pittance of respect paid to a younger female. In addition, fortune and rank are not numbered amongst my attributes, the possession of which might have afforded me some modicum of respect. I suffer from the worst combination: that of being past the age of childbearing and poor. Well, not so poor, for I have been fortunate in some ways, too, but poor relative to my expectations when I set out in life.

Luckily for me I am not friendless, or my life would have a much worse aspect. At present, I live with my niece, Milly, who I brought up from before aged two and her lovely husband Ambrose Fulton. They have one child, Aloysius, and are on the cusp of having their second. My nephew, Mr Edward Hardcastle Huntington, is my only other close relative. He and his wife, Jemima, are currently also staying with us at Frobisher Manor. They are visiting from their home, Willow Park in Sussex. They are visiting so that Milly and Jemima could share their confinement, for they were due to give birth within a week of each other. We don't normally live in this manor, but as Hatfield was torn down by a rampaging, and to all accounts monstrous, machine, we are renting here, thanks to the good graces of Sir Giles, who recommended us as tenants.

I own that Edward and I have not always been on the best of terms, but I take leave to explain. My sister, Edward's mother, said that the cottage in Kingsfold Village, where Milly and I used to live, had been left to me by our mother. However, when my sister sadly passed away at too young an age, I found to my chagrin that the title was in her name and was not mine at all. I only learned this when my nephew informed me of the fact, and this upset me greatly, for instead of being self-sufficient, I had to rely on my nephew's good graces for my home and had also been reliant on my sister's for years. The anger I felt at the time was overwhelming and I fear I was not kind to Edward and we argued terribly. Our estrangement was not so bad until I also made the unfortunate blunder of suggesting, perhaps too strongly, that Edward take his cousin, Milly, to wife. He did not take this well and kept his distance.

Alas, until Edward requested me to come post haste to Willow Park, the estate he inherited, and take charge of his then ward, Jemima Hardcastle, we had not seen or spoken to one another for at least a year. If not for all the shenanigans orchestrated by Jemima and the resulting contretemps, we would not have rescued Edward and defeated the foul beast Geneck, and I would not be here with Milly and Fulton today, living a life in which I feel valued. Edward married Jemima, and they are important to me as well.

It is worth adding that I now see there might be more to Jemima, who once I took for a snooty upstart and troublemaker, than I once thought. While some of my opinions about this young woman have proven to be true—she does indeed attract trouble and mayhem with uncommon regularity—she is also intelligent, agile and brave to a fault. I own that I have warmed to her. Upon reflection, I fear I may have envied Jemima's abilities and her situation in life, but if I had my life over, I would employ some of her tactics to gain the upper hand in certain situations.

As for friends, we have a small circle: Sir Giles, stalwart gentleman and magistrate, who has been kind and solicitous, and Mr Ferdinand White, a friend of Jemima and Edward's who visits often and unexpectedly. Jemima calls him Uncle Ferdy, for she has known him since childhood, but I am uncertain if there is a blood connection; perhaps there is one on her mother's side. From what I can gather he was a close friend of Cousin Wilbur, Jemima's father, and that would account for the degree of familiarity. I find him amusing company. The Heatons, of course, but they live in town and only visited recently to heal poor Ambrose after that awful towering machine ripped off his mechanical arm, flung him to the ground and left him for dead. Luckily, Edward was able to build him a new prosthesis and with Jasper Heaton's help, reattach it.

I have been hinting at writing down my history for months now. At first it was but an idle fancy; my skills usually lie elsewhere. I enjoy making things of beauty, and while I can do that with silk and fine fabrics, I have no idea how to do so with words. Without too much determination, I had started to write when I met with an early-morning caller and, unexpectedly, had to face my past head on. This was what had me pacing and agitated.

Now my tale is waiting to be untangled like a knot of threads in Jemima's sewing basket. My story is a puzzle of intertwined memories and feelings bound together in a clump in my mind. One tug and it could unravel easily, I suspect. I fear, then, that instead of fine words that paint an exquisite picture, you will get a child's finger painting that sketches out my past in a crazy, haphazard fashion.

In spite of it all, as I sit down at my table and take up my pen, I find that now that I have started, I cannot stop. Memories burn across my mind and I feel a great impatience to write them down. Alas, one cannot rewrite the past, but one can look back and, perhaps, cast it in a different light, make excuses or ponder the 'if only I had done this or said that'. However, too much reliance on such thinking might lead one to regret. And regret my past, I cannot do.

Thus, I will begin at the beginning, as one is meant to do in these situations. I will try to be truthful in this record of my life. It is not a confession, as I am not on my deathbed, but a story told from my perspective. And in so doing, I will finally let my secrets into the light.

# CHAPTER 1

I was born in 1818 in Sussex, the year after beloved Princess Charlotte died in childbirth, along with her stillborn son. My parents had a healthy child in me, at a time when the nation was still mourning a great loss, and thus I was cherished.

While I was still a babe in arms, my elder brother Brandon passed away from some terrible contagion. He would have been five years old. My parents valued me and my younger sisters even more, I believe, after that loss.

It would be good to say I remembered Brandon in life, but I do not. However, I often saw Brandon when I was a child, and when I related these visitations to my parents, they grew upset. For example, on one occasion I was dunking my toast soldiers into my soft-boiled egg, reciting: 'In out, in out, take a bite.' And when my mama asked me why I was eating in this manner, I told her that was the way Brandon liked me to do it. Her reaction scared me to death. She screamed and then fainted. Father came running, and my nurse scolded me. I was forbidden to mention my brother again.

It was hard. To me he was there, smiling as plain as day, talking to me and keeping me company. Of course, being a child I couldn't help but mention Brandon again. I told my father how sad Brandon was that his cricket set sat alone in the closet and that he wished Father to play cricket with me on the grass while it was sunny. Father's face grew red and the next time I saw the closet open, the cricket set was gone. Some nights later, in my room waiting to fall asleep, Brandon arrived and told me his cricket set had been given away. I exclaimed that it was a shame and bade him not to be sad about it. He replied, "'Tis all right. Another boy is playing with it now. Go to sleep, dear Pru. I will watch over you."

Eventually, I stopped telling my parents the things Brandon did and said, since it upset them so, and by the time I was eight or nine, Brandon no longer visited me. Either he was a ghost, or I had a healthy (or from my parents' perspective, an unhealthy) imagination. Given what I know now, I understand I had a talent— though an unnurtured and neglected one.

There, judge me if you dare!

I set down my pen. It was a fine, clear day, and I was in the morning room, alone with my thoughts, the rest of the house still abed. I poured myself a second cup of tea and reached for the last muffin, which I liberally covered with jam and had just brought to my mouth when the footman entered.

"Yes, John?" I tried to mask my impatience at this interruption as I lowered the muffin to my plate and turned towards him.

The footman bowed elegantly. "Good morning, ma'am. Sorry to disturb you so early, but Sir Giles is at the door."

Sitting bolt upright, I nearly choked. Sir Giles here this early?

The footman continued, "Sir Giles has brought a bushel of apples and a basket of flowers from the hothouse."

After a deep, calming breath I responded, "That is kind." But I wondered. Sir Giles had been increasing his visits of late, and had extended several kindnesses of this nature to our household. I was touched by his thoughtfulness, but what was it in aid of?

"Is he coming in?" I asked.

John shook his head. "I have delivered the apples to the kitchen as he instructed and the flowers to the housekeeper for arranging. Sir Giles asks if you might have time to join him for a walk in the garden."

A walk? Whatever for? I looked longingly at that muffin. "Why does he not come in?" I had to own it was strange for him to arrive before midday, which was the polite hour for visiting.

The footman inclined his head. "Those were his exact instructions to me, ma'am. He refused my entreaties to enter when I told him you were awake and downstairs in the morning room. He said he was happy to wait until you had finished eating breakfast."

Swallowing another mouthful of tea, I said, "Please let him know I shall join him shortly." When John had left, closing the door behind him, I tried to deduce what was going on with our dear friend Sir Giles. He had been most considerate during the stressful time when Hatfield had been attacked by a monstrous machine, even finding our current house for us to lease while our companions were away seeking those responsible and now while Hatfield was being rebuilt. He was the most conscientious gentleman and very attentive, often pre-empting our needs. I found him most congenial company on many an afternoon when the household was busy on other tasks and he sat with me while I sewed, apparently most content to say nothing and observe.

Realising these ponderings were fruitless, I downed the last of my tea, quickly ate my muffin, and then wiped my hands and mouth on a serviette.

My cornflower-blue wrap with the silver fringe was draped over the chair by the door, and as it was warm out, it was sufficient to drape around my shoulders. A glance in the mirror showed me my lace cap neatly affixed to my head, with its trailing ribbons falling delicately on my shoulders. A poked bonnet would be too much bother and would require me to return upstairs to my bedroom.

I patted the pocket of my gown and found a pair of gloves, which I slid on. Then I contemplated my reflection in the mirror, and was pleased with what I saw. My dress was a deep burgundy brocade, with a ruched satin panel on the bodice and rich Chantilly lace gracing the sleeves. Lace and frills distract me from the ravages of age on my face, and beautiful fabrics from my ever stouter figure. Jemima liked to tease me about disappearing doilies, and I take those little quips as they were meant—as affectionate teasing.

It had been such an outrage to my senses to wear borrowed clothes in the days after Hatfield was destroyed. At least most of my wardrobe was recovered quickly because I would have been mortified to continue on for weeks in such a fashion. God forbid I should ever be called scruffy!

Preparations complete, I went to the front door. John opened it for me on approach, and I stepped outside. It was a fine day, not too bright. The front garden was not so large as Hatfield's, as we were in the village, but it was closed off from the street by a tall stone wall. There was a large oak with some beech trees behind it and a row of silver birch and hazel. Flowerbeds with white, bright pink and purple cyclamens skirted the neat little path, which gave the impression of whimsy as it wove this way and that. When my gaze fell upon Sir Giles, his almost black eyes flashed with recognition and, dare I say, delight. I took the opportunity to admire the man. He was still sprightly for forty-three, and he dressed neatly, without being flamboyant about it. He was intelligent but not showy or overbearing, and prepared to let others display their wit. I liked that about him. My heart gave a little jump; thrill or fear, I could not tell. Was I anticipating bad news, or good? I wish I knew, for it was a most uncomfortable feeling and my breakfast turned to lead in my stomach.

Sir Giles walked up to me and bowed. "Good morning. Thank you for joining me." He placed my hand in the crook of his elbow. "Shall we walk this way?"

My heart fluttered a little at this overt display of gallantry. While I admit I had flirted with Sir Giles on occasion, I had detected no particular regard in him for myself; his acceptance of my attentions was good-humoured and tolerant. You might think it very *de trop* of me to flirt with a gentleman, for as you know with a reputation as an older spinster, I was sure no one would take me seriously. Or so I thought. My present company was making me doubt myself. We kept walking along the garden path, commenting on the weather, the green of the garden and the health of the house's occupants.

Sir Giles' mood appeared buoyant and the smile he flashed me was eager and open. My heart beat hard in my chest as uneasiness sped up my spine. We reached a small, enclosed space in which was situated a bench seat and a statue of Cupid surrounded by Michaelmas daisies just coming into bloom.

"Would you care to sit?" Sir Giles said, indicating the bench.

"Why, thank you." I was out of breath, not from exertion but agitation. My cheeks felt hot, and I was certain I was blushing like a schoolroom miss. My impulse was to run back to the house because I feared what was about to unfold. However, I valued Sir Giles as a friend and could not hurt his feelings by behaving in such a brusque manner. Nor could I climb on my high horse and call him impertinent. He was a gentleman of sense.

I sat, but he remained standing beside me. I cast a glance at him, hoping to ease my anxiety. He was a magistrate, and it occurred to me that he might have some news that he wanted to share, me being the oldest person in residence, rather than going direct to Fulton or my nephew Edward. As I considered this, I calmed myself. Knowing that those dear to me were all safe within the house, I thought his news might be related to the incident that had destroyed Hatfield. Yes, that must be it. Sir Giles looked up at the sky, then at the ground, which he scuffed with the toe of his boot, and then sighed.

"Whatever is amiss, Sir Giles?"

Sir Giles proceeded to take up my gloved right hand. Before I had a chance to digest this move or even protest, he blurted out, "Mrs Wainwright. Prudence. Do let me tell how much I adore you."

I gasped. My heart sped up, and it was difficult to breathe.

With my hand still in his, he continued, "I wish you to marry me, if you will."

My mouth fell open. I shut it and heard my teeth click. Trying to calm my racing heart, I took a moment to respond. "Marry you?" I managed at last. My mind went white. Marriage. At my age? Was I dreaming? "Become your wife?" I replied stupidly.

"Yes, that is usually what happens when one marries." He chewed his lip in agitation. When I did not speak, he checked himself. "Surely you have been expecting a proposal. I know you enjoy flirtation, generally, but I thought there existed between us a genuine affection and respect."

I tried to focus. I tried not to faint. I could imagine Jemima making a mockery of this situation. *That is what you get, Aunt, if you feed puppies at table. You can never get rid of them and have to banish them to their kennels.*

I cleared my throat. My cheeks were definitely aflame as I struggled to find an answer. Was this my own fault? Had I engaged a man's feelings, trifled with his affections? Oh dear. "I do have an affection for you, and the deepest respect and gratitude for all your solicitous attentions to my family in our hour of need, but...but..." There was nothing for it. I had to speak plainly and honestly. "I was not expecting a proposal, Sir Giles. I thought I was beyond such attentions. Why, I am getting long in the tooth. I am plump and I have no money of my own. I do not consider myself marriageable."

Sir Giles shook his head and flapped his hand as if throwing off my excuses. "I don't care about money. I have enough of my own. Despite what you say, you are an attractive and intelligent woman who would be a prize for any gentleman worth his salt."

I coughed and tried not to laugh, for I did not think Sir Giles would respond well to mirth at that moment. "You should qualify that statement, sir. Gentleman of a certain age, surely." I saw that my comment caused him grief and so I squeezed his hand. "Truly you do me a great honour, and I am sensible of the—"

"Pfah!" Sir Giles said, and squeezed my hand in turn. "Enough talk of honour. What about love and desire? I have both for you."

My mouth fell open. Love and desire were things buried deep in my past. Those emotions and needs had not featured in my life for many a year. Yet, I could see he was sincere, and that gave me pause. I said carefully, "I have not turned my mind to matrimony at all. You have surprised me with your proposal, and, at this moment, I can barely think of an adequate response. Please consider, sir, that my family needs me."

Sir Giles' eyes glittered as his gaze fixed on me. "Indeed, I am sensible of that fact, and would have no qualms about you spending time with them and staying near to them. Their comfort before my own, I vow."

My mind and my heart caught up with me. Sir Giles was in earnest, and I was in a quandary. I did care for Sir Giles. He was an excellent gentleman, wonderful manners, great dexterity of mind. He had survived Jemima and her interesting ways with his sanity intact. How could I wound him? It would not do just to fob him off with gratitude and a refusal. I had to tell him the truth, and I arrived at that thought just as he sank to one knee at my feet. With my hand still in his, he urged me, "Please consider my proposal, Prudence. I have a large house just outside the village, servants; your every need would be met. We could stay in London a few times a year. Shop in the best warehouses."

I put my hand over his. "Giles, I am so flattered by your regard for me." I took a breath, my stomach full of butterflies. "Believe me when I say that I have a strong regard for you. However, I cannot marry you..."

"Do not say—"

I lifted my other hand and touched his lips gently with my forefinger. "Please hear me out." His eyes grew sad, but he nodded once, even as he clung to my right hand. His disappointment was palpable. Not having entertained the idea of marriage for more than twenty years, I was surprised how sanguine I was about it. Nonetheless, I was sad that I had to refuse him.

"I cannot marry you for the reason that I am already married."

He let go my hand and stood hastily, then turned away from me so I could not see his face. "How can that be? Where is your husband?"

Tears blurred my vision. I did not mean to weep. I had barely thought about Leighton in years. "I do not know where he is. I cannot even tell you if he is still living."

Sir Giles turned back to me. "I know you call yourself Mrs Wainwright. I thought it was an affectation of older spinsters. I did not realise that there was a Mr Wainwright."

Drawing my handkerchief from my pocket to dab at my eyes, I replied, "There is no Mr Wainwright."

"What?" Sir Giles exploded. "Are you trying to bamboozle me like your niece, Mrs Huntington?"

At the mention of Jemima's name, I nearly dissolved into a fit of hysterics. Imagine if Jemima heard of this morning's proceedings. She would doubtless derive much amusement at my expense. "No. I am not. I am telling you the truth. If you have time, perhaps we could go for a walk, and I can explain. Part of it, at least."

Sir Giles looked at the sky and nodded. "It is a fine day, and I have time. My morning was to be devoted to you. Do you need anything from the house? Shall I inform the footman of our outing?"

I dried my tears and realised my hands were shaking. "I can manage as I am. If you would be so kind as to inform the footman so my family do not worry, I would appreciate it."

Sir Giles strode back along the path, giving me precious moments to order my thoughts and recall the details from my past. Memories I thought I would never have to revisit would have to be unearthed, bringing with them emotions that I had kept buried for years. All of the morning's lightness dissipated. As much as I did not want to face my past, I owed Sir Giles the truth.

Upon his return, we set off around the garden in companionable silence. My knee ached until the movement soothed the pain away. How unfair it was to be old when there was so much of the world to see and so many interesting things to do.

Sir Giles' voice brought me back to the moment.

"You said you were married but you don't know where your husband is or if he is alive." Sir Giles' voice was soothing, and I chanced a look at his face. So many emotions played over his features, but I did not know him well enough to understand them all. That I had shocked him was obvious. I knew my family would feel similarly, as they did not know my full history either. Charity, my next youngest sister, who was Edward's mother, was the only one I'd told, and she had never spoken a word of it, I was sure. Faith, my youngest sister and Milly's mother, passed away before she knew the whole.

I took a breath and began. "It might surprise you to know that I was once a bold, headstrong young woman, not given to heeding my parents. I had a modest dowry and, being tall and well formed, I had many suitors. Charles Ingleford Leighton, from Canterbury, in

Kent, was the least suitable of them all. I was young and, dare I say it, very ignorant. I was flattered by his attentions and thought us friends. How wrong I was. Only in hindsight did I see that I was manipulated, that by befriending him and being open, I gave him an opportunity to force me to accept his marriage proposal."

Sir Giles stiffened as he swung towards me. "Do not say he forced himself upon you?"

Not able to bear his look of outrage, I kept my eyes forward. "Not exactly. Let us just say that a situation occurred that might have impinged upon my reputation had I not agreed to marry him. My younger sister's hopes of a good marriage would have been adversely affected, as well. Charity was much in love with Theo Huntington, and I could not jeopardise that."

"And were you in love?"

"No, I was not, and despite what my parents told me, I never did come to love my husband, and I was sure that he did not love me. My dowry was his object."

"These are heavy tidings indeed."

"My father agreed to the match and made a marriage contract that would secure my future. He consoled me that at least Mr Leighton was not vicious and seemed amiable. However, events soon overturned my father's plans. The money held in trust to provide for me and for any children of the marriage in the event of my being widowed had to be used to pay my husband's debts.

"Upon marriage, of course, my money became his, and he quickly put it to use. I tried my best to make good of what was a potentially bad situation. I managed our house and within a year I was expecting a child. However, there arose another issue with his debts, and all my money was gone. My father liquidated some shares and paid the debts yet again, under the proviso that Charles find employment. Indeed, my father found him work with the East India Company. After my son was born, we sailed to Calcutta."

"You have a son? And have been to Calcutta?" Sir Giles' surprise was evident. "Where else have you travelled?"

"Singapore is as far east as I have been."

"You have visited Singapore?" Sir Giles was wide-eyed. "When?"

"Yes, I lived there awhile around 1840–41. I stayed longer than I expected to, in fact, because one day, after accepting an invitation to tea, I returned to our accommodation to find I had been abandoned."

"Abandoned?" Sir Giles paused in his walk and faced me. "You were abandoned in Singapore during that lawless period?"

"I was."

"There appears to be a lot to this story, Mrs Wainwright." Mr Giles appeared quite flabbergasted.

"Oh, there is, Sir Giles. Let me give you the particulars. I last saw my husband in 1840 before he sailed from Singapore to either Australia or China. He was accompanied by my son, James Ingleford Hardcastle Leighton. I could find no trace of them at the port, so I fear they used different names so I could not follow them. One of the great sadnesses in my life is that I do not know what happened to my son, either."

With a frown, Sir Giles regarded me. "Surely you must have noticed your possessions being packed away."

Emotions roiled then and I held them tight. "I did not know they were leaving. If my husband packed anything, he did it in secret. He abandoned me in Singapore with nothing but his debts and some of my personal effects. I became homeless and penniless that very day."

His cheeks grew red. "This is a terrible tale. No gentleman would behave this way. The man is a scoundrel." Sir Giles drew out a pencil and a small notebook and wrote a few lines. "Did you ever hear from him again?"

"No, I never heard from him or my son, James, again."

"You didn't try to track them down?"

"Of course I did," I replied hotly, but then softened my tone and breathed out slowly. "I made enquiries. More than one ship sailed that day, and none reported having my husband and son aboard.

The two most likely were headed to China and Australia, but my enquiries yielded nothing. You must understand that I had not the means to investigate further."

"I see." Sir Giles slid his notebook into his breast pocket, and I kept my gaze fixed ahead. I could not bear to see the judgement and disbelief that would be in his eyes. "I cannot deny that my hopes have been dashed at hearing this news. However, that is my problem, and you are blameless." His voice quavered.

I dug around in my pocket for my handkerchief. "I am truly sorry for any pain I have caused."

Sir Giles cleared his throat, adjusted his cravat and straightened his shoulders. "Pray excuse me, Mrs Wainwright. I have recalled an engagement. Perhaps when next we meet, I can hear more of your tale? In the meantime, I must bid you adieu. Please convey my apologies to Mr and Mrs Fulton, as I will not be able to dine with them this evening as previously arranged."

I blinked at this sudden change in Giles' demeanour. "Of course, I will convey your apologies." I lifted my hand to shake his.

He bowed over my hand. "Please give my best wishes to the Huntingtons as well."

"Of course." My voice was rough, clogged with emotion and surprise.

He met my eye, and I could see that my revelations had shaken him. "To you I wish the best of health. We will see each other again soon, I am sure."

Then he was off, striding down the path we had ambled so companionably only minutes before.

I stood still for a moment, taking stock of all that had transpired, and then I burst into tears. I took off my gloves and clutched at my handkerchief. Thank goodness I was in the garden and there was no one about to witness my distress. After a time, the tears subsided, but not so all the turmoil my revelations had evoked. Thoughts and feelings and scenes from my past swamped me, and in their wake arose a burning desire to write them down.

I needed to order my thoughts. I roamed the garden, thinking about Sir Giles and the effect of my revelations. He had seemed quite appalled by my outrageous tale. Did he even believe me? I had revealed just the bare bones to him, so surely, he deserved the whole of it—and so did my family. How else might they understand what had happened to me? I saw that my story could not be truly understood if I did not paint the full picture.

Straightening my shoulders, I returned to the house and was admitted. I informed John that Sir Giles was no longer to dine with us that evening, and returned to the morning room, where I gathered my writing things and then retreated to my bedroom.

I had always liked this room. As well as a bed, I had a worktable and chairs and also a desk in one corner by the window. A small pale pink settee made the room cosy. At my desk, I drew out some fresh paper, used my knife to sharpen the tip of my quill and began to write in earnest. I did not know then that it would take me many, many weeks to write it all down, and even more time to amend, add forgotten points, and explain my actions and feelings at the time and also now, looking back on them with the benefit of hindsight. That was the hardest thing to do: to reflect on my life of then and now and reconcile the two. However, I will note that I felt lighter as the years of memories filtered through me onto the paper. My heart, though, sometimes grew heavy with loss, then beat swiftly as if reliving the moments, or calmed as if relieved of all its burdens.

# CHAPTER 2

In the evening a few days later, we were all gathered in the drawing room. A storm hurled rain against the windows and made the fire in the grate flutter. Although it was late summer, the air was chill. As well as writing my memoir, I had been thinking on Sir Giles and feeling confused and sad. Even the embroidery for the table runner failed to keep my attention. The poor man. I had really surprised him.

A giggle drew my gaze down. My little nephew, Ally, wriggled in my lap, smiling as I pulled faces and made his toy rattle. His dark eyes sparkled, and his chubby hands grabbed at my fingers. Across from me sat Milly and Jemima, looking very round with child, and chatting. Fulton and Edward sat together on the settee, sipping tea and reading the papers. A languid, carefree evening.

Needless to say, the imminent arrival of two new additions to the family was a waiting game. Not that they were due at that moment, you understand, but in the next week, or two, or three, the mysteries of birth being difficult to predict. Jemima and Edward were visiting so that the two families could share the moment with one another, the couples having grown very close during the terrible time when Hatfield had been destroyed, and Fulton so terribly injured. Edward and Jemima had arrived in the nick of time to save the poor man. Such mayhem. Such upheaval! It was a wonder we still had our wits.

The nurse came to collect Ally and I removed to my little work desk by the window. Sitting apart from the others, I could be an observer and auditor. The footman brought in a large box and placed it by the settee. "Oh, the samples have arrived," Milly said as she peered into the box. She drew out a rich green brocade. "What do you think of this one, Aunt Prudence?"

Jemima sat up straighter and drew a hand along the fabric. "It's very rich."

"You have a good eye, my dear," I said. "They will go well with the carpets you have chosen for the drawing room."

Milly smiled broadly. "I am glad you think so." She drew out some more samples.

"I do not like this brown," Milly said as she ran her hand over the fabric. "It is rather thin too. I think that one is a definite no."

When all the samples had been viewed and discussed, Milly put them aside and got laboriously to her feet.

"Excuse us if you please. It is time to put Ally down for the night. He likes me to be there," she said, and Fulton rose as well and took her arm. He bowed as he left the room.

Jemima and Edward chatted quietly, and I was able to focus on the task at hand. Surrounding me in a semicircle where Edward had dumped them were stacks of family Bibles. It was too bothersome to carry them upstairs—too many trips and the Bibles were unwieldy, heavy and dusty.

The first Bible, a black leather-bound tome tooled in gold leaf, creaked as I opened it, the threads in the spine protesting. After finding the pages I wanted, I heaved another book open and withdrew some yellowed papers containing birth records from a sleeve in the back. I turned them this way and that, wrinkling my nose at their vinegary smell and noting small holes where some insect had nibbled the edges.

"Mmmm." No one was paying me any mind. What are family trees to young people these days? Drawing up my family tree was a peripheral task, not central to my memoir, but a way of laying out how we were all related.

After picking up a roughly drawn family tree from the first Hardcastle family Bible, I frowned. This was a tangled mess of births, deaths, marriages, name changes and so on. It was almost enough to make me scratch my head—a disgusting habit—and took a lot of concentration to make sense of. There was the notation of my parents' marriage and the birth of my elder brother, Brandon. Tucked in behind was the record of my baptism.

A moan rose up from where Jemima lounged on the sofa, her aching feet elevated. She shifted position, favouring one side and then the other, unable to get comfortable. Edward applied cushions at regular intervals, trying to soothe her. It was good to see him so attentive as he usually seemed to me to be oblivious, his head buried in one of his journals, scribbling away at pace. You might wonder if I had tried to read these journals, but you would be disappointed. The truth was, I could never find them. I knew my nephew had special talents; you cannot be around these relatives of mine and not notice. Often, when he thought I was not looking, Edward made strange gestures with his hands and murmured things. And then something would happen, such as a large journal would disappear or reappear, as if out of thin air. It was the worst-kept secret that my nephew, Edward Huntington, was a gentleman and a magician.

There were other things that defied explanation. Jemima had been at death's door with heart failure. Next thing, she was back again full of life and my nephew had had a hand in that. If you listened hard enough you could hear the whirr of her ruby heart. And Fulton was miraculously hale and hearty after being ripped apart by that machine that demolished Hatfield. His prosthetic arm was replaced again by my clever nephew. My sanity is intact, so I can only conclude there was some supernatural force at work there. It ran in my family, as I well knew, for there was something special in me, too, a spark—but that is a story for my memoir.

Another exclamation from Jemima stole my attention. "Oh, fiddle, this baby will not stop kicking me in the ribs and 'tis making me most annoyed." She tugged two cushions from behind her back and tossed them to Edward, and he in turn tossed them to an empty armchair.

I wanted some peace and quiet so I could work on my family tree. "Try walking around, Jemima; the movement should soothe the baby and get it away from your ribs."

Jemima sat up, eyebrows raised. "Oh, that is sensible advice, Aunt Prudence." I could see the question in her eyes. What would an old spinster like me know about it? I kept my face impassive and Edward assisted her from the settee. "I wish I had thought of that on the train journey here. Bounced around in my seat like a sack of potatoes. Most uncomfortable. However, coming by carriage would have been even worse."

"Indeed," put in Edward. "The train shortened your suffering."

Jemima grinned at him. "I am sorry for making you bear my complaints. I am usually quite indestructible."

Edward smiled at her with real sincerity. "And I know it, Jemima. I just wish I could do more to alleviate your discomfort. But we are settled here now and in good company."

A low rumble rattled the windows and the rain grew heavier. The storm was settling in for the night.

At that moment Milly returned, Fulton on her arm. "Walking is very therapeutic. Alas this storm makes a turn around the garden impossible. But this room is large enough," Milly said, having caught the end of their conversation. "Take Edward with you for support."

Jemima picked up her shawl and chuckled. "Marvellous idea.

Edward, do offer me your arm. I would like to take a turn around the room."

Edward stepped forward and guided the cumbersome Jemima between the items of furniture, and soon her complaints subsided. Meanwhile, Fulton led Milly to one of the settees, made her comfortable, then announced, "As Ally is asleep, I have some business that needs attending to. Please excuse me. I shall not be long." He bowed and left again.

Milly leaned awkwardly over the end of the sofa and fished up her sewing basket. Soon she was industriously sewing a baby gown in the finest lawn fabric. It was delicate and pretty; a gift for Jemima, I knew. Jemima could not sew if her life depended on it. She knew it and I knew it, but we did not discuss the topic due to past disagreements.

I considered my two young relatives. It was hard to tell who would be the first to start labouring. I had placed bets with their husbands, so I would win either way, the thought of which brought a smile to my lips. This was to be Milly's second child and Jemima's first. Jemima complained of the discomfort most often. Even with her extraordinary abilities, she moaned about aching feet and heartburn like every other expectant mother. Not only did she have some Hardcastle talent, her ruby heart was imbued with some of Edward's magic, which spilled into her apparently. Then, she absorbed all that terrible emerald fire from the monster Genek so that she radiated magic. Even I could feel it sometimes, like a vibration in the gums. I understood from dropped bits of conversation that she was learning how to use it so she could be a magician too. Also, I overheard Fulton tell Milly that Jemima survived being burnt alive in a furnace, when they fought the evil magician who sent the huge machine to destroy Hatfield and steal Fulton's arm. So if anyone could survive childbirth, it would be Jemima.

The rib-kicking complaint was a new one, though. Milly, on the other hand, bore her discomfort quietly. However, having supported her through the birth of Aloysius, I knew she had a good set of lungs, a strong grip and great determination. I was immensely proud of her: she was an excellent wife, who could manage the household well, and was much loved by her husband and friends. Her achievements exceeded mine, which was gratifying, as it meant I had brought her up well.

Looking down, I opened up another of the Bibles that Edward had transported from Willow Park and studied the first few yellowed pages, webbed with wiry scrawls. A few loose, brown-edged leaves fell onto the desk. These I scooped up and gently coaxed open, then read the dates and names. My brow furrowed. "This cannot be right."

"What, Aunt?" Jemima asked as she passed the side table and reached for one of the sweetmeats stationed there. The titbit slipped from her fingers, caught the edge of the table and disappeared under the settee. Try as she might, she could not bend to retrieve it.

"Just take another one, Jemima," I murmured. "The servants will find the other one, I'm sure."

Jemima did just that and then collapsed back onto the settee, which gave me pause. Jemima being compliant was always an astonishment.

"What has you looking so puzzled?" Milly said, lifting her head from her sewing.

"It is this entry, my dear." I waved the aged fragment. "Someone must have made a mistake. It is written here," I said, bringing it close to my face once more, "that Wilbur Hardcastle was born in 1760. It cannot be your father, Jemima, but I did not think there was another Wilbur in the Hardcastle line."

Jemima pursed her lips and her gaze narrowed. "Father *was* born in 1760, actually."

I fell back in my chair, doing some swift mathematics in my head. "Do not be ridiculous. If he was born in 1760, he would have been eighty-four years old when you were born."

Jemima nodded vigorously. "Yes, he was. Mama was much younger than him. About fifty or so years younger, I believe."

"You cannot be serious. I met Wilbur and he did not look that old." At least, I was sure I had met him, only the circumstances of our meeting were shrouded in mist. Did I travel to meet him in a carriage or did I visit him in another fashion? In spirit like my conversations with my brother. At that moment, I wasn't quite sure.

A sad, far-away expression came over Jemima's features. "He looked old when he died," she said in a low voice. "It was an amazing transformation. I was only thirteen at the time, but I remember thinking that a month earlier, he had been the picture of health. Of course, he had grey hair and wrinkles, but he was always so full of energy, and he walked around like a man of twenty-five. I was called to his bedside, when old Mr Cready found him. It was said he had passed in the night. I would not have known him but for his signet ring, for he was wasted and thin, just skin and bone."

"He looked old when he died? What a preposterous thing to say." My mind was racing. It was an odd thing for her to say.

"Not so preposterous in this family. Edward said he was a magician, which I didn't know when I was a child."

I bit my lip, considering that this made perfect sense.

"He met with foul play," Edward said as he bent to pick up the dropped sweetmeat. My nephew then took up the plate of sweetmeats and sat in the chair next to the settee.

"What?" Jemima launched out of her seat. "I was told there were no suspicious circumstances. I railed against the undertaker when he tried to take his body away. It was natural, theysaid. No blood. No injury. Everything was in its place."

Edward looked stricken. "I had meant to tell you. It is just with one thing and another, the time has never been right." Lifting his gaze, he met Jemima's shocked expression. "I am sorry, my love." I could hear Edward's true affection for his wife in his voice.

Jemima, though, stood rigid, vibrating with anger. "Tell me what?"

Edward's blue eyes were bright but solemn, his mouth a hard line.

"That your father was murdered, most likely by the brothers from the *Societas Magicae.*"

The *Socieitas Magicae* were a brotherhood of magicians, some plain evil, who had plagued Edward in their search for the secret texts in my nephew's possession. They also lusted after his inventions, trying to steal the ruby heart from Jemima while she lived and one even stole Fulton's arm, ripped it from his body, all to find Edward's secrets. Mr White was one of the good ones. Now it seems the connection even extended to Cousin Wilbur.

I dropped my pen in shock. "Edward!" Even a halfwit knows you do not tell an expectant mother such horrible things. "I do not think—"

"No! Edward...that, that cannot be! It is..." Jemima's voice rang with hysteria. Tears trickled down cheeks that had ripened to berry-pink. I feared for her health and that of the babe.

Realising his mistake, Edward did his best to calm his wife, taking her into his arms and caressing her.

I realised too that it was not my business and that there probably was never going to be a good time to convey such tidings.

Jemima sobbed. "Do you mean...you mean that he was...he was taken from me deliberately?"

"We can talk more about it later, my love. Now is not a good time. Think of the baby."

"But I want to know now. All this time I have been denied the truth. It changes everything."

"Now, Jemima. Do not be rash. I should not have said anything at all. I am thoughtless. You were talking about him, and I blurted it out. I am sorry. Please forgive me."

Jemima wiped her tears with the handkerchief Edward offered

and rested her head on his shoulder. Once her breathing calmed and the hiccoughs subsided, she said in a distant, unemotional way, "Of course I forgive you. But please tell me what you know."

Edward took a breath. "All right. Your father told me in a letter what was likely to happen. He said if I am dead, they have murdered me, and he bade me to keep the secret texts safe. He stole them and they wanted them back. My later interactions with the *Societas Magicae* confirmed your father's suspicions that something evil lurked within the brotherhood and keeping the text would keep everyone safe."

Sitting forward and absently rubbing her distended abdomen, Jemima asked, "Do you know who in particular did the deed or must I torture Uncle Ferdy to find out?"

"No. It was an official act of the brotherhood, and there are records of the decision and who carried out the deed. At least, there should be. As there was a lot of damage to the priory, those records may have been lost."

"Uncle Ferdy will know. I am positive of it." Her tone held the gilt edge of the sword of justice. "They were close friends. My father's only friend besides me."

"I am sure Brother Ferdinand will tell you all he knows," Edward agreed. "Consider, though, that the perpetrator may already be dead. Geneck did kill a lot of the brotherhood that dreadful night."

The massacre at the priory in Kent had been big news at the time. I did not know all the particulars of that evening, except for what was in the papers afterwards and what I had gleaned from listening in to conversations. Geneck had wiped out nearly all the brothers, decimating their number and leaving blood, limbs and entrails in his wake. In London, in the lead-up, I helped fight Geneck's human followers, even though I was not entirely in Edward's confidence. Luckily, I have some defensive skills—a way with everyday items with which I can defend myself and others. A quick study, Milly learned from me and together we did our fair share to keep our friends safe.

Jemima stood up and called out, "Uncle Ferdy? Uncle Ferdy! I need you."

Blinking away my surprise, I buried my head in my birth records in case Jemima remembered I was in the room. Milly looked up from her sewing and tilted her head to the side, owl-like. "Jemima. Are you well? Should I order a tisane for you?"

Jemima jerked and wiped her eyes "Oh, sorry." She smoothed her gown and sat down again. "I beg your pardon."

Fulton came back in and stood looking at the tense gathering. "Is everything all right?"

"Yes, we are fine," Jemima responded. Fulton inclined his head and came to sit by his wife.

An awkward silence ensued.

Jemima sat there, straight-backed, with clenched fists resting on her knees. Mr White did not magically appear. After a few moments, Jemima nodded her head decisively. "Right then. I shall hunt them down..." Rocking forward, she tried to stand and then fell back once more. "As soon as this baby is born."

"Hunt who down?" Fulton asked.

Edward shook his head, perhaps hoping to cut Fulton off, and reached over to pat Jemima's hand. "Perhaps not directly after the baby is born. It will need its mother."

Jemima met his eye and smiled through her tears. "Well then, you will get me the information I need, will you not?"

Edward's face was serious, but he inclined his head. "Of course. And when you are ready, we shall investigate the matter together."

Milly leaned in to whisper in Fulton's ear, and he nodded, understanding dawning in his eyes.

Jemima and Edward considered each other for a few moments and then stared at the empty plate. Jemima said brightly, "Did you leave any of those marzipan balls for me, Edward?"

Edward picked up the empty sweetmeats plate and shrugged. "I am sorry. No."

Milly climbed out of her seat. "Never mind, Jemima. I shall ask John to fetch some more from the kitchen."

Thereafter, there was peace in the room. Jemima was presented with more sweetmeats and swatted Edward's hand away from the plate. "You have had enough, husband."

For the third time, I tried to continue my perusal of my very convoluted family tree. Two other Bibles provided notes, diagrams and crumpled old brown baptism records. This time, I was able to work for a while in silence, but soon my neck began to ache, so it was some relief when it was time to dress for dinner. I went to clean the ink off my fingers and make my toilette. Then I joined Milly and Jemima for an excellent meal of fricassee of chicken with five side dishes, including my favourite devilled mushrooms and dressed eggs. With business to attend to, Edward and Fulton made themselves scarce when dessert was over.

After dinner we women retired once again to the drawing room. The fire had a fresh log added to the glowing red coals. I fetched my own work basket and made myself comfortable. After a while, the men rejoined us and, after he'd sat down next to Milly, Fulton glanced over at me. "You look worried, Aunt Prudence."

The knowledge that my cousin Wilbur had been murdered had shocked me, and I found I could not stop myself contemplating it. This magic business seemed fraught with danger. I tried to recall when I had met him and could not quite place the year or even the occasion. However, I didn't want to discuss this further in Jemima's presence, so I replied, "Oh, well, this family tree is difficult to unravel. It is so complex, and Edward's is equally so. His father, although a Huntington, was actually a Hardcastle by blood. The reason Theo had a fortune was that his grandfather—at least I think it was the grandfather—took his wife's name, so they became Hardcastle-Huntington and eventually just Huntington. It was through that line that Edward inherited Willow Park. My line was also a Hardcastle line, which intermarried with the Smythes and became Hardcastle-Smythe. Both families being of proud lineage, they chose to keep both surnames. My youngest sister, Faith, married Reverend John Jones and became Mrs Smythe-Jones. Those are Milly's parents."

I paused for a moment as a ghastly thought arrived in the front of my mind. "If Cousin Wilbur was born in 1760 and Jemima is his only issue, that would make Jemima something like my fifth great-aunt." My heart gave an uncomfortable lurch.

Jemima stared at me, wide-eyed, and then a huge grin spread across her face.

"Are you going to call me Aunt Jemima now, Aunt Prudence?"

I narrowed my eyes at her. "Absolutely not, you upstart of a girl. It is just a family tree. I am still older than you, and seniority counts for a great deal, thank you very much."

Jemima chuckled. "Oh, thank goodness for that. Having you call me 'aunt' would be disconcerting to say the least."

"Indeed. Quite preposterous." I checked my notes. "Edward has double the Hardcastle blood, for he is one on both sides."

Jemima frowned. "Both sides? And our child? What an extraordinary thing to be thrice a Hardcastle."

Edward's eyebrows rose. "I had not thought of it like that."

"The family's gifts will run deep, I suspect."

Regarding her husband warily, Jemima slowly shook her head. "It does not change anything, does it? The baby will be all right."

"It does not change a thing," my nephew said staunchly. "However," his cheeks grew pink, "we might prepare ourselves for a *very* Hardcastle child."

Jemima nodded. "Oh yes, I suppose we must."

Memories flooded into me then, of the journey I had begun when I was an unremarkable young woman and the adventure that had brought me here to this moment with these special people, my dear family. Memories that I must examine now that I had told Sir Giles my secret, one that only Edward's mother knew.

My story was pressing against my mind, and I felt an even greater urgency to write it down—for Giles, for my family, and for myself.

Returning to my room, I prepared my paper and readied my pen once more.

# CHAPTER 3

***K**ent, 1836*
My first ball! How deeply the memory is embedded in my mind. It was the moment I stepped out into the world as a woman of marriageable age, albeit accompanied by my mother.

My excitement had been building for months and I did what I could to contain it. As the eldest daughter I had to maintain a certain amount of decorum and dignity, for not only was my own reputation at stake, but so too those of my younger sisters, Charity and Faith. Faith was a good three years younger than me, and still in the schoolroom. It was Charity, though, whom I was most concerned about, for she was only a year my junior and we debuted together.

Charity squeezed my arm as we waited to enter the ballroom behind the other girls, who I judged to be far prettier and more expensively dressed than us. However, I was so excited I did not care that their silks were finer, or that they wore more jewels. I was just happy to be there, finally.

Charity and I were coming out together because I preferred it so. The custom was for the eldest daughter to appear in society first and marry before the younger came out—securing a husband being the sole reason for a debut, of course. Mother would have let me debut on my own, but Charity was my dearest companion, and why should she have to wait for her turn? I felt it a boon to savour the experience with my beloved sister.

Then as now, a gentlewoman had to marry and marry well to secure her own happiness and prospects and those of her family. This may seem rather mercenary these days, though I think it is still the norm to take pecuniary matters into consideration when considering matrimony. At the time of my debut, I knew my future life depended on how well I performed socially. To fail was unthinkable, and the alternatives, such as earning my keep through a profession, were out of the question. To work for a living would see me forever shunned by my social circle and bring shame on my family. While I am not averse to employment, and I do what I can for charity, my mother would have had conniptions if I had suggested I earn my own bread. I might as well have told her I wanted to be an actress, or a scandalous novelist, instead of a respectable housewife. So, in that time and in that age, that was my goal and my reality.

The queue moved forward. I heard the swish of fabric as our gowns brushed against one another. Hand in hand, Charity and I strode up to be announced.

"Mrs Hardcastle-Smythe, Miss Hardcastle-Smythe, Miss Charity Hardcastle-Smythe," the master of ceremonies declared.

Mother inclined her head, and we dutifully followed suit, trying to keep from tripping over our hems as we gaped with wonder at the general awe and splendour. Overhead, dazzling chandeliers brimmed with candles, and flowers overflowed from vases set on the wall and against the columns. People thronged. Voices murmured as everyone talked together. The gentlemen were dressed so fine in their coat-tails and breeches and the women in their gowns, their headdresses flowing. Music and chatter filled the air, fans swishing, eyelashes batting and teeth smiling. Oh, the wonder of it.

Women wore their sleeves so big, and the lace trims were so delicate, I was grateful that Mother had allowed us to wear the latest trend. We may not be wearing the most expensive fabrics and the finest lace, but our dresses were modish. My ballgown was of the softest pink, and my wide silk skirt swept the floor gracefully. Charity wore a similar gown in pale blue that enhanced the colour of her eyes. My own brown eyes and slightly darker complexion did not compare to my sister's beauty. Poor Faith, who was at home with our governess, was even more sallow than me. However, I had a good height and figure and kept my posture upright to show my décolletage to its best advantage. A few glances in that direction through quizzing glasses made me shiver. How rude I thought them, and how exposed I felt. It was all so new to me to be the object of a man's eye—and other women's, particularly the mamas who looked down their noses at every girl who was not their own daughter. At least my mama was not so mean. She was too busy looking at us and smiling, unable to hide the admiration in her eyes. It was truly wonderful to be so loved.

Like rose petals clinging to a bud, we surrounded mama as we stood next to a column, watching the rest of the young women being announced. When that part of the evening was concluded, the musicians struck up a familiar tune and the dancing began.

"I am afraid to dance," Charity whispered to me.

"We have practised, dear sister. You shall delight all those who behold you."

She squeezed my hand. "But to dance with a gentleman who I do not know. How will I do that? Where should I look?"

A laugh bubbled out of me. "You could stand up with me, if you prefer."

"Oh, you," Charity grumbled. "You are meant to provide advice."

"That is a little hard, because I am as unused to dancing with strangers as you are."

"But you always know what to do."

I considered the dance before us and the various attitudes of the ladies and their partners. "Be polite, Chari, and respond to questions if you are spoken to. If you are required to look at your partner, perhaps fix on his shoulder rather than his face. Although, this dance is quite intricate so I do not know how you can talk and follow the moves."

It was growing warm in the ballroom and Charity and I fanned ourselves as we watched the current set. Eventually, Mama tapped me on the forearm with her own fan. "You girls wait here a moment. I see an acquaintance of mine."

"Yes, Mama," I replied dutifully, and watched as my mother made her way through the people fringing the dance floor to approach a trio of refined ladies. When she reached them she spoke a few words, and then gestured to us with her fan to join her. It transpired that my mother had not just one acquaintance but three, all former school friends whose own offspring were in attendance. Soon there were daughters and sons, nephews and nieces and cousins to whom we were introduced.

My head was awhirl as my dance card filled up quickly, as did my sister's. I never thought a ball could be so much fun or that I would meet and dance with so many young men.

A dashingly handsome man with bright blue eyes and soft curls requested two dances with Charity. My sister's blushes told me she liked the look of young Theodore Huntington. As she disappeared into the throng, my own dance partner escorted me to the set forming up.

"Is this really your first ball, Miss Hardcastle-Smythe?" Mr Leighton asked me. Mr Leighton was a friend of one of my new acquaintances. He was perhaps an inch taller than me, and had straight black hair that shone in the light. He also had side whiskers, which was an affectation I was not sure I liked. His dark hazel eyes glowed with warmth, though, so I did not take umbrage at the bluntness of his question.

"Why do you ask? Am I out of step?" I said as we commenced dancing.

Mr Leighton chuckled. "Not at all," he replied, his voice deep but gentle. His eyes twinkled mischievously. "You exude such confidence I fear you must be a veteran of at least twenty such gatherings."

I laughed as he swung me into the turn. The compliment hit its mark, and I was charmed to be so acknowledged for the many weeks of practice I had endured. I had worked hard to be accomplished and elegant in my moves and felt immensely proud that I had succeeded.

"And what do you do with your time, Mr Leighton?" I asked, rather boorishly. We had exhausted the general topics of conversation, and this was the fifth set in our second dance. After this we had to part ways lest we set tongues wagging. My next dance was promised to a serious curate, who spoke with a lisp and had bright red lips set in a pale face.

"This and that. I have no occupation, and I must own to being sadly lackadaisical with my time. I like to read and ride." Before I had time to digest his comment he asked, "And you, Miss Hardcastle-Smythe, how do you occupy your time?" He flashed me a grin. He meant to prick me, as he knew that no lady present would have an occupation, as such.

"I play a little, sing poorly, and while I learned to paint with watercolours, I prefer embroidery and sewing above other things. A terrible bore, I am sure."

"Proper employments for a lady of your station."

Although perfectly correct, this comment did not humour me. How terrible to be categorised by who I was, who my parents were, what my dowry was. At that moment, I hated that society expected me to merely become some man's wife, the mother of his children and his housekeeper. It made me want to scream, but what else was there for me? I loved my parents as they loved me. I would not knowingly act against their expectations. I lacked the backbone for defiance, in any case. My parents doted on me and gave me ample leeway. But I could not stay with them forever. I had to pursue my own life, and this entrée into society was the first step.

I had, of course, been circumspect with Mr Leighton about my daily occupations, not yet knowing how they would be received. When I read about science in secret, my father turned a blind eye. When I snuck books from his library, he knew what I was about and left tomes of what he thought might interest me out on the side tables, so I did not have to go looking for them.

My most pleasing pastime, however, was designing clothes, not just for me but for others. I offered advice, sewed for my sisters, embellished bonnets and embroidered nightgowns and petticoats to make them pleasing rather than merely functional. It was more than just dressing well; it was about loving beauty. However, I did not think a man would understand my love for fashion, so I did not speak in detail of this, either.

Before we parted ways, Mr Leighton lifted my gloved hand and bent over it. Not quite a kiss, but the gesture was there. "Do forgive me if my comments offended you. I enjoyed our time together."

In that moment, I understood that Mr Leighton's life was also dictated by custom. He was expected to marry, preferably a woman with money, and then become a father to continue his line. As a man he had more freedom to choose than I did, and he could earn a living if he needed, without risking his reputation.

I acknowledged his gallantry with a curtsey. "Thank you, Mr Leighton, for the dance. Please enjoy your evening."

Before the next dance I was able to cast an eye around the room. One or two gentlemen stood out. A dashing man whom I had admired from afar proved to be an earl. He caught my eye and inclined his head. Although when we were introduced, my dance card was full, so I could not accept his entreaty. The other man who caught my eye was rumoured to be a rake. Tall, thin and blond, he stood about with a quizzing glass, sneering at everyone. "I see you looking at Mr Arthur, my dear," Mama whispered in my ear.

"Is that his name? The tall blond gentleman?" I responded in a low voice.

She lifted her fan to hide her mouth. "Yes, he is a merchant who trades in wool. Mrs Graves told me that he is from the colonies. Made his fortune in New South Wales and is extremely good with sheep."

I studied the man. "If he is a colonial, Mama, why does he look like he looks down on us all? Surely they have little polite society in the antipodes."

My mother waved her fan slowly but with feeling. "I have no idea. Mrs Graves had it from Mrs Weatherby that he is looking for a wife, one robust enough to live in Australia."

"I do hope he does not choose me," I responded with a laugh. "But if he is looking for a wife, why do people call him a rake behind his back?"

My mother blushed. "Do keep your voice down."

"I am sorry, Mama."

Despite her admonition, she whispered, "Apparently he has tried his luck with a number of widows."

"Oh, I see, and they did not suit? A widow can marry, can she not?"

"Indeed, but these were some years older than he." My mother's words were clipped, and I realised it was not a topic she was comfortable with.

"Not strong enough to shear sheep, I suppose." I laughed and blushed.

My mama tapped me on the arm and jerked her head in the direction of the man we had been discussing. "Oh, dear me, he is coming in our direction."

She gave him a cold nod of acknowledgement and thankfully he passed us by.

"While you may look strong enough, my dear, I fear you are not quite what Mr Arthur fancies."

"Thank goodness for that," I replied. However, I pondered the colonial man. He was indeed attractive. If I had caught his eye, I might have considered moving to Australia, despite his penchant for widows. But the truth was, I loved my family too much to be really tempted. How could I leave them? How could I not visit with my mama every day and Charity and Faith and my father? No, I could not do it. Oh, little did I know that my worst fears were to be realised and I would be separated from them.

The curate came to claim his dance, and the rest of the ball passed in a haze of merriment. The strongest memory I had was the joy in Charity's face as she danced and later spent time talking to Theo Huntington.

❧

Two weeks later, we attended the Suttons' dinner. Mrs Sutton was one of my mother's dear school friends and was keen to host the young people and make it an event to be talked about on the best of terms. Mr Leighton was also invited. While he acknowledged me with a bow before we gathered for the meal, he did not pay me any particular attention. The after-dinner entertainment was a trial. While I was not the first invited to exhibit, I was still required to sing, and I was extremely nervous.

Charity played for me, but that did not stop the quaver in my voice. I chose an old ballad and was relieved when some people joined in for the chorus. However, I knew my limitations, and it was a great relief when I was allowed to regain my seat. I am sure I blushed for an hour after my terrible rendition of 'Scarborough Fair'. However, I was mollified by the fact that two other young ladies made a terrible hash of their performances, so I was not the worst. Why Mr Leighton chose to speak to me again after that embarrassing moment I do not know.

We had gathered for tea, and he came up to me. "It is pleasant to see you again, Miss Hardcastle-Smythe. Did you miss me?"

I tapped his shoulder with my fan. "Do not be so impertinent, sir. But I am pleased that you still wish to speak with me."

He lifted his cup and took a sip, his eyes dancing. "Are you going to send me on a mission then, to make you a cambric shirt?"

Speaking in kind, I replied, "It depends on how well you sew."

He passed off his cup to a passing servant. "It is your hobby, I understand. Did you make this exquisite piece of fluff yourself?"

He was referring to my gown, which was exquisite, and there was nothing negative to be said against it.

I frowned, detecting both flattery and censure in one sentence. I had designed the dress, but alas, my mother would not let me wear clothing made by my own hands. She said the rumours would sink us all. People would say we were too poor to afford a seamstress or a mantua maker. Besides, my mother had added, it was too close to employment, and, as I had heard so many times before, a lady did not work for a living. "No, it is not of my own making."

His forehead furrowed. "Are you sure? It bears a marked similarity to the ballgown that was your attire when last we met."

I cast a meaningful glance around the room. Most of the dresses had similar features: wide puffed sleeves, lace, and low-cut bodices for evening wear.

"Ah," he replied as he tracked the direction of my gaze. "I take your point. I only wished to congratulate you on your talent in design. Did you perchance have a hand in that?"

I was charmed. Mr Leighton had redeemed himself. "Yes, I designed the dress, and the dressmaker followed my direction. The fabric that I desired did not exist, so I had to make do with this cream satin brocade."

"Excellent. It is good to know if fate ever dealt you a bad hand you could earn a living and feed yourself by dressmaking and so forth. I have no such skill."

Blinking in surprise, I replied, "I do not mean to boast, sir. But I am well provided for should I marry or not."

A faint blush stole across his cheeks. "Forgive my impertinence."

Mr Cook then joined us and that was the end of the tête-à-tête.

THAT SUMMER, MR LEIGHTON JOINED A NUMBER OF GATHERINGS that I attended. It was the ones he did not attend that gained my attention, because I was at times lacking in company. He was easy to talk to, and we had found a comfortable space between us. It was not a romance as such. If I had romantic thoughts, they were for Earl Sommersby, who, although somewhat shorter than I was, cut a dashing style with his tailored coats, broad shoulders and the delightfully arranged curls around his face. Unfortunately for me, aside from our first introduction at the ball where I'd had to refuse his offer to dance, the earl took no notice of me. If he had been interested in an acquaintance, he no longer was, and I wondered if the difference in our heights had something to do with it. Out of all my male acquaintances, Mr Leighton had been the most consistent.

One day we were invited to a picnic in Kensington Gardens. Charity and I were very excited. Mr Huntington was there, and he and my sister were now inseparable. Charity could talk of no one else. How handsome he was, and how clever, for Theo Huntington invented things—what exactly, I was not sure. I was certain he was going to propose to her, for I noticed him staring at my sister with an earnest expression as if hanging on her every word. She, I knew, was deeply in love with him, and I feared what would happen if matrimony did not eventuate, for it would have destroyed all her hopes and dreams. Mr Huntington was always civil to me, though it was obvious I only had half his attention whenever we tried to converse. When we did, he often asked me about my sister.

"Would you care to take a turn with me, Miss Hardcastle-Smythe?" Mr Leighton asked politely. He had doffed his hat and bent over my hand in a gallant but extravagant fashion. I knew I was not in love with him; I thought us friends. He did not excite any passion in me like the earl who did not notice me. As I had nothing better to do, I allowed Mr Leighton to help me to stand and away we went, still in full view of the rest of the party. My parasol kept the sun from my face, as I could not bear to get even browner, and for good measure we stood in the shade of a large plane tree.

"Are you enjoying the picnic?" he asked me.

"Why yes, it is most diverting sitting out of doors. I used to like such gatherings when I was young. Mama used to take us to picnic in the garden."

He laughed lightly. "I have something of importance to ask you."

"Really?" I had no idea what he could say to me.

"Miss Hardcastle-Smythe," he said, and grabbed my hand. "Prudence. Please make me the happiest man in the world, and do me the honour of being my wife."

I dragged my hand back, astonished. "Your wife? But surely you are not in love with me, sir."

"Why do you say that? I know we get on well. You like me, I know."

I was in a quandary. I did not want to marry Mr Leighton, but I was certain it was up to my father to refuse him. Having never been proposed to before, despite being on the marriage market, I was completely in the dark about how to accept or refuse a proposal. True, it was expected that Theo Huntington would propose to Charity at any moment, as their affection was obvious to everyone. This had been much talked of, and both my parents and my sister had already agreed to an acceptance, should the offer be made. In my case, no such plans had been anticipated or devised. Would I not get into trouble for refusing an offer without considering my parents' views? I longed to be able to confer with my father. I checked over my shoulder to see if I could get my mother's attention, but Mama was deep in conversation with one of her friends.

"Have you spoken to my father?" It wasn't the most romantic of replies and the only thing I could think of at the time. I did not want to hurt the man's feelings by rejecting him outright. I thought I had acted correctly in deferring to my father. In hindsight, I should have flatly refused and walked away.

"No, I thought I would ask you first, as it concerns you the most."

"Indeed, how kind. However, I could not go against my father's wishes, and I must not entertain a proposal of marriage without considering his advice on the matter."

"But do you love me?" he asked.

I searched my feelings. "I like you and I consider you a friend," I said carefully. "However, I cannot say that I am in love with you, Mr Leighton." I tried to be kind as well as truthful. "Nor am I of a mind to marry you. I am very sorry."

He grabbed my hands and kissed my wrists above my gloves. "Sir, you must not." I looked around me in case anyone saw. Hitherto he had not touched me, except to dance. "Stop!"

I was unsettled, distressed and embarrassed.

"Come over here behind this tree. I will make you desire me."

He pulled hard on my hands, nearly toppling me. I resisted.

"No. Please, Mr Leighton, let me go."

With a glance at the rest of our companions, he let go. "I beg your pardon, Prudence." He bowed his head, although his cheeks were pink, with anger or shame I did not know. I was quite beside myself. "Do let me call you Prudence. I only wanted to share this burning passion in my breast. I think of you night and day and long for when we can be together forever."

This latest speech upset my equilibrium. I did not know where to look. "That is...you should not use my Christian name, sir. I do not give you leave. I fear that your confidences are unsettling to say the least. I like you, sir, but I do not suffer from a burning passion."

I turned on my heel. Mr Cook was heading towards me. Perhaps I walked too quickly, as my cheeks were flushed. Mr Cook put out his hand to stop me. "Are you all right, Miss Hardcastle-Smythe? Is there something amiss?"

"Oh no, I am fine. Everything is fine. I am a little overheated. Perhaps I should sit in the shade."

He turned and held out his elbow. "Let me escort you back to your mother. She has been asking after you."

The rest of the picnic went off well. I ate so much my corset creaked. It was not hunger that drove my appetite, but anxiety. I did not set eyes on Mr Leighton after our discussion. As my mother was enraptured with Theo's attentions to Charity, I did not get the opportunity to speak to her about the incident, and so I bided my time. The opportunity for discussion would arise if Mr Leighton spoke to my father.

However, as the days passed, he did not call on us nor speak to my father. While I had been flattered by Mr Leighton's attentions, I was relieved my refusal had put a stop to his pursuit of matrimony. When his name was mentioned in company, however, my ears pricked up. While I did not know the particulars, I had heard that he had only a small fortune and was on the hunt for a rich wife. I was not rich but nor was I poor. This put his proposal in a different light, making me believe that he had a genuine affection for me.

My future earnings were in the six per cents, and that would make a comfortable income for any future family. Father had invested well and took good care of us all. He neither gambled nor spent an inordinate amount of time at his clubs. He preferred his library, taking tea with my mother and being with his daughters. I admired my parents' relationship. They loved each other as they loved us, and I could only wish for the same. Mother did warn me that not every wife was as fortunate as she. She told me several times that she and Father were of one mind and that they talked often about everything that mattered. My mother urged me to watch out for signs that a man might be cruel to a future wife, as some wives were not respected by their spouses. In the limited company I was exposed to, I did sometimes observe these traits. Occasionally I witnessed snubs, such as a man who had been dancing with a young woman one week ignoring her the next, causing tears and recriminations. I overheard snippets of nasty comments at times when men grouped together. They were not usually men of my acquaintance. Those with weaker minds were unable to disguise their nature and thus were easier to spot. It was my observation that people, both men and women, put on a façade in company so it was not always easy to see their true selves.

At the next dance party, Earl Sommersby asked me to dance the waltz. My mother flinched and narrowed her gaze, and I saw the refusal on her lips. She did not approve of the waltz. But when she saw who had sought my hand, she acquiesced. It was obvious that I liked the earl. The music filled the air. When we joined the dance, I nearly fainted after he took me in his arms. He did not speak to me but for the merest small talk. "You dance well, Miss Hardcastle-Smythe." And later, "The floor is rather full this evening." And then, "Be careful," and turned me out of the way of another couple. I did not speak a word myself, as I was concentrating on my steps. I just smiled and nodded like a simpleton. I would treasure every word he said, the scent of him and the feel of his body when we accidentally bumped against each other.

Afterwards, he took me back to my place beside my mother,

bowed and took his leave. There was a twinkle in his eye, and I blushed.

It had been nice to admire the earl from a distance, and I made sure to save my dance card with his name on it in my journal. But to my mind, he was unattainable. An earl for Miss Hardcastle-Smythe? Of course not. Charity was the one with the looks and the charm, and she was madly in love with Theo.

Later that evening, Mr Leighton approached me as I left the retiring room. I had needed to reaffix the ostrich feather in my headpiece. I had not been aware he was in attendance.

I pulled up in surprise. "Oh, Mr Leighton. How do you do?"

He put my arm in his elbow and led me away from where my mother awaited me.

"What are you doing? My mother is expecting me." I tried to extract my arm, but he held it firmly. "Mr Leighton! Stop," I hissed, though I smiled at people and tried to hide my struggle. I could not draw adverse attention.

He turned to me and grinned. "Did you enjoy your dance with the earl? Did you find yourself titillated?"

"Sir, please unhand me. If you must know, the earl was a gentleman."

Next thing I knew Leighton had pulled me into an empty room and pushed me up against the wall, crushing his lips to mine. I would not call it a kiss. "There, does that not excite you?" he breathed in my ear.

I pushed with all my might, but he held me firm. "Let me go."

He studied my face and saw that I was serious. "I beg your pardon," he said in a loud voice. He stepped back, a blush staining both cheeks. "I don't know what came over me. I thought you liked me. I thought you welcomed my advances. Did you not say you loved me?"

"I said no such thing, Mr Leighton. I said I liked you but that was before you, you—"

"Prudence!" My mother's voice echoed around me.

"Mother!" I responded, giving Mr Leighton a huge shove. He stumbled back and pretended to be appalled.

Mother came into the room and stopped still. "You, sir, explain yourself."

He bowed. "I beg your pardon, Mrs Hardcastle-Smythe. Forgive me, I could not resist your daughter's charms."

Anger coursed through me. "I do not have any charms, sir. You drew me here against my will."

"I have spoken to your daughter about my love, my passion for her."

My mother's angry visage turned to me. "Have you encouraged this man's attentions?"

"No. I have not."

"Did he declare himself?"

"Well, yes, at the picnic but I told him—"

"Your daughter gave careful consideration to my proposal, ma'am. She urged me to talk to her father. Alas I have not been able to avail myself of his time."

"That is not how it was. Mama—"

My mother's shoulders squared. "Call tomorrow at ten o' clock and you will be admitted." To me she said, "Come along, Prudence, I fear this ball is at an end."

In the carriage, all my mother's ire spilled out. "How could you act so disgracefully? What about your sisters? Charity is in love with Theo Huntington, and he is this close to proposing." She raised her gloved fingers to emphasise the point. "Your behaviour has jeopardised that."

Charity was sitting across from me, bawling into her handkerchief. Our sudden departure meant she had not been able to dance with Theo again.

"Mother, believe me, I did not intentionally encourage Mr Leighton. I considered him a friend until he spoke of his burning passion. I was surprised. I did not accept him, Mama. I told him quite clearly that I did not love him and nor did I wish to marry him. I told him he must speak to Father and not speak to me first. Did I do wrong?"

"You should have rejected him outright, my dear. Made your intentions clear."

"I thought I made myself clear, Mama. I thought if he did speak to Father, then Father would speak to me, and I would tell him that I did not love Mr Leighton and I did not wish to marry him. When he did not come to see Father, I assumed the incident closed. He took me quite by surprise tonight."

My mother gaped at me. "You do not want to marry him?"

"No, I do not. After how he behaved tonight, Mama, I am even more certain."

I think my mother finally understood what I was saying. "But you allowed yourself to be compromised by him."

I squared my shoulders, spared a look for Charity. "Mama, I did not. Before you interrupted us, I was going to punch him on the nose."

My mother sighed. "That would not have made the situation any better. I fear I made a mistake. I should have accompanied you to the retiring room."

"Is it bad, Mama?" As I had been so focussed on the moment, I did not take note of who had witnessed or heard the altercation. Mr Leighton had made no attempt to be discreet.

She put her arm around me and squeezed lightly. "I was so pleased the earl asked you to dance, so proud, even it if was that distasteful waltz."

I sank back in my seat. "I was so anxious not to make a mistake, I barely spoke a word to the earl the whole dance. He must think me a terrible bore."

"Quite the opposite. His cousin, Mrs Tallforth, said he spoke warmly about you, despite your height."

"Really? Oh..." My spirits soared. I hadn't dared to hope the earl would have renewed interest in me given the presence of so many prettier and wealthier young women, and many with better standing in society than me.

A frown marred my mama's face and my heart dropped to the pit of my belly. "But if word gets out about Mr Leighton's amour, then your reputation will be ruined and no one will propose, let alone the earl."

Tears stung my eyes and, try as I might to quell them, they fell. Charity had sniffed and blown her nose.

"It will be all right, sister dear," Charity said now.

My mother held a handkerchief to the corner of her right eye. "I believe you, even though you have been cosy with Mr Leighton previously. People have talked on it, even thinking an engagement imminent. I did not realise it was you, Prudence, that had been observed in the park behaving inappropriately with Mr Leighton. Why, Mrs Hutton was talking of it the other day at the Ladies Charity Group. All of us thought that the couple must marry. Believe me, one bad word from Mr Leighton about you and you will be utterly sunk if you do not marry him. They will call you a jilt and a flirt. My goodness...so distressing."

"I wanted to tell you about the incident at the picnic, Mama but...well...we are all so focussed on Charity."

My mother threw her head back, as if begging for strength from the Lord. "You failed to mention his proposal then?"

"Yes. I am sorry."

I looked between them, seeing the hard look in my mother's eyes and feeling the truth in her words. "But to judge me for this would be unjust. I have done nothing wrong."

Looking back, I understand that my naivety made me vulnerable. I was overly friendly with Leighton, and I should not have shown him any preference at all. I was flattered by his attention; it felt good to be admired, to have someone smile and welcome me to a room. To have someone talk to me about things other than day-to-day trivialities, the weather or the food. Looking back, I can see the faults in my behaviour. I had not paid proper heed to my mother's lectures.

"Yes, my dear. Gossips will not care about that. The more unfair it is, the more they enjoy talking about it. A stain on your reputation will affect your sisters and the whole family. I fear you have no choice now. If he comes to speak to your Father, then we must accept."

To my dismay, Mr Leighton did come to speak to my Father early the next morning. While he did not give his immediate consent, he began looking into Mr Leighton's background.

Rumours of our amour had circulated. Mother's visitors were full up with the news and pre-emptive congratulations. I had been seen embracing Mr Leighton at the ball and identified as the young woman who had been seen holding his hand at the picnic. It was very likely these stories about me were helped along by Mr Leighton. I felt so penned in.

The conversation with my father was not pleasant. While kind as always, he acknowledged the difficulty of my situation and apologised for the lack of guidance on his part. They had been focussed on Charity's match and had assumed I knew better. I felt more and more obliged to acquiesce to Mr Leighton's proposal. Mother was adamant that while I did not love him, I could very well learn to love him as he seemed a gentle and kind sort of man. "How well does anyone know another when they marry? You could be pleasantly surprised," she said.

While I had always considered my mother's advice, that day I learned that she was not infallible. She loved me dearly, but it was Charity who put the sparkle in her eye, and the marriage to Theo Huntington was almost a certainty but for me and my scandal. My parents were too liberal to force me to marry against my will. But for the love of my sister and regard for my family, I decided to accept Mr Leighton, all the while hoping he found another woman. My hopes of that were dashed by the increase in rumours about our liaison. Mr Leighton became as trapped as me by the gossip.

## Kent, 1837

In the lead-up to our wedding, Mr Leighton was ever polite and solicitous towards me and never gave me cause to complain or start an argument. Believe me, I tried. However, I did not get to know him either. It was a shallow kind of relationship and I felt there was a barrier there to knowing the true Mr Leighton. Father said he could not find fault with him in the responses to his enquiries, other than that he had insufficient income to support a family. Given the situation, Father used my dowry in his calculations and said if Mr Leighton was modest in his expenditure, we would be comfortable for our married life. As it was, I married a man I could only tolerate and did not love. My sister was, therefore, able to make a fantastic match with Theo Huntington, a second cousin, who was dashingly handsome, exceedingly clever and had a good income. They married within the month, and Charity was expecting Edward before I had set a date with Mr Leighton.

After our honeymoon, I could barely stand to have Charles—as I now called him—near me. If I had known what was in store as part of my wifely duties, I would have run screaming from the church. Actually, now that I think about it, I would never have entered the church in the first place. My mother consoled me and told me I would get used to it. She advised me to be compliant and not resist and then my life would be smoother. When I asked her about her and my father, she said they got along well on that front. Then we both blushed and drank tea. My mind would not entertain the thought.

Charles was an indifferent companion, often out on business. While I had a husband, I was often lonely. I could not say outright that I was ignored. We shared meals and discussed family news. But he was not kind. After a while, married life became tolerable. I suppose one can get used to anything. I think for a time my spirit was so worn down that I made good of a bad situation, to the point where it felt normal and natural to be in a loveless marriage. I ran our rented house to the best of my abilities and soon found myself with child. The idea of becoming a mother was a solace. Mother comforted me and exclaimed at how full my life would be, and how happy Charles would be to be a father.

To my surprise, Charles lost his temper when I broke the news. "How could you let this happen? Surely you take precautions?"

I did not know one could take precautions against pregnancy. "How will we manage the extra expense?" he said before storming out of the room.

I could only gape at the closed door. Surely there was enough money for us all?

### KENT, 1839

Late in my pregnancy, I answered a knock at the front door. Charles was out and the housekeeper was needed in the kitchen, so I happened to answer it.

Two men with surly expressions stood there. My gaze shifted between the one with the thick, black moustache and the one with the scar that made his mouth lift in a kind of half smile. "May I help you?"

"Is this the residence of Mr Charles Leighton?" the moustachioed one asked.

"Yes, I am afraid he is not at home."

He shoved some papers at me. "Give him these. We shall be back to collect the rest of the money."

The men turned to leave, and I fumbled the papers as I stepped back inside. In the dim hallway I read the figures and realised they were gaming debts. A sharp pain hit me in the side and I stumbled to the settee.

Charles had lost so much money through gambling. A gamester! He had kept this vice secret because Father would not have permitted the marriage if he had known. My father would not have entrusted me to a man so weak as to lose his household's entire income within a mere two years. Father abhorred gambling and strong drinking and I had the same values.

The housekeeper found me, distraught in the drawing room. The tears of anger and shame had turned into cries of fear as my pains came on. I was going to give birth. Charles was nowhere to be found so the housekeeper sent for the midwife. My son, James, arrived the next day and still Charles had not come home.

It was some days before I could inform my parents of this terrible state of affairs. I sent a note around to my mother:

*The baby has come, Mama. Please come visit me as soon as you receive this.*
*Pru*

When Mama arrived, she kissed me on the forehead, asked me how I did and then went to the cradle. With the baby in her arms, she took a chair. "What a joy to behold, my dear. Such a wonderful head of hair." She played with his fists. "Strong too."

"Mama, I have something to tell you…" I related everything that had happened with the debt collectors and Charles being absent.

My mother thought I had lost my senses. "That cannot be so. Are you certain?"

I handed her the bills. "My word, that must be all your capital." She lowered the papers. "I shall send for your father. He will know what to do."

She called the housekeeper and asked the houseboy to go over and bring my father.

"What am I to do, Mama? How shall we live?"

She gazed fondly at James. "Two grandsons." With a sigh, she put the baby back in the cradle.

"Father will help you, I am sure." Then she wiped the tears from her eyes.

My father burst into the room. Mama informed him of my news. He had no time to view his grandson. "I will make enquiries. Obviously, my initial investigations were somewhat lacking. Mr Leighton has imposed on us under false pretences."

My Mama moved me and my son to our family home to recover from the birth. Charles had still not returned before then or communicated with me in any way. Eventually, Father came to my room, his face as solemn as I had ever seen it.

"What is it?"

He wiped his eyes with his handkerchief. "I have sought Leighton out and also spoken with the bank and my solicitor. All your capital is gone. He has liquidated all the shares, and the cottage in the country that was in your name has been sold. There is nothing left."

"We have no money? Nothing?"

"It is worse than you think, my love. He did all this within the first month of your marriage. You not only have no capital now, but you owe money for gambling debts, and the rent on the house, the salaries of the servants and payments to your other suppliers are in arrears."

"We have been living on credit all this time? Oh, Father!"

He drew out a list from his pocket. "I have an accounting of what is owed. Approximately a hundred pounds for your food and the servants' wages. The rent I have paid, as the landlord was most distressed. I never suspected for a minute what Charles was doing. The gambling debts are too awful to contemplate."

The thought of leaving him was strong in my mind. Mother looked upon me with pity. I would become a pariah if I left my husband. If Charles never came back, then the shame would be on him, but still I would be a source of gossip.

I had been residing at my parents' house for a month or so when we had the first word of Charles. He had returned to our house, demanding to know where I was. He soon found his way to my parents' home. Meanwhile Father had made meticulous enquiries and discovered some other most troubling information. It appeared that Charles Leighton was a fortune hunter who had been courting a woman whose wealth was rumoured to be five times my own. When things had become more serious, her family had become suspicious and taken her away to the north. When he met me, Charles had been in desperate financial straits. I saw now that he would likely have done just about anything to force me into marriage. I was a dupe, an easy target. I knew I was no great beauty or heiress, but to be a mere consolation prize—a means to an end—was dispiriting in the extreme. No wonder Charles was indifferent to me after the honeymoon. He had already liquidated my assets, so I was of no further use to him.

I was the mother of a young baby, with a wastrel of a husband, no money and insurmountable debts. I had no brother to fight for me, but I did have a wonderful father. What transpired between my father and Charles, I do not know. After the initial interview, Charles returned to my parents' house the next day, ostensibly to greet his son. I wished him miles away but as his wife, I was powerless to stop him.

My son, James, was my delight and my solace. He was a healthy baby, with dark eyes like my own and a head full of thick, dark hair. He had a lusty appetite and strong arms and legs, which he thrust about energetically. He had to be swaddled to keep him in his cradle. A bonny child such as ever there was, even if I do say so of my own offspring. Caring for my son for those few weeks in the sanctuary of my childhood home soothed me. I grew in strength and then courage.

When I finally had a conversation with Charles, it was heavy indeed.

He threw himself at my feet. "Please forgive me. I am so sorry. It will never happen again. Do come home with me."

"I will never forgive you," I replied. "You have ruined everything."

"I was weak. But now I am strong. I will do better for you and our son."

"It is hard to believe you, Charles. We are better off without you."

Charles cheeks grew red. "No, you cannot deny me my son. Think of what your friends and acquaintances will think if you don't return home."

A shudder overtook me. He had played the winning hand. I felt like folding in on myself. Seeing my reaction, Charles took my hand. "Your father is helping us. He will guide me, and I will be compliant."

Overwhelmed, I ran from the room. If I did not return, he could take James from me and I would be ruined socially and my standing in society meant a lot to me.

After urging from my father and mother, I reluctantly agreed to return to the marital home. At our parting, I cried, my mother sobbed, and Father loomed. Charles was oblivious to our suffering. Looking on, he smiled and flattered and pretended all was well. I wanted to be sick. I wanted to scream, but that was not possible. To show such emotion, such a lack of decorum, would sink us all in society's view.

A few weeks later, I was visiting my parents and sipping tea while Mama cuddled with James when Father said, "I have finally settled Leighton's debts. It meant liquidating some of my investments, but you shall have a fresh start."

"You did what?" I blurted out, raising my voice to my father for the first time in my life.

Father grew flustered, using a finger to ease his cravat away from his neck. "I had no choice. He was set to desert you and little James. I could not allow that when it was in my power to assist you."

"But that debt was huge. What of you and Mama? You have reduced your own income."

We were all poorer after Charles was done with me.

"A few economies will see us all right, my dear. We will be well."

"How will we go on?" I asked, half to myself. It was one thing to clear Charles' debts, and it was another to continue living. "While I am grateful you have assisted us, how will we live?"

My father lowered his chin to his chest. "I paid his debts on the condition he find employment, and with his promise that he is to live within his means and never gamble again. He swore to me he would abide by our agreement."

"He is to work for a living? What kind of work can he do?" I asked.

"I have given him a reference to a friend of mine in the British East India Company. I fear that you will need to go to India."

"India?" This was a place I knew little about, a place far from my precious family. A place where people sickened from the heat, disease and who knew what else. "India?" I repeated, feeling the tears readying to fall once again. Oh, I had cried so many tears because of that man.

Later I asked Charles for more information. "Is it not hot there and full of savages?"

Charles nodded. "Yes, it can be. I understand that some parts can be cooler at certain times of the year. You will need to study up on that so you can prepare for the journey."

Our destination was to be Calcutta, a place quite settled but still growing. Fort William had been built and many other British women lived in that city with their husbands and families. Some were company men and others were in the military or government.

Father and Charles managed to pack up our belongings and pay out the lease. We could only take limited luggage with us, as Charles' position was junior, the salary just enough to keep us in a certain style in India.

Determined to learn what I could about what was to be my new home, I returned to my parents' home to read as much as possible. My father had an extremely good library, and he borrowed some books from his friend in the East India Company to expand my knowledge. A book by Emma Roberts on travelling to East India provided a lot of detailed advice and guided my preparations. In the end, I knew more than Charles, but I kept that a secret. I would not allow him to try to demean me further.

I have often thought about those days and asked myself whether I was an ignorant girl who did not see Charles' manipulation or whether I should have fought harder to break off the engagement. I was not oblivious to the entrapment, and neither were my parents. We were held firm by society's expectations and false assumptions as to Charles' true character. However, hindsight is a marvellous thing, and makes one think one was wiser than one really was. If I was incandescently angry at Charles, I cannot recall it. I had made my bed, as they say, and had to lie in it. Perhaps a bitterness settled in my heart. The only women I knew to be happy in their marriages were my mama and my sister Charity. Many of my other acquaintances let slip their discontent with their husbands' treatment of them, either ignoring them, scolding them, abusing them and so on. I was not the worst off, believe me.

With a sigh, I leaned back in my chair and glared at the pages I had written. I thought my writing would be more elegant, more refined. However, it was very late, past two o'clock in the morning, and my back ached from hunching over the desk.

My head foggy from fatigue, I was about to go to bed when I heard a noise and then a voice somewhere in the house. Peeping out into the hallway, I caught another, deeper, voice, coming from downstairs. Drawn on by curiosity, I held a candle aloft and crept down the dark stairs and along the hall. The door to the drawing room was ajar and light flickered from within. I snuffed my candle and pushed open the door.

Draped in a fine frippery gown was Jemima, and she appeared to be haranguing Mr Ferdinand White.

"You will tell me who killed him. I know—Oh!" Jemima turned as I entered.

"What are you doing up?" I asked in return. I smiled at Mr White. "How nice to see you again, Mr White."

He grimaced and I realised that he was imbued with an arsenic-green glow. Jemima held him with her power. I had heard Fulton and Edward discussing the emerald fire that Jemima held within herself, but had never seen it. Ringed in viridescent light, Mr White was held immobile, and it could not have been comfortable. My teeth were set on edge by the vibrations coming from Jemima. Narrowing my gaze, I raised an eyebrow at Jemima. "What are you doing to Mr White?"

Jemima set her lips in a straight line and glared. "Nothing much," she said when I did not back down. Another breath and she sighed. "Have it your way."

The glow faded and Mr White sagged as if he had tired of fighting. For her to aim her power at her uncle was surprising. She was normally so even tempered, except when fighting monsters.

Mr White turned to me and bowed. "Thank you for your intervention, Mrs Wainwright. There has been a misunderstanding."

"No, there has not," snapped Jemima. "You know who killed my father. You never even told me the truth."

"For that I apologise, but I have only ever acted to keep you safe. It will serve you no good to know their names. Names are powerful things. Just thinking of them could draw them to you. I was on my way to warn you of some impending danger when I received your summons. Can you not understand the risk? In your current state, you are vulnerable."

Jemima jerked her chin and scoffed.

I myself grew perturbed. "Are you saying that the assassins that killed Cousin Wilbur might come here?" I asked. I could not say—come here to kill Jemima—not when she was so full with child and emotionally vulnerable.

Mr White nodded vigorously. "Indeed. There have been ripples of disquiet amongst my fellows. Rumours that those powerful magicians who once served the *Societas Magicae* are seeking power, seeking Jemima."

"Why now?" I asked, casting a sideways look at Jemima.

"The amount of power she possesses is a serious temptation to these magicians. They covet what she has. Indeed, some murmur that for a mere woman to have such power is a waste. They believe her to be too ignorant to use her powers and want them for themselves."

"I will crush them," Jemima said in a low voice. "Cowards that they are."

"Jemima, that is not a very ladylike thing to say," I reproved.

Jemima scoffed. "As if I—"

"You should care," Mr White said. "You are in a delicate state. Now is not the time to draw attention to yourself. When you are ready, I will stand with you. Wilbur was my friend too."

My gaze shifted to Jemima. Her expression was militant. "Let them come!" she replied, fists clenching. In the next breath, she squeaked and rubbed her rounded abdomen. "Sorry, the baby kicked."

Mr White had tears in his eyes. "Oh dear, Jemima. Take care. There is more than just your own life in the equation now. Despite what you think, you are not indestructible."

Jemima yawned loudly. "I think I have proved that I am. I survived the furnace and came out unscathed."

"You have proved yourself physically strong and impervious to fire. However, there are other ways to defeat a magician. Do you think your father let them willingly drain him of life?"

That won him a hard glare from Jemima. I had never seen her out of countenance with Mr White before. She turned her back on him. "You can leave,now, Uncle. I will not try to stop you. However, I will not be happy to see you again unless you give me the information I require."

Mr White nodded solemnly. "Thank you. My thoughts and prayers for your health and safety. I will do what I can to keep you safe, as I promised your father I would."

Jemima turned back, eyes flashing. "Fiddle. Where were you when Edward sent me to school? You did not intervene then."

"It was in your best interests to go there. Admit it—you enjoyed school."

Jemima clenched her fists again. "Go. I will admit nothing." Lifting her elegant robe clear of the floor, she made to move away. "Aunt, could I prevail upon you for some warm milk? I do not wish to wake the housekeeper, and as you are still up..."

"Indeed, I would be happy to. Please do not hurt Mr White while I am gone."

Off I went to the kitchen, relighting my candle from a candelabra in the drawing room as I exited. When I returned with the glass of warm milk, Jemima was dozing in a winged chair and Mr White had vanished.

Together we walked up the stairs. "Why are you awake, anyway?" Jemima asked me. Outwardly she appeared calm, but I sensed tension running through her. The news about her father's murder had really unsettled her.

I looked down at my ink-stained hands. "I was writing."
"Ah...messy work. Good night."
"Sleep well, Jemima."
We parted in the hall outside her room.

# CHAPTER 4

The next day, I was going through some papers when Jemima waddled up and leaned on the desk as if she was carrying the weight of the world. Then she yawned loudly and that started me going.

"Did you get enough sleep, Jemima?" I asked as I wound the string around the bundle of my old letters I had been perusing and placed them back in their box.

Jemima straightened up. "Yes. It is hard to sleep generally."

"Did you tell Edward about your meeting with Mr White?"

Her face clouded. "Yes, after a fashion."

"What did Edward say?"

Jemima rolled her eyes. "The same as Mr White. I am to be quiet and timid and wait."

I rolled my eyes. "They were not his exact words, surely."

She let out a pained sigh. "Oh no, Aunt. His used different adjectives. You know I think I liked you better when I thought we were not blood related. It is most extraordinary."

I sat back a little, not quite meeting her eye. "Extraordinary? How so?"

"We are so different. I could never be...Oh."

"What?" I looked her up and down, but she did not appear to be in pain.

"Forgive me, I just realised what I was going to say would sound rude and I was not trying to pick a fight with you."

"I am glad to hear it."

I waited for her to continue but she stepped away from the desk and then flomped down on the settee, letting out a pitiful moan. As Jemima was impervious to harm, or so I had overheard on a number of occasions, I figured her need for assurance and comfort sprang from elsewhere. I had my mother to comfort me when I was expecting James. Jemima had no mother. Although Milly was her bosom companion, Milly had a husband and a child herself and was in the same expectant situation, so she did not have the capacity for devoted attention. I saw it was up to me to fulfil the role of older, female bosom companion.

A stool stood near the settee, and I pulled it over and sat down. "What is wrong, dear?" I said in my tenderest voice.

Jemima, who had her eyes closed, slitted them open. "Could you bathe my forehead in lavender water? It aches so much."

With a smile, I inclined my head in the affirmative and went to organise a small bowl with warm water, lavender essence and a cloth. I commenced soothing my discommoded niece.

"Edward is working on something complex, he says..." Jemima commented as I finished bathing her head. By complex, she meant spells. He researched them and then wrote the pertinent bits down.

"Most annoying for you. Your comfort should be paramount," I added. "Can I do anything else for you?"

"Not really," Jemima said. "Once Edward starts a project it is quite hard to cry off. Besides, he just thinks I am capable of anything and does not notice that I need him."

My head inclined slowly. "You are normally proud of your self-sufficiency, my dear, so it is easy to see why he thinks that way."

Jemima leaned forward, took my hand and held it firmly. "But this is different, you see. The enemy is within me. How is it to get out? I did not think of that before."

Swallowing my mirth, I patted her hand. "Well, a woman's body is a marvel, my dear. It makes way for the baby. You and I are evidence of that."

"Does it hurt?" she asked me.

I tried to make my tone calm. "Yes, I believe so. But they say when you see your baby, you forget the pain of its birth."

While I had had a son in wedlock and had no reason to be ashamed, I had kept up the pretence of being a spinster for a long time. My son was lost to me, and I would rather no one knew about my life before I went to India, except in the most vaguest of terms. I had yet to get to that part of my memoir where I needed to explain it all. I would rather not complicate things now so close to Jemima's confinement by blurting out the fact that I was a mother. With the anxiety over a potential threat from rogue magicians, there was enough to think about. At this stage it was only Sir Giles who knew I had been married and had a child.

"I cannot help but worry. Milly did say I would scream loudly, and it is not ladylike to do that."

I could not help it; I laughed. "But you have never concerned yourself with being ladylike before."

Jemima sat forward again abruptly. "Well, I have had time to think, sitting around like an overstuffed turkey waiting for slaughter, and I think there is merit in this ladylike business after all."

For the first time, I saw the panic in her eyes. I shifted my position to sit next her and threw an arm around her shoulder. "All will be well, Jemima. You are young, strong and healthy. You are supported by your husband, your friends, a midwife, and a doctor is on call if needed."

She clutched at my hand. "Will you stay with me during the birth?"

How could I look into those brilliant, pleading blue eyes and say no? "Of course, if you wish it."

"I do wish it. Somehow, I know I will need you." She clasped my hand tightly. My heart lurched with a strange emotion. Being important to Jemima was not something I had expected. We had often clashed, but I believed my instinct was right: she needed a mother figure in her life right now. "Do you think ill of me for being horrid to Uncle Ferdy?"

"No, I think you feel strongly about the circumstances of your father's death. At the same time, I think you must listen to his warnings."

"He came when I called him, but I would not let him leave. That was wrong of me. If you had not interrupted, I am not sure I would have let him go until I got what I wanted."

"I see. Well, that did not occur. However, what of his warnings? Does Edward know of this potential threat?"

Jemima shifted. "Not exactly. As I said he is rather caught up in his..." She waved her hands

"I think you should tell him as soon as you can even if you do have to interrupt him. He will know what to do."

"All right. I shall. Do you think Uncle Ferdy will forgive me for being so wretched to him?"

I stroked her head. "I am sure he already has." A feeling of warmth and, dare I say it, love, filled my breast. With a kiss on her forehead, I urged Jemima to lie back and relax, and soon her eyes closed. When her breathing deepened, I knew she slept. I remained by her side. After a while, as if she had some inner clockwork mechanism, she sat up, checked her watch and said, "It is time for afternoon tea, Aunt Prudence. Will you come through with me?"

"Why, yes, thank you." My voice was thick with emotion. This had been a first step into a deepened intimacy with Jemima, and for some reason it seemed to be a momentous occasion.

In a daze, I followed Jemima into the drawing room. My life had taken an interesting turn of late. I wondered whether this change had started when I decided to write my memoir or whether it was the awful events at Hatfield. Surely the latter, because without those events I would not have met Sir Giles, nor had a reason to become acquainted with him. Rather than humouring an annoying older woman, he had truly desired my company and conversation. He had a discerning eye and a satirical turn of mind. He picked up on my subtle quips. As I reflected on that, I could see that he had always treated me kindly, with tenderness and respect. He had sent us food from his estate: game, fruit, vegetables and so on. After his proposal I viewed those past interactions differently.

Edward came into the drawing room behind us with a distracted look. "It is that time already?" He kissed his wife on the cheek. "You look rather well, Jemima."

Jemima rolled her eyes. "I am alive and breathing, so that will have to be sufficient for good health."

Milly came in with Ally and the nurse, followed immediately by dear Fulton. Ally took a few steps and made it to the settee, where he walked along it before toddling over to me.

"Squee!" I said as I took him up and lifted him high before settling him on my lap.

"He has a present for you, Aunt Prudence," Milly said.

I looked at Ally, dark eyes meeting mine. "What have you got for me?"

Ally opened his mouth. "Pudu. Puuduu."

I blinked, uncertain. Milly chuckled. "He is saying your name. His 'rs' are not what they should be."

I met Ally's eager eyes. "How do you do, Ally? Can you say Aunty?" I looked to Milly. "Prudence is such a mouthful."

"Tanti," Ally said, eyes nearly crossing with the effort of saying the word.

"Well done!" I said. Milly and I laughed together. "Such a clever boy."

Fulton rubbed his hands. "I hear Cook has made us a special treat."

Milly laughed. "The last of the summer berries in tarts."

"Sounds marvellous," Jemima said, her cheeks pink with delight.

I sat down to join them, partaking of the tarts and pouring the tea. I looked at the two expectant mothers and felt compelled to write about my own experiences. I wanted my family to understand me, to know my secrets, all of them.

When afternoon was over, I went straight up to my room to continue work on my memoir.

# CHAPTER 5

**C**alcutta, *1840*

Two months after Queen Victoria married Prince Albert, we departed for India. We left behind a country full of hope for the might of the British Empire. The journey was long, through cool climes and hot. We skirted the coast of Spain, kissed the top of Africa, crossed the Equator near Cape Verde and thence sailed down into the cool of the Cape of Good Hope. South Africa was in the throes of winter when we stopped at the cape and traversed its waters, passing from the Atlantic to the Indian Ocean. The temperature grew warm again as we travelled north-east. What with the seasickness, keeping a baby entertained, listening to

Charles' complaints and missing my parents terribly, the journey was almost intolerable.

Charles spent most of his time on the deck with the other men. In my cabin on the poop deck, I was within reach of the cuddy where the food was served. I had a cot, a couch, a small table and my washstand secured to the wall. During heavy seas, we did not get swamped with water, but it was always noisy. People worked above the cabin and the chicken pen was just outside. All day and night there were men calling out, the sound of rope scraping along the deck, and people stomping about. Eventually I grew quite inured to it.

It was hard to launder clothing on the ship, and sometimes when we called at port for water and supplies. Generally, I did not go ashore as we were in port for such a short time and there were people bustling around, unloading, loading and nothing much for a woman to do. When I did disembark, there had not been enough time to have our clothing laundered. The only thing I managed was to slip letters into the post bag that went ashore. On the journey, I wrote to my parents, my sisters and a few friends. Luckily, I had heeded all available advice and brought many changes of linens, made with cheap muslin, as well as thinner dresses to endure the hot weather and flannel for layers when it was cold. The journey took one hundred and five days, and we arrived in Calcutta at the end of August 1840. The air was thick with humidity, for the monsoon— the rainy season— held sway.

Calcutta was a shock. I was immediately hit by the smell, and I could hardly believe the mud and the great number of people flocking around the docks. I own that I employed a handkerchief over my nose, for at first the reek near made me faint.

Calcutta sits on the Hooghly River, so as well as docks there were markets, and tanneries, and effluent everywhere. Uniformed British soldiers, native porters and food hawkers abounded. While it was a relief to be off the ship, I felt overwhelmed by the chaos at first.

Fort William dominated the banks of the river and wooden sailboats peppered the waterway. Cows walked amongst the people in the Esplanade parklands. Everything was new to me, and despite the stench, the noise and the ceaseless activity, I found it interesting. The rain soaked everything, however, so I was keen to have a roof over my head.

Thankfully, we had a suite at a hotel that was quite within our means. Our meals were included in the monthly fee, and servants too. Yet there was no escaping the heat. I quickly learned what 'monsoon' meant. It was hot and humid before the monsoon rains began and my skin felt coated in oil. All I could manage was to stay as still as possible. When the monsoon arrived, it was wet as well as hot. I had never seen anything like it before nor have I since. On our first night in our hotel, the rain fell so hard that the noise kept me awake. The breeze drummed up by the rain provided relief from the humidity, yet everything felt wet almost all the time: my skin, my clothes, the bed linens. Little James fretted, and both of us had a painful red rash, which I believe was called prickly heat. It was the most dreadful affliction, like thousands of needles sticking into your flesh. The barest touch hurt us.

Meanwhile, that first night while I lay there unable to sleep, Charles drank with some other young men in the hotel's main room and was gone by morning, out into the muddy streets, leaving me to adjust to my new home alone. After the voyage and his now habitual neglect, I was quite resigned to this fate.

At the start of the following week, Charles commenced his new job, and I tried to make the best of our situation in the hotel. The servants did not speak much English and there were many miscommunications. They called me "memsahib" and that drove me to distraction. It seemed like an insult to me. I would rather have been called "ma'am" or "Mrs Leighton" than a word that seemed to aggrandise me and disparage me at the same time. However, they were kind, and they loved James. My favourite was the woman who helped me with him. She doted on him as if he were a prince, and he lapped up her attention. In the short time we were there, James thrived despite the heat and the rash, and I delighted in playing with him and teaching him to walk and kick a ball.

The food was not something I took to at first; it was all spicy and full of pulses that disagreed with my digestion. However, we were not starving. We stayed in the hotel, as houses were difficult to find in Calcutta and, in any case, expensive to rent. We were in no position to purchase one, either. The hotel served our budget well enough and afforded me some companionship, as there were other families living there. Mrs Evie Turner was the person I took to most. Some of the others were a bit rough around the edges, to put it politely—dressed in a slovenly fashion, often intoxicated, their language and accents not refined.

Mrs Turner liked to stitch, so we sat in the afternoons drinking tea and embroidering. She had arrived some three months before us and filled me in on what was in store for me. She introduced me to a lovely network of women who organised social events, card clubs and so on.

Some of the British people were downright nasty about Calcutta, the food, the Indians, the servants and each other. The constant talk was about their "native" servants. Some had nearly thirty in their employ due to issues with their different religions. There were Hindus, Muslims, Christians and others. The Hindus would not touch beef. The Muslims stopped to pray during the day and would not touch pork. Due to castes some servants would only do certain chores and not others. While I found this confusing, it also fascinated me. All these people living so close, so different in their beliefs and culture, and then more so because they were different to mine. Previously I had not understood that the world was not all white and Christian. Sadly, I realised that I had a narrow view of the world and that it was time I opened my mind, listened with my heart and tried to understand those things that were new to me. Some amongst the group of women were enlightened and made astute observations about India and Britain's role, but sadly I was not in Calcutta long enough to deepen my acquaintance with them.

Not even a month had passed when it became apparent that Charles did not take to the work. Soon after, I learned that the work did not take to him, either.

"I have been singled out for a special honour," he told me one evening before he was heading out to spend time with his friends. Needless to say, we hardly socialised together.

"What honour is that?" I asked.

"I am being transferred to a new settlement. A place called Singapore."

"Singapore? Where is that?"

"It's further east. Closer to China than England. Rumoured to be untamed and wild and as hot as Hades."

"That sounds most disagreeable. Should I not return to England with James? The climate here is intolerable as it is and James would thrive better at home. I could wait for you there." There was a moment of hope when I thought I might free myself from him and return home to my parents. No one would think it objectionable that I had not found India to my taste and did not want to undertake further travels.

He turned to me then, his mouth so tight and angry, I drew back. "Go back to England without me? Absolutely not. I will not have you embarrassing me by returning to your parents' house, making it look as if I cannot support my family."

Thinking quickly, I responded, "I only meant for a holiday. You might not like Singapore and then you could come back, too. We could find something else. A small cottage in the country, a simple lifestyle."

He stood up. "No. We go to Singapore as a family. No more discussion."

Afterwards I found out in a letter from an acquaintance that Charles' performance as a clerk had not been exemplary, and he had gambled with the soldiers stationed in Calcutta. I understood by then that Charles was not a man of his word. Father would have been appalled. However, without funds and Charles' permission I could not return home, despite him not living up to his promises to my father and to me.

One day not too long before I left, instead of going to play cards, I used a break in the relentlessly wet weather to go to the market and explore the growing town. The smells were a mixture of sewage and spices, human industry and incense. It was difficult to see such poverty but also interesting to see the temples. One man, a priest of some kind, gestured to me. "I tell your future, Miss?"

"Mrs, actually." Not really paying attention, I was going to keep walking, yet the effigies sculpted onto the temple behind the man caught my eye.

He came closer. "I know you are special, have special power inside."

I sighed, as it was not a very original sales pitch. But as I was enjoying my adventure, I decided to go along with it. "How much?"

He tilted his head again in that Indian way. "Two pence."

I felt around in my pocket. For some reason I could not explain, I did not care if this man, this priest, perhaps a Brahmin, told me lies. At least with my coins, he could buy some food and not go hungry for a day or two, and I could escape my current problems and indulge in the fantasy he wove.

He took me to the side of the temple entrance, and someone brought me a flimsy chair to sit on. The priest burned incense and chanted, seeming to go into a trance, and the sounds of the market fell away, as if someone had muffled the outside world.

"You come from cold place," he began.

Being white I was obviously from Britain, where, compared to this crushing heat, it was cold. "But your heart is not cold. One day you will find a fire in your heart, love for a man who is very different from you."

"What?" I struggled to make sense of this, telling myself that it was just common nonsense that could be told to anyone with a spare coin or two.

"But you will love others, too, bring them to your breast to cherish, and you will protect them with your inner light."

I clasped my fingers together, caught between outrage and intrigue. I should not have listened to his talk. I readied myself to leave, not caring if I gave offence, when his next words stilled me.

"You have a son. He is everything to you. But you must learn to live without your everything."

I met his eye, and he stared at me, looked into me, and my heart thumped and my breath grew short. "Is he going to die?" That got me. He got me.

His voice grew quiet. "No, not soon. Only when it is his time."

With a heave of breath, I calmed myself. This was just fancy talk to bamboozle English folk. Why was I even listening to this tripe?

"You have special gift. I can see it there within your spirit. You do not know how to touch it. You were born with this gift. The gift is in your family."

"No. I have nothing special inside of me." Anger grew in my breast. Life had proved that there was little that was remarkable about me. I was trapped in a loveless marriage where all my husband wanted was money. Now that mine was exhausted, I felt surplus to requirements, except I had a son to care for.

He tilted his head from side to side, but slowly. "You think that, but I see it."

Suddenly uncomfortable, I rose. The sound of the market intruded again as if I had broken the bubble of quiet the priest had created. "Thank you. I think I have heard enough." I handed over my coins, even gave him a little extra, and headed back to our hotel.

Despite knowing that it was all a tale made up to glean money from foreigners, some of the priest's words haunted me. I kept thinking that the cold place was in my heart. James was my only light. For my husband I felt nothing, not even tolerance, and I found I was always bracing myself for the next misfortune. Charles was not physically violent towards me. His ways were much more subtle than that. He had taken to criticising me at every opportunity, withholding affection and kind words, restricting the housekeeping money, and saying things about me to James that were unkind and untrue. "Your mother thinks you are stupid, James. You mother thinks you are ugly. Mother is always angry at Papa." Despite all of this, I never spoke ill of his father to James. He was still too young to understand any of this, but he would learn soon enough.

As part of our preparations for our journey to Singapore, I had to sell most of my jewellery to pay what I could of Charles' debts. All that was left was my wedding ring and a thin gold chain with an amber cross, which had been my mother's. At Charles' insistence, I dispatched a letter to my father. "See what funds you can get from them. If they love you, they will help us."

Too angry to speak, I inclined my head and took a seat at the table to write. While I informed my parents of our transfer to Singapore, I did not mention the debts or Charles' further request for funds to be dispatched. My parents were getting older. Father's health was not good. Mother had written of a stroke of the heart, and I could not add to their burden by mentioning my circumstances or, more importantly, my husband's. Just thinking that I would not see them again brought me to tears. Instead, I filled my letter with hope and news of James. I told them how excited I was to travel to Singapore and what a good thing it had been that Charles had got a job at the East India Company.

Again, the journey aboard the clipper was not a comfortable one for me, but at least it was relatively short. Charles was so angry all the time. He spent most of his time on the deck, even sleeping there, and he would not speak to me, as if I were the one who had lost all our money, as if it were my fault we did not have enough left to pay our debts. With James nestled beside me, we travelled across the water to this newer outpost, even further away from my home and my family. How I wished we were going in the other direction so I could see my ailing father and my ageing mother once more. I dreamed that I was heading there and that I would see my treasured sisters' countenances again. In my dream I heard Charity chatting merrily to her husband, and when I came to Faith, I saw her praying with her husband. I saw my mother walking down the hall, candle in hand, sadness in her expression. She was stooped and walked slowly.

"Mama!" I called out.

"Prudence?" my mother said. "Is that you?" Then, as if realising I was not there, she shook her head and kept shuffling down the hall.

It was so real I could almost smell the damp from the English rain. When I woke, I was disoriented, as if I had really been back home and not on that rocking vessel. Misery enveloped me and I gave way to tears and wished that my life had gone differently.

As I gazed at my son, though, I could not regret him. He was as the charlatan priest had said: my everything. Without him, my life would not be worth living. Picturing myself alone with Charles, trying to exist with him without our child, was a nightmare. If not for James I would have left him, and if my family had turned their backs on me, so be it, I would have worked for a living. When I thought of my husband, I was sad. How could a man who started out with so much potential waste it? If only he could have controlled his gambling, he could have made something of himself. He was intelligent. It was as if he cared for no one but himself.

At my lowest moment, I thought I could see clearly that I had been a mere means to an end. Charles had never had any real affection for me. Now his indifference and that lack of love and affection was killing me inside, chilling my heart, and the only warmth I had was for James.

The words before my eyes blurred and I allowed myself the indulgence of tears. I had never really mourned the lost opportunities of my life. It was hard to imagine what my life could have been like without Charles Leighton in it. But what was done was done; I could not allow recriminations. I put up my pen, exhausted, and went to bed.

# CHAPTER 6

"Sir Giles has been absent from our table for a few days, Aunt. Has there been a grisly murder in the neighbourhood for him to investigate?" Fulton asked.

We were all at table for dinner.

"Pass the potatoes, please," Jemima said to me.

I flicked Fulton a quick look and then handed up the requested dish. "I cannot tell you. I am not the man's keeper."

"Did he not visit the other morning, early?" Jemima said as she cut into a potato. That young woman was always sniffing out gossip. She'd probably found out from the footman.

"Yes, we had a quick stroll through the garden."

"He did not stay for breakfast?" Edward asked. "He usually eats whatever meal is being served. Very unlike him to take himself off without being fed."

Rolling my eyes was natural in response to this comment. Edward focussed on the most mundane things. "He does not eat here *all* the time, Edward. You exaggerate. I believe he had business elsewhere."

Milly's eyes shone. "Did he leave any messages for us?" Milly had grown fond of Sir Giles and he had always behaved nicely to her.

My expression hardened. My own dear Milly was trying to trick me into revealing something personal. What they suspected, I did not know. Surely Sir Giles' proposal was as far from their minds as it had been from mine. "The usual," I replied lightly. "He hopes you and Jemima are well and sends his best wishes to all."

I didn't know when it had become easy to lie. The family continued their meal and the conversation turned to more trivial matters such as what to do with the excess number of squashes in the garden and whether it was prudent to donate some to the poor. This appeared to be the consensus, so Milly wrote a note to the housekeeper with instructions. As the Harry started to clear our dishes, the other footman, John, came in with a letter on a tray and presented it to me. He then presented a small parcel to Jemima. The envelope was addressed to me in Sir Giles' elegant hand. My cheeks warmed as I picked it up. I dared not look at my audience as I opened it.

Dear Prudence

I send this note to advise your household that I will be absent from Kiddlington for a number of weeks. Please do not concern yourself with my wellbeing. I have some business to attend to in London and hope to see you all again soon. May I take some inspiration from the Bard and say:

Shall I compare thee to a summer's day?

Though art more lovely and more temperate.

Your affectionate friend,

Giles Seaforth-Black

Jemima's gaze locked onto mine after I had read the note through. My cheeks grew heated at the words from the sonnet. Surprised, too, for I had never taken Sir Giles for that kind of thing. I was flattered as well because I couldn't recall ever being sent lines of poetry before. After clearing my throat, I advised them of the contents meant for them.

The men left the table, acknowledging the tidings from Sir Giles before they went away. Milly stood up. "I hoped it was a love letter," she said. I fixed Milly with a glare and she backed away to the door. "I have something to attend to just now."

Jemima giggled and my quelling look did nothing to discourage her.

"Have you upset him, Aunt? Driven him from our table?" Jemima's eyebrows were climbing in query or amusement, I did not know.

"Impertinent girl!" If I could have reached, I would have nudged her foot with mine.

Jemima smiled. "I have touched a nerve, have I not? All that flirting has finally caught up with you."

My fists clenched on the tabletop and I tried not to rise to the bait. It was so close to the truth, I could have died of embarrassment. As it was, I held it together. "He has business in town, which is nothing to do with me. As he converses with me most often, it is only natural that he correspond with me to put our minds at rest. Fulton was just remarking on his absence."

Jemima played with the small parcel.

"What is it that you have there?"

Jemima peered at the box, which was just bigger than a hand. "I do not know." She peered at it. "It looks to have been redirected from Willow Park, for that is Mrs Eddington's handwriting."

The housekeeper had sense at least. "Well, are you not keen to see what it is?"

As well as being curious, I wanted to turn Jemima's mind away from my personal life.

Jemima undid the string and the paper and unwrapped it. "Oh, how darling. It's a silver rattle for the baby. I wonder who sent it." She reached in and picked it up, giving it a little shake. At the same time, I stood up from my seat, for I sensed something terribly wrong. "Jemima!"

My stomach churned and my feet felt like lead. Looking at the child's toy made me quite bilious. However, my warning was too late. There was a zap, a smell of sulphur, and Jemima froze. "Jemima?" Her expression blanked, as if she was caught in a moment between breaths. She didn't respond. Then she began to tremble, fell back in the chair and slid off to the floor.

I raced to the door. "Edward! Edward!" I called in a panic. "Come quickly!"

Jemima appeared to be having a seizure, the rattle caught in her clenched fingers. As she was not prone to such attacks, I guessed that it was the silver toy in her hand. I reached out to touch her, and as I did, a vibration ran through me. Whatever was in that rattle was coming through to me.

"Let it go, Jemima!" I urged. Either she didn't hear me or couldn't heed me.

Edward rushed through the door. "Jemima!"

He stopped and stared as I quickly filled him in on what had happened. Edward waved his fingers, chanted and then plucked the rattle from Jemima's hand, dropping it as if burned. However, Jemima stayed as she was.

Just then Mr White walked in and issued a caution. "Be careful."

Edward stepped back to give Mr White some room. Mr White rubbed his chin and then studied the rattle now lying on the floor. My eyes narrowed. Had he already been in the house or had he just arrived?

Jemima was pale now, nearly lifeless. "What is wrong with her?"

Mr White acknowledged me with a nod. "I know this work. It is not a fatal hex. Just a nasty nip."

Edward's neck grew red. "Nip? This is my wife and child."

Mr White waved his hands, an intricate pattern like lace. Jemima sucked in a breath and blinked.

Edward inclined his head. "I see how you did that. Interesting."

"Edward?" Jemima said, struggling to sit up. "Why am I on the floor?" And she peered at us all. "Why are you all gathered around me? Uncle Ferdy? What do you do here?"

Mr White leaned down and helped Edward place Jemima on the chair. "You were hexed. One designed specifically for you."

Then he scooped up the magical item and placed it back in its packaging.

My understanding of hexes was rudimentary. I was not a magician like my nephew but I knew they were bad and that they could do different things. "The baby?"

Edward put his hand on the front of Jemima's gown and closed his eyes. "The baby is unaffected. It is moving around and kicking."

Edward went to inspect the package and the rattle, moving them with the end of a pencil drawn from his inside coat pocket.

Mr White began to speak. "I did not think that they would go this far, dare so much. I told you, Edward, that there are some who are jealous of Jemima's power. They are outraged that a woman could have such a vast store and not deserve it. Their thoughts, not mine."

"Are they the ones you warned me about?" Edward asked.

"These are but troublesome youths. I will deal with them. The others are far more dangerous. They would not stoop to a prank. This was vicious but not deadly, as Jemima is too strong."

"How do you feel?" Edward asked Jemima.

"Like someone thumped me. What happened? Aunt Prudence did not plant me a facer, did she?"

I scoffed.

Edward took her hand. "The rattle had a hex on it."

"I was hexed? But who would...ah."

Edward nodded. 'The rogue members of the brotherhood."

Jemima looked at me and then so did Mr White.

"What is it?" I asked, suddenly very uncomfortable.

"Aunt Prudence, I swear you have a kind of halo around your body, like a light." Jemima narrowed her gaze.

Mr White lowered his eyebrows. "Interesting. Tell me, Mrs Wainwright. Do you have any particular talents? Like talking to the dead?"

A gasp escaped me. I considered lying, but I was curious that they could see something, something that I was not conscious of doing. "On occasion. Also, the living."

Jemima frowned. "Living?"

"Oh, people who are living but are not present in my vicinity. However, it is not a reliable talent, so I would not even think to mention it."

Mr White studied me further and I began to fidget.

"You can speak to dead people? Like a medium?" Jemima grinned.

I rolled my eyes. "I am no circus freak. I do not hold seances and the like. I have very rarely had conversations with people who are no longer alive."

"Most interesting. A relative of Wilbur's, you say?"

"Yes, as it happens."

"I see. I will have to keep an eye on you." Mr White returned his attention to Edward. "I think perhaps, with Mr Fulton's permission, you should set some wards. If a few envious young magicians can deliver a hex, then you are not safe."

"I will start straight away."

"Good. And I must leave you. Jemima, Mrs Wainwright, I will take my leave."

Edward turned to me. "May I leave her in your care, Aunt Prudence?"

I had been mulling Mr White's comments and then focused on my nephew.

"Of course, I will watch over her." Mr White left the room and Edward followed soon after.

"Watch over me?" Jemima said, scorn in her voice. "I want to grab those magicians by the throat and wring their necks. Attacking a woman with child?"

She made to get up as if she was going to tear out of the room and go after them.

"Jemima, love, there is nothing you can do at present, is there? Your time is close now."

Jemima sat back on the settee, wrestling her distended abdomen. "You are right. No point going on the attack now. It must be defence that we turn our mind to. Edward is setting up a perimeter with wards and they are very effective. I shall turn my mind to giving birth."

Milly entered the room and came forward with arms outstretched to clasp Jemima's hand. "Edward said there had been an attack. Are you all right?"

Jemima threw up a smile. "Yes, fine now. Just do not touch that silver rattle. It was meant for me so I do not think it can harm you. We should let Edward deal with it."

"Indeed," I said. "Perhaps you and Milly could go into the drawing room and read and sew."

Milly took Jemima's hand as if she was going to escort her. Jemima stood, at first a bit unsteady, and then took a step. "I could do with stretching out on the settee and napping and reading. Will you join us, Aunt?"

Jemima was much more herself.

"That is a very kind invitation. But I feel I must work on my memoir just now."

Jemima grinned. "Indeed, you must. I cannot wait to read it."

"How is the work going, Aunt?" Milly asked. "Will you talk about my mother and father?"

"I will, of course."

They left the room, seeming at ease, and I was left to my own devices.

Afterwards, I was back at my desk writing furiously. With every thread I pulled, the weave of my story became looser. I knew the unravelling could not be stopped.

*ingapore, November 1840*

Singapore was as hot as Hades, just as Charles had said, and humid to boot. To make life interesting, it had two monsoon seasons, and we arrived before the north-east monsoon, which accounted for the humidity—that, and the fact the island was close to the Equator. Calcutta would have been cooler in the winter than Singapore ever could be.

I must have fainted three times before we were installed in our accommodation. We had a room at a lodging house that was set aside for employees of the company. Housing was in short supply, but we were eventually to move to a little bungalow, so it was only to be temporary.

Overheated, squashed into a single room with our travelling chests, a toddler and an indifferent husband, I was so depressed I did not get up from my bed the first few days. With a small advance on Charles' salary, my husband had to find a Malay girl to help with James. For a time, I was quite ill. Some said it was the malaria or some other tropical illness. Even when I was on the mend, the heat prevented sleep, and I spent my days in my nightgown by the window, hoping for a breeze.

Singapore had a mix of peoples: some Indians, Chinese, Malay and a small number of white people. It was full of bustle and commerce. Our Malay girl, Dewi, cooked for me, but I could not stomach the spices. In the end we determined that besides plain boiled eggs, I could eat rice and steamed vegetables and the exotic fruits available in the market. Bit by bit, I pulled myself together, ashamed of my surrender to despair. This was my life, and I had made all the decisions that had brought me here. There was no one else to blame.

By the time I had recovered, Charles was absenting himself for days at a time, so it was just James, me and Dewi. This continued for about six weeks, and I kept my peace. When Charles did return to change his clothes, I did not yell or cry and I tried not to argue. However, angry words were very much on my lips when he came home one day reeking of smoke and drink.

"Give me that amber cross you wear," he demanded.

My hand went to my last piece of jewellery, besides my wedding ring. "But why? Have you not been paid?" The truth slumbered there. I had a strong suspicion he had been gambling again, and I was to suffer the consequences.

"Don't ask daft questions. Just give it to me. Oh—and I have a treat in store for you."

With tears pouring down my cheeks, I undid the necklace and

handed it over. It was worth little but, having been my mother's, it meant much to me. "A treat?" I asked glumly.

"Yes, you have been invited for tea tomorrow, at the Resident's House. His wife wishes to meet you." The Resident was the title of the chief administrator of the British East India Company in Singapore.

"He has a wife? But we are not acquainted." Being so ill since my arrival, I had met no one.

He tapped his chest. "I am acquainted, and that is sufficient to garner you an invitation. Perhaps then you can stop lying around here moaning about the heat."

"It is extremely hot, though, you must own," I objected.

"You get used to it. I have."

"I wish it would be so." Already I was thinking about my wardrobe and what might suit such a gathering and not overheat me too much.

He left soon after, not before taking up young James and swinging him around to make him squeal and laugh. While Charles had been generally indifferent to me, he had been increasingly involving himself with James. Playing with him and even feeding him while I was too sick.

I had no way of knowing that what came next would change the course of my life and wound my heart immeasurably.

To prepare for my morning tea invitation, I set about choosing my outfit. I absolutely could not wear a petticoat, but I was able to take a light summer dress I owned and add a layer to the hem to give the appearance of a petticoat. Then I fashioned a roll of fabric around my hips to fill out my skirts. I hoped this was enough to pass myself off as decently dressed. My corset was hard to do up as I had lost so much weight since leaving England, and even more since my illness. My breasts had shrunk to almost nothing and my arms were like sticks. However, I managed. Charles' "treat" extended to ordering me a carriage, and I had a few coins in my pocket as I set off.

After my illness, my nose seemed even more sensitive to the stench in the streets, which near overwhelmed me as we went. A handkerchief over my nose did little to keep it out. This was the first time I had properly left our lodgings since my arrival. Street hawkers called out their wares and strong, spice-filled aromas lay like a miasma over everything. Rows of shophouses huddled together, with crowds of people buying and selling under verandas. I had heard there were gangs roaming the streets and crime was rampant. How the East India Company coped with this I did not know.

Mrs Church's bungalow was situated amongst others of a similar style near Fort Canning. When I was admitted, I saw that there were other ladies in attendance. I quailed. The opportunity to socialise had been thrust upon me and I did not feel up to the task.

"Is not this place vile?" said one of the ladies, wife to one of the clerks, who came up, took me by the arm and led me inside. "How are you bearing up?"

"The heat is certainly challenging," I agreed.

"You came out from India, did not you? Surely you were used to it there."

"We were not long in Calcutta before my husband was assigned here," I replied. "It was humid and wet, being monsoon season. I believe, though, that one can escape the heat in the hills. I was not so fortunate."

"Are you coming to watch the cricket on Sunday? It is where everyone gathers and is a place to socialise. It is nice to have some society."

With a flick of my fan, I responded, "I would love to, of course. Some horrible illness has kept me at home until now." My interlocutor stepped back as if wary of me being contagious.

Another lady sauntered up, smile plastered onto her face. "So, you are the elusive Mrs Leighton. I have been dying to meet you. Your husband is all the rage in the officers' mess. A mean hand at cards, my husband tells me," she said. My stomach dropped. It seemed my suspicions about Charles' return to gambling had been correct.

"I know nothing of such things," I replied, hoping to stifle the topic. I offered up a smile, but the woman seemed disappointed with my response and turned away.

A quick survey of the room and I felt out of my depth. The women were nice enough, and I heard there were social activities that the wives organised to keep up a middling social congress. Yet all I could think about was that I was here in Singapore with limited funds and was dependent on a man who had proven to be most unreliable. There was another half-written letter to my parents in our accommodation, full of lies about happiness and largesse. How could I wound them with the truth?

Oddly, Mrs Church did not come over to greet me. Indeed, she barely spoke to me, although in fairness she was much occupied. I began to wonder if I had been invited after all and began to suspect that Charles had sent me here to humiliate me. At least some of the other ladies were not indifferent to me. I was particularly gratified when a lovely lady with dark hair and a modish gown came to sit by me. Her name was Mrs Dent, and she said she had come from Newcastle. Her accent was detectable, even though I was sure she had been privately schooled in elocution. "Do you sew, Mrs Leighton?" she asked me.

With a smile I responded, "Indeed, I do. It is my delight. However, I have been ill since we arrived here and have hardly set a stitch, except for the most urgent mending."

"You are feeling better now, I hope," Mrs Dent said in a tender voice. I felt she was sincere in her well wishes.

"Thank you. Indeed, I am much improved. This invitation to tea which Mrs Church has extended is most welcome." Mrs Church must have heard her name mentioned, as she turned and inclined her head in acknowledgement. I continued, "I have met all of you, which is delightful. Alas, I have been so secluded I would not have thought there was another lady about."

Mrs Dent sipped her tea and then lowered her cup. "There are not many of us, but we have some decent society here."

Mrs Dent was excellent company, and she kept by me for the rest of the afternoon, which I most appreciated. "We must meet sometime and sew together," Mrs Dent said.

"That is kind of you. I am afraid that our accommodation is very incommodious at present. We are waiting on a bungalow."

Mrs Dent chuckled. "No bother. I shall invite you to my bungalow. I wish to show you some lovely silk that I bought at a terribly good price."

"That is most generous. I would love to see your new fabrics."

We continued to discuss haberdashery, and I found myself feeling a little brighter. Then our host invited us all to tour her garden. While we walked about the abundant ferns and flowers, we received a lecture about life in Singapore, including how everything centred around the smooth passage of commerce, how the British Empire was at its height and growing, and how much money was to be had.

Money. I hardly needed a reminder about how important that was. My heart sank every time I thought about Charles gambling again. It seemed no matter how bad things got, he would never learn. He was heedless and reckless, and I despaired of him.

When I took my leave, the Churches' manservant summoned a carriage for me. As I took the bumpy ride back to our accommodation, I ruminated over my predicament. I was pleased that there was pleasant society here for me. I truly liked Mrs Dent, and some of the other women were delightful, too. I could live here, I thought to myself, now that I was well. But Charles' gambling habits were a big problem, and, I was sure, would continue to be. The spectre of disgrace, due to my husband's debts and dissolute ways, loomed large. How was I to navigate this strange life of mine in tropical Singapore? I was on the precipice of both potential happiness and complete and utter misery.

As I alighted from the carriage at our accommodation, I was

met by the landlord. He seemed neither Indian nor Chinese but a mix of the two, and his tanned complexion and accent were not British. "Mrs Leighton?"

"Yes, sir. Is there a problem?"

He bowed. "I am afraid there is the matter of the unpaid rent."

"My husband—"

"Has vacated your room, madam."

"What?" I was at a loss. "Do you mean he has taken our son out?"

The landlord shook his head. "After you departed this morning, Mr Leighton and your small boy left. He dismissed the maid and sent her away in tears. A carriage came to collect him, and some of your possessions were loaded onto it. Mr Leighton said he was due at the port."

"No, that cannot be possible. He works for the company."

"Be that as it may, Mrs Leighton. Your husband deposited your travelling chest as security and said that you had the means to defray the debt."

My heart was beating so fast I nearly keeled over. "I am sorry, but I do not understand you. You say my husband and child have left this accommodation—left Singapore?"

"Yes, he said that he was booked on a ship that left on the morning tide. There is the matter of your rent."

A faintness came over me. My vision went black and as I descended to the floor, a hand guided me to a chair. A glass of tepid water was put to my lips. "Mrs Leighton?"

I took a sip and opened my eyes. The landlord looked concerned. "You have been unwell, I know, Mrs Leighton. I take it you did not know that your husband was leaving?"

"No. I do not know what to do."

"You have the money to pay your bill?"

I blinked and looked up at him. "I have no money. I cannot pay the bill. Perhaps the company...?"

The landlord shook his head. "While we prioritise company

employees for our rooms, there has been no payment from the company. When I spoke to Mr Leighton about that, he said that he would cover the rent."

My mouth flapped open as I tried to think. "What shall I do?"

"You cannot stay here. Your room has been let. Perhaps seek help from your friends and return when you have the money to pay what you owe."

"But my things, my clothes..."

He shook his head. "I am sorry, but they must stay here as surety."

Surging out of my seat, I tried to push past him further into the house, but he was strong, and he turned me towards the door. "Leave now. Do not make a scene."

There was nothing for me to do but walk to the port and find my husband. I had a few coins so I hailed a cart. However, at the docks, which were chaotic to say the least, locating him proved impossible. Eventually I found a clerk who informed me that two ships had departed that morning: one bound for Australia and the other China. He could not tell me which ship my husband and son had boarded, as their names were on the manifest of neither.

Disbelief and shock kept me searching. Surely Charles, useless as he was, had not abandoned me and stolen my child? Yet, as the sun set, I was left in no doubt. He had indeed abandoned me in Singapore, with little more than a few pennies to my name, and no clothes or possessions of any kind other than those on my back.

I stared at the words I had written, tears blurring the words. Emotions I had not felt in years had built up inside of me. Unshed tears came out in huge sobs. My son, my everything, had been taken from me then. There had been no time to truly mourn what I had lost. Despair had driven me to a dangerous place, and it had taken all my strength merely to survive.

# CHAPTER 8

Yesterday, Edward had set the wards around the house. Wards were not explained to me, but I understand they were to prevent uninvited guests, most particularly intruders. After the hexed rattle, it was a relief to go to sleep without worry. The morning passed off with the usual routine. Once again, I was in the drawing room with Milly and Jemima, enjoying some time together in a leisurely fashion.

"Surely pregnancy was devised by a man," Jemima said as she turned again on the settee, trying to find a comfortable position.

"Why do you say that?" Milly asked as she sat at the table, sewing.

"Because it is impractical, uncomfortable and, by all accounts, the birth itself is painful. In addition, men must bear none of it! If a woman thought this up, she would have arranged things better."

As I was sitting at the table too, I could not help but comment. "Surely you are arguing that God is a man, or male, because it was he that invented pregnancy."

Jemima glared at me. "Your argument is flawed. There is no proof that God invented anything."

Milly gasped. "Jemima, you must not say such things. People believe very strongly. Society would not approve."

Milly's father had been a vicar, and her mother, Faith, had been pious as well. Milly herself had been raised by me, and of course we attended church in our small village, but religion hadn't featured very heavily in our lives. For me it was more about being involved in the community, rather than faith. Despite this, Milly had a soft spot for the church and Godliness, perhaps feeling it brought her closer to her absent parents, and so she was truly alarmed by Jemima's comments.

With a sigh, Jemima surged to her feet and waddled across the room. Turning to face us, she tapped her chest. "I have faced death. I walked through fire. It hurt a lot, but I survived. I do not think that was part of God's plan, if there is a God. But sure as hell this pregnancy thing is someone's idea of torture."

Milly put down her needlework. "I said you would yell just as much as me when the time came. However, we are not giving birth yet, and already you have a mountain of complaints."

"It is because I look and feel like a mountain! Besides, the baby is kicking me in the ribs and it is extremely tiresome, and I wish it would stop. However, I realise that making it stop involves pushing it out, and that is the part that has taken up a lot of my thoughts."

"How would you make it better?" I asked, amused at the turn of Jemima's mind.

Jemima glanced my way, a smile playing about her lips. "Well, firstly, I would make it so men would have babies. Or, like a marsupial, the mother could give birth to a tiny baby and then it moves to a pouch to grow. This makes giving birth a minor affair, with limited pain and discomfort."

"Who would have the pouch?" Milly asked, and I could see by the quiver of her lips that she was suppressing laughter.

"The father, of course."

"Have you been reading Darwin again?" Milly asked with a knowing air.

As I had read Darwin myself, I kept quiet about it. God forbid that Jemima acquire the notion that I was a science-reading bluestocking. There would never be an end to it.

A groan escaped Jemima as she took a turn around the room. "There it is again," she said.

Milly sat up straight, eyes on Jemima. "Are you starting?"

Jemima turned. "I cannot say. I had a twinge, but that is the least of my complaints. Would you mind if I rang for a jug of hot chocolate? And maybe shortbread?"

Milly stilled and frowned. Then, shaking herself, she replied, "I have to speak with the housekeeper so I will see to it. Apparently, the butcher had trouble delivering our order. Something to do with the wards. Edward was able to fix it. Such a terrible thing to attack an expectant mother."

Jemima frowned. "Very rude, indeed." Jemima ran her hands over her midsection. "Thank goodness the baby was not harmed. A peculiar sensation to be sure."

Milly shuddered. "I am glad I was not in the room. I fear I would have become hysterical." She walked to the door and paused. "Aunt, will you sit here with Jemima until I return?"

"Of course, my dear. I could do with some hot chocolate myself."

Jemima lifted a hand. "In that case, Milly, you best order two jugs. I intend to drink one on my own."

"Jemima! Are you sure you are not...you know..."

Jemima shrugged. "I am sure I want hot chocolate and shortbread. Do not let Edward know, for he will come and steal it all." She lifted a finger to her lips to make a "shush" gesture.

Milly's laugh tinkled as she left the room. Jemima and I eyed each other.

"Is there anything I can do for you, dear?" I asked.

"Not really. Except tell me it will be all right in the end."

Giving her the once-over, I sighed. "Jemima, you are the

likeliest of persons to have it all work out in the end. You are young, you are fit, you are...you."

Jemima had tears in her eyes. "Thank you, Aunt Prudence. Your confidence in me is inspiring. Shall we play some cards?"

"Of course, my dear." Jemima fetched the cards, and we played Concentration, a card-matching game. Her eye and hand were much quicker than mine and she beat me several times. I had to admit that my mind was engaged elsewhere.

We drank our hot chocolate and chatted to Milly. Jemima fidgeted and rubbed her belly. When Edward came in and was prepared to entertain Jemima, I made my way to my room to write some more. I was fairly certain Jemima was in the early stages of labour.

With my pen at the ready, and a small glass of port to hand, I bent to work, recalling that terrible night, alone on the streets of Singapore. The anger, the sadness all roiled within my breast. As I put the pen to paper, I tried to be objective and let my story flow.

### SINGAPORE, NOVEMBER 1840

I wandered the streets in a state of shock. Other than the women I had met that very morning, I had no acquaintances amongst the British in Singapore, and thus nowhere to seek shelter. There was the church, I supposed, but I was not quite desperate enough to seek poor support and ruin my reputation. So stupefied by despair was I that I could not think clearly that night. The port had been a dead end. My son was gone, to who knew where, torn from me by an unfeeling man.

Tears bathed my face. My emotions overwhelmed me as I stumbled to the edge of the river. A bridge stood before me, leading away from the part of town I was familiar with after my short sojourn. There were junks— wooden boats particular to this part of Asia— on the water. The swell smacked against their hulls and the voices of their occupants echoed in the dark night. Pots clanged as meals were cooked. A dank, watery smell filled the night, and something that had the odour of effluent wafted on the breeze.

I found myself wondering what it would be like to drop into the polluted river and sink below the surface. My love for James was too strong to ever do such a thing, but for the first time, I considered it. With no help to be had and misery in my heart, I crossed over the bridge to the edge of Chinatown, where warehouses and shophouses fringed the riverbank.

Often, I have wondered what I intended to do there. Find a dark doorway in which to sleep for the night, perhaps? Rational thinking was beyond me. Thoughts of the morrow were snatched away by grief and tears. All I wanted was to hug my son to my breast, touch the top of his head and kiss his dark curls.

On the far side of the river, I walked blindly. Vacant with loss and despair, I was out of my mind. It was like there was a huge blank wall in front of my eyes that I could not see past. A kind of stupor came over me. I gave no thought to the dangers I might face, and might not have cared in any case if they had come about.

In this unfamiliar part of the town, I soon found myself in a bad situation. There were many people in the streets, working, socialising, selling food. As a lone British woman, I stood out. Even though I ducked and weaved through the shadows cast by the hanging lanterns, and kept behind the columns of the shophouses, trying to be unobtrusive, I drew attention. My clothes were in disarray, I had lost my shawl, and my shoes were ruined by mud and filth. The more distressed I became, the more I ambled about as if intoxicated. It was only a matter of time before I garnered the wrong kind of interest.

People either shied away from me or stepped closer to stare right into my face. Some even tugged at the sleeves of my gown, but I ignored them. When the fabric eventually ripped, I took fright and surged ahead blindly, ducking into the first alley I came to. Surrounded by tall shophouses on both sides, I faced a dead end. Why I thought I could huddle there for the night, I did not know. In those days lawlessness reigned on the streets of Singapore— secret criminal societies, opium dens, prostitutes and other iniquities I could not name—so my only thought was to find some shelter.

Unable to bring myself to remain there in the dark, however, I turned to make my way out of the alley and found I was not alone.

Five men stood in my way, dressed as coolies in thin trousers and shirts, some with dark stains. Blood, I guessed. I doubted they were indentured labourers, with their fierce looks and menacing postures. Blocking my exit and sneering at me under their conical hats, even though the sun had set, it was clear they meant to do me harm. Thus disguised, they were safe from ever being identified. I doubted I would live to bear witness to anything they did to me.

As one they moved, surrounding me. Kicks and punches flew. I thought that I would die as the blows fell. I tried to duck and weave to avoid the blows, but I had never been attacked before and had no idea how to protect myself. When one was close to me, I instinctively pushed and shoved, screaming my terror. One man tilted to lift his leg and kicked me in the head in a smooth move that toppled me to the ground. "Stop, please," I cried brokenly as I tried to push myself into a sitting position. "I have no money."

Blood dripped from my nose and a split in my lip. Dazed, the world around me spun in a slow circle and darkness gathered at the edge of my vision. I could feel consciousness slipping away.

Beyond my heaving breaths and the sound of blood pumping in my ears, I heard another voice. My heart leapt with hope that someone had come to intervene. Yet, no one called for the men to stop, no one stood between me and my attackers. I crawled to my feet only to be felled again, a sweep of a leg dropping me to the ground once more. I heard chuckles and comments laced with scorn. The men's laughter at my plight wounded me as much as the physical punches. My hip hit the ground and my knee scraped. Pain shot at me from everywhere. Perhaps I hit my head, I did not know. But something within me told me not to give up. Determined, I used the wall to brace against as I dragged myself to my feet and faced my attackers.

In the blood haze, I saw there was indeed someone behind the men. He was dressed similarly to them, so I thought he was Chinese as well. He spoke gruffly to them, words I did not understand. My heart lifted at the thought of rescue, that somehow, I was worthy of a reprieve. However, my attackers ignored him.

Something inside me started to build. Was it not enough that I had suffered at the hands of my husband? That I'd been left alone in a strange country with no money and had my child, my delight, stolen from me? It was so wrong—so unfair. The feeling inside me grew warmer, and then red-hot, and with some surprise I realised it was rage. I had never been governed by my feelings before, but now I let them come forward, let them grow, and it was a great relief. Yet this feeling in me was strange, almost tangible, and to my amazement it grew into a light that was just outside of my body, right where my heart beat in my breast. The ball of light grew denser. It was pure, cleansing, and I was fascinated by the sight and feel of it. I had passed beyond being frightened and dwelled in a space that cocooned me. Was this me leaving my body? Was this me dying?

The men attacking me drew back and cried out in fright. The light hung there, pulsating, eager, still growing in size. Experimentally I pushed it out, and then I fell back, as though a cannon had been fired from within my body.

Darkness surrounded me. I waited for the men to come at me

again and finish the job, to send me to the death they intended. But it was quiet. There was no movement. My eyes fluttered open and I saw the men lying motionless in the alley before I passed out.

❦

THE FIRST THING I SENSED AFTER THAT WAS THAT THERE WAS A man squatting beside me, gently touching my arm. "Miss?" he said in accented English.

I tried to focus on him, at first in fright, and then I relaxed. It was the Chinese man who had tried to intervene. I wondered if he had dispersed the men and saved me.

"Can you move?" he asked.

"I think so."

Gently, he assisted me to sit up. I wept with relief and wiped the tears away with the handkerchief I had in my skirt pocket. I was sore all over, but I was alive when I'd thought I was going to die. How had this miracle occurred?

"We must move quickly," the man said. "Come. Their friends will be here soon. On your feet."

With a shake of my head, I tried to take in the scene. The men who'd attacked me lay in a circle around me. They were still unmoving. "What happened? Are they dead?" I felt hysteria rise in my chest. Who was this man that he could lay them out like that?

"No time to check. We must get you out of here."

The stranger was about my size, except thin and wiry. However, the hand he held out to me was strong as he assisted me to stand. Once I gained my feet, he steadied me as the world spun. There was fresh blood on my handkerchief. Dark smudges stained my bodice, and my skirts were torn. My hair had come out of its pins and hung loose around my shoulders. My face hurt as much as my ribs and my thighs.

The stranger looked me in the eye, exuding a calm I could only envy. "What your name, Miss? Can I walk home?"

108

Blood dripped from my nose afresh. I tried to stem it, but my handkerchief was already soaked. The man handed me a folded clean cloth, and I held it to my face. In the back of my mind, I wondered what that white light had been. Had it come from this man? Perhaps I had imagined it. The light had given me such a good feeling, but I could not explain it at all. "My name is Prudence," I replied softly. It was forward of me to offer my Christian name, but I was not going to use my married name. I had too much anger in me for that. "Thank you for helping me."

The skin around his eyes crinkled as he studied me. "So, this thing, this power, it is Prudential Light?"

My jaw fell open. "It's what?" I had not a clue what he meant, but slowly my mind began to work. My eyes fell on the unconscious men surrounding us. I remembered the light; I remember pushing something out. I had been so afraid. Could it have been me all along?

The man looked around quickly . Perhaps more people were coming to investigate. I had been screaming. He turned to me. "You need help. I take you home. Where you live?"

I could hardly speak. "Nowhere." I wanted to explain myself further but could not get the words out.

The man blinked at me. "Nowhere?"

"Yes."

He looked me up and down, and I could see he was puzzled. "How?"

My reserve vanished and all my woes came pouring out of me in an incoherent wash. I explained what had happened earlier that day, ending with, "My husband took all the money, and my baby, and I cannot return to our prior accommodation."

The man pulled back as if stunned. "Your child?"

"Yes. They left on a ship this morning, without my knowledge."

"Your home?"

I shook my head. "It has been re-let because I have no money. I do not even have my possessions."

The man stared at me as if he did not quite understand me or, perhaps, believe me. It was a relief to be rescued by someone who could speak some English, though. He had a strong accent, and his grammar was not perfect, but it was better than my non-existent Chinese.

He turned sideways and gestured back along the alley to the street. "Come, I get help. My name is Chen. Chen Yu Tang."

I nodded gratefully. Clutching his arm, I limped along beside him. Glancing sideways as discreetly as I could, I noticed he was handsome. He had rather large eyes and an interesting face, flatter than mine, with lightly tanned skin. I had not seen many Chinese men up close until now, but he looked different from the coolies and the men I'd seen working the docks hauling sacks.

I remember the heat and humidity felt like a blanket smothering me. Everything hurt when I moved, and blood trickled down my forehead. We hadn't gone far when Mr Chen unlocked the door to one of the shophouses that lined the street, lit a small lantern and helped me inside and up the stairs.

When we reached the room at the top, he pulled out a wooden chest, dusted it off and helped me to sit on it. "You safe here."

The room was full of boxes of different sizes. Downstairs was a shop, so I deduced that this must be where he stored his goods.

With his handkerchief pressed to my head wound to staunch the blood, I tried to calm my frantic heartbeat. My nose had started to bleed again, and I felt around the bridge to see if it was broken. Although it hurt, it was not too swollen. I had been lucky, for some of the blows to my face had made stars fly in my vision.

Mr Chen headed towards the stairs. "I go to get help. Make no sound. Do not answer door."

I nodded. "Thank you, Mr Chen."

"I must take light. I sorry." He bowed politely and was gone, taking the lantern with him. As the darkness and silence folded in around me, my tears flowed. I had never felt so lost and alone and miserable in my life. The loss of my money felt like a penance, but it was nothing to the gaping hole in my heart that was my lost child. I felt I would not survive the emotional and physical pain I endured in that moment. I knew then what it was to be utterly alone in the world.

It must have been about half an hour later when I heard a scratch at the door. I ceased whimpering and listened. Were those men coming after me again? I held my breath, my heart beating so hard I could barely hear the door open. Then a light appeared in the stairwell. I clutched my skirts, trying to stop the scream in my throat.

"Miss Prudence?" Mr Chen's voice echoed up the stairs. My name in his mouth sounded like "Miss Pludens". I let go of my skirts, though my hands still trembled.

"Yes, I am here."

The yellow glow from the little lantern grew larger as he entered the room, revealing the shadow-shrouded figure of Mr Chen and a second shape, smaller and thinner. "This is Mrs Li. She look after the sick."

The old lady addressed me, but I did not understand a word. She took the lantern and placed it on another tea chest situated near the door. She started gesturing to me.

"Mr Chen, I do not understand her," I said apologetically.

"She wants you to take off clothes so she can see injuries."

"Undress? But...I...er..."

Mr Chen bowed and disappeared into the dark recesses of the room. The sound of boxes and chests being dragged about filled the space. He returned a few minutes later with a robe. When he handed it to me, I could see it was made of the finest cotton, dyed a dark colour. "Thank you."

He bowed. "I have made a room for you. There is a bed. You can sleep after. Can you change into robe by self?"

I looked to the dark space. Mr Chen went to a shelf in the wall and came back with a candle, which he lit and handed to me. "Mrs Li will call when ready. She need me to speak her words."

He bowed to me and gave a deeper bow to Mrs Li before moving away. In the poor light, I shuffled to the room he had made for me. It was small, with a narrow camp bed set against the wall under a window. I began unbuttoning my dress and removed the padding that I had used to make the semblance of more petticoats. Mrs Li had followed me, speaking all the while in her language. The woman gestured to me, and it looked like she was telling me to turn around. This I did, and she unlaced my stays very efficiently. Next, she lifted my shift and I put my arms into the sleeves of the robe as I stepped out of my bloomers. I felt exposed with just the fine fabric between me and the rest of the world. However, as it was oppressively hot in the dark room, it was a relief. My underthings were damp with sweat and my outerwear stained with blood, dirty and torn. It would do.

Mrs Li called out, and Mr Chen returned. They exchanged words.

"Mrs Li says she bathe your hurts in water with herbs. Chinese medicine. You will allow?"

"Of course. Please thank her for me."

Mr Chen left the room and returned with a small, steaming cauldron. Mrs Li accepted this from him and gestured for me to sit. She bathed my head wounds first. The warm herbed water was soothing, though I winced as Mrs Li's brisk movements brushed over my injuries. While she worked, I could feel her assessing my injured nose and the cuts on my face while Mr Chen held up the lantern.

"Your nose is not break, she says."

I blinked, once again feeling tears threaten. "That is a relief." Then I realised that I had but a few coins to my name. I met Mr Chen's eyes. "I have no money to pay her."

"You no pay."

Mrs Li spoke again, and with my back to Mr Chen, she drew down my robe to expose my shoulders and arms. These she bathed, and while she did so, she spoke to Mr Chen.

"She says you must drink tea to help hurts. I bring from her house."

"Very well," I said, turning my head and looking at him over my bare shoulder. "I will take her medicine with thanks."

While Mr Chen was gone, Mrs Li ran her hands over my body, bathing where there were scratches and pressing in the places where I was bruised. She studied my pulse, too. I felt very exposed and embarrassed to be examined in such a way, so I was relieved when Mr Chen returned and I was once again wrapped in the robe. By then, I was sitting on the bed, exhausted from Mrs Li's ministrations and the night's adventures.

The tea the old woman gave me tasted horrible, but Mr Chen encouraged me to drink it all. "Chinese medicine good. Yes? Very long time use."

With a nod I drained the cup. However, the old woman poured more out and pushed the mug at me again. I thought I was going to vomit. However, I forced it down. It was the least I could do after the woman had cleaned all my wounds.

She spoke to Mr Chen again and there was some vigorous back and forth. Mr Chen turned to me with a slight bow. "Mrs Li said you have good luck. No bones break. No bleed inside. You will get good soon, but you must rest. She come back tomorrow."

"But..." I was going to explain that I had no idea where I would be tomorrow, but Mr Chen forestalled me.

"You stay here. There is bed. It is not the best, but it is safe."

"I don't know how to thank you," I said weakly.

Mr Chen waved this away. "Only one rule to keep safe."

"What rule?"

"Stay inside, stay quiet. If anyone but me and Mrs Li come here, hide."

"Why hide?"

"Best no one know you be here. Yes?"

I tried to frown but winced instead. He was probably right. My husband had left me in a difficult situation. Debts had to be paid. I had been beaten up in Chinatown, where no English lady should set foot at night on her own. I might have somehow injured those men who attacked me, so their friends would want to find me, too. And I had endangered Mr Chen by being here. Would anyone understand that a Chinese man had offered to help me? That his intentions were honourable?

"You are right," I replied. "It is best to keep my being here secret for now."

Mr Chen indicated the bed. "Best you sleep. Feel better in morning."

There was a sheet and a thin blanket, but the room was hot and stuffy, so I lay on top of them. A window above let in a whisper of breeze. Even the robe felt too hot on my skin. I allowed myself to relax; everything hurt more now that I was calm and safe.

Mr Chen spoke some Chinese words and then took the candle and blew it out, leaving me alone in the darkness. Outside my makeshift room, he and Mrs Li spoke some more, and then they made their way down the stairs and it grew quiet.

It was hard to sleep. I ached. The heat was unbearable. My life was a shambles. I cried for James, wondering how he was and whether his father was taking care of him. Why had Charles taken James? He had barely paid the boy any attention.

Something in the tea was making me feel drowsy, I thought. I found if I did not move, I could bear the heat well enough. A dog barked and voices echoed somewhere outside. Eventually, I must have drifted off to sleep.

You must think it odd that I would go off with a stranger, particularly one who was so different from me. But I had no friends and the only acquaintances I had met that very day. No one I could trust, and even if I had, how could I have borne the shame of what had happened to me? It was better this way, because I was anonymous. It was also freeing, because the normal strictures of society did not apply. It was just me, Mr Chen and Mrs Li, dealing with an unusual situation.

# CHAPTER 9

My notion that Jemima was in labour was correct. In the early hours of the morning, Edward knocked on my door to alert me that the midwife had been sent for. "I shall attend on her."

When I arrived, Jemima was complaining loudly and the midwife was being abusive.

"Now, Mrs Huntington. Less yelling, if you please."

I sent the woman a glare. "What Mrs Groot means, dear, is that you need to conserve your energy."

Jemima gritted her teeth through a particularly bad pang. "What do you know? You have never had a baby!"

With exaggerated patience, I replied, "I have been present at a few births." I took her hand and she squeezed it. Watching her suffer was not easy and her pains appeared particularly strong. A few hours of intense contractions and nothing seemed to be moving. I checked my watch at it was already ten in the morning.

The midwife examined her and shook her head. "It will be a while longer."

"How far along is she?" I asked.

"Not very far," she replied.

I took a cloth and wiped Jemima's forehead. I was concerned. By my reckoning, Jemima had been in labour sixteen hours.

"Perhaps, she should move around the room," I said to Mrs Groot.

The snooty midwife ignored me. "Everything is under control. I can manage without you, Mrs Wainwright."

My smile was meant to smite her.

Jemima was prone on the bed, as was the custom, but I sensed that this position was not helping the baby move.

"You should get up, Jemima, and walk around," I urged when the midwife left the room to gather more towels.

Jemima glared at me. Then her jaw clenched as another contraction hit. "I cannot possibly walk. I can barely lie down."

I put my hand on her head, stroked her hair and spoke soothingly. "It will help. If you move, the baby might, too."

"I don't want to." Jemima's tone was petulant.

I sat on the edge of her bed and took her hand in mine. "Trust me. Please."

To my relief, she squeezed my fingers and nodded. I assisted her to stand. A pain came then, and she buckled, but I held her upright and urged her to walk. We walked a few circuits of the room as her pain eased. With her hands supporting her belly, she let go of me and walked by herself.

"I think you should give birth standing up," I said.

Jemima flung her head back. "What? Are you out of your mind?"

I could not suppress a smile. Jemima certainly had spirit. "Impertinent girl. I know what I am talking about." How to tell her that I knew this from personal experience? I thought of some way to explain myself that would make sense to Jemima's logical mind. Only my sisters knew of my marriage to Charles. Edward would not have remembered as he had just been born. And as James was taken from me, none of my other relatives knew about him. "Other cultures do things differently. I think your baby is quite big, and using gravity might help it to be born faster."

The midwife returned, but stopped in her tracks when she saw Jemima up and walking. "What on earth are you doing, ma'am? Mrs Huntington, you should be in bed." She turned to me. "This is your doing. You are interfering. I must ask you to leave."

Jemima turned to her. "Wait. This is helping."

The midwife sneered. "I am a professional. I have birthed many a wee babe."

"That may be," I replied. "But everyone is different. If it is helping Jemima and you can find no medical reason not to let her walk, then..." I left that open to her interpretation.

"I must insist you leave the room, Mrs Wainwright."

"Only if Jemima wills it."

Keeping quiet, I waited for Jemima to decide. If she wanted me gone, I would go without argument. But Jemima kept walking, and she did appear less distressed.

"I wish you to stay, Aunt," she said.

I kept a tight rein on my pleasure at this statement so as not to raise the ire of the midwife. Despite my experience, I was no expert, and no matter how irritating the woman was, I did not want to risk her walking out. If anything went wrong, we might need her.

The midwife looked between us, her expression mutinous. "Well, Mrs Huntington," she said finally, "if walking is helping to ease your pain, you may continue. However, in my experience, the mother must rest in bed in a darkened room, with no visitors, no stimulation at all."

The labour progressed much more quickly after that. Soon, the midwife was urging Jemima to take to the bed. "Your time is near. You are trying to push." She had her arms around Jemima.

Jemima untangled herself. "No, I wish to remain standing."

"What?" the midwife replied. "You do not have the strength for that and I cannot support you."

"What should I do, Aunt?" Jemima asked.

"Perhaps find something to lean on, to support you," I said quietly.

With a nod, Jemima wrapped her hands around the bedpost. When another pain hit, she squatted, holding on and making a guttural sound. I lifted her nightdress so the baby could arrive unhindered. With a dark glare at me, the midwife scrambled onto her knees and hurriedly grabbed a towel. After a few moments, she exclaimed, "I can see the head. It's coming fast."

I sat on the bed next to Jemima, soothing her and giving encouragement. "Not long now, Jemima. You can do this."

The midwife looked up at us. "Push hard with the next contraction, Mrs Huntington."

To Jemima I said, "You can do anything. Breathe."

Jemima continued, gripping the bedpost like her life depended on it. I continued to rub her lower back and speak soothing words.

"Now push, Mrs Huntington. Push."

Jemima pushed and screamed and pushed again, and suddenly the babe was crying in the midwife's arms.

"'Tis a boy, Mrs Huntington."

Jemima sagged and I held her up as she wept. "I need to kneel, I think," she said, and I helped her to the floor.

The midwife was examining the child. "He is fine and healthy, Mrs Huntington."

Jemima looked over at the red, squalling creature. "Trust a man to give one such trouble."

The midwife cut the cord and bundled the baby in swaddling, then placed him in the cradle so as to attend to the afterbirth and cleaning. The baby cried in protest, and it was a strong cry.

Jemima suffered the rest of the ministrations without much complaint, and then allowed herself to be tucked into bed.

"There you are, Mrs Huntington. All done now. You must rest, unless Mrs Wainwright objects?"

I met the midwife's combative look and smiled. "Of course. I do not object. Rest is the best medicine."

While I helped make Jemima comfortable, the midwife fetched the baby. "Here you are," she said, and laid the boy in Jemima's arms. I checked my watch and the baby had arrived at ten minutes to five in the afternoon.

My stomach rumbled. I hoped for a good dinner, as I was famished.

Jemima gazed down at her son, touching his forehead and nose and then his chin as if considering whose likeness he had. She sighed and leaned in to kiss the baby's head. Then she looked over to me. "Will you fetch Edward, now, Aunt Prudence?" she asked calmly. "We are ready to receive him."

"Of course, my dear. He is likely wearing a hole in the hall carpet."

Jemima nodded and then grabbed my hand. "Wait. I want to say I am sorry for my cross words. You were helpful. I do not think I could have done this without you."

Tears threatened, but I held them in. With a smile and a nod, I went to fetch the new father.

On opening the door, I paused. Standing in the hall was Milly.

"Is she all right?" Milly's eyes were wide.

I gave her a hug. "Indeed, hale and hearty." Milly looked pale. "Are you feeling out of sorts yourself?"

"I am fine. I was just concerned. I told her she would scream as much as me. It cannot have been easy for her."

"As you know, there is suffering but, in the end, when the babe arrives safe, it is all forgot. Where is Edward?" I looked around. "I thought he would be here waiting."

"He is in the library with Ambrose. He could not bear Jemima's cries. I think Ambrose has him half drunk." Milly slid her arm through mine, and we walked together down the hall.

It was new to us all, seeing Jemima in pain. "Typical," I replied. "Men like to cause pain but are rarely around to witness suffering. It is a woman's lot in life to bear it all."

Milly raised an eyebrow. "That sounds a bit harsh, Aunt. Are these musings due to assisting Jemima give birth or from pondering your life for your memoir?"

I gave a little chuckle. "A bit of both, I think. You stay here while I go down to fetch my nephew."

Edward was very merry when I found him in the library. Fulton held his port wine better than my nephew.

"Edward my dear, congratulations: you have a fine son. He is waiting to meet you, and your wife deserves love and gratitude for all her suffering." I sent him one of my disapproving stares.

Edward stood up, swaying a bit. "Is she feeling better?"

I repressed the desire to roll my eyes. He was a good lad but a tad lacking in nous. "She just pushed your son into this world after a long labour, so I think she is feeling much better, yes."

"Right then," he said, and ambled towards the door. Catching Fulton's eye, I shook my head. A walk in the cool evening air would have been better than getting Edward drunk. What use was he like that?

Following Edward upstairs, I was able to witness his reunion with his wife and his introduction to their son. Edward was gentle and sweet and Jemima too exhausted to notice that her husband was in his cups. Or if she did notice, she did not mention it.

"What shall we call him?" Jemima asked.

I knew they had a few names picked out, only they had not decided yet.

"Louis Theodore Wilbur Hardcastle Huntington. What about that? I think we have covered everyone," said Edward.

Jemima smiled lovingly at him and then at her baby beside her on the bed. "I like the name Louis. Yes, Louis it is. And thank you for Wilbur; I think my father would have liked that."

Louis was a name we all liked. I thought if I consulted my family tree, I would find a Louis or two in there. Theodore for Edward's father. Wilbur for Jemima's and, well, that old Hardcastle name was not going to die out. The whole thing was a mouthful but would look impressive on Louis' stationery when he grew to be a fine young gentleman.

Patiently I waited for my own opportunity to hold the baby. Milly cut me out of line by sneaking into the room instead of resting. I finally managed a cuddle while Jemima drifted off to sleep and Edward dozed in the bed beside her.

The midwife finished tidying the room and prepared a trundle bed for herself, as she was to stay a day or two and tend the new mother and baby during the night. "I shall pop downstairs and have a bite to eat while the mother is resting. Please do not tire her out, or the baby."

The midwife left the room before I could comment that it might be difficult to tire out someone who was asleep.

Looking down into Louis' face, memories of my own baby son flooded back to me. "Hello, young Louis. I wonder what delights are in store for you." I looked into his eyes, and something stirred within me. A fierce protective feeling, and, as my Prudential Light came forward, an answering vibration came from young Louis, as if he too had the family gift. That was the second time my Prudential Light had surfaced in recent days. After all the trouble I had in Singapore trying to summon it at will, I was annoyed that it just surfaced as if it had a will of its own. I knew it came forward when I needed to protect myself, but now I had more people that I cared about, that I wanted to protect, so maybe that was why. My emotions were heightened. Just as I detected my talent, it faded. Just as Edward jerked awake.

"What was that?"

"Nothing," I said. "Just a candle flaring."

As Edward was sleepy and tipsy, he went back to sleep.

I kissed the top of Louis' head. "Welcome to the world, Louis Theodore Wilbur Hardcastle Huntington. You are going to be an interesting one to watch."

If Edward was a gentleman magician and Jemima had extremely powerful magic herself, then their child was going to be exceptional. He had the family talent within an hour of his birth. I wondered what shape his gift would take. Mine was the restrained Prudential Light, a vague power that opened up like a parasol when me and mine needed protection. Apart from talking to the dead and sometimes the living at a distance, I could not do much more than that. I could not direct it at will. Louis would have much more ability than me because his parents would be able to teach him. Who knew what greatness he would achieve?

# CHAPTER 10

After all the excitement of the birth, fatigue hit me hard and I lay down to nap. A few hours later, Milly sent the maid up with some soup and bread, and this I ate while it was still warm. The house was quiet as night fell, and I had the urge to try to write some more of my story.

**Singapore, 1840**

I awoke the morning after the attack to bright sunlight streaming through the window. Aches and pains bothered me, but I was awake and ready to face the day. Blinking a few times, I saw that my "room" had been created with walls of wooden boxes.

Rolling over, I saw on an upturned crate next to me a fan made of paper, a pot of warm tea and a small cup. Next to them was a bowl of broth with a piece of green vegetable floating in it, a ball of what looked like meat and some flat things I had never seen before. I later learned they were called "noodles".

After picking up the bowl and inhaling the aroma, hunger flared in my stomach. I had not eaten since the tea party the day before, and even then I had only partaken of some sandwiches and a piece of cake. The delicious soup soon disappeared, and I drank the tea and took up the fan, for already the room was warm from the moist hot air leaking in through the window. The small rectangle of light was too high for me to look out of. The scent of the sea where it met the river drifted in and the noise from the boats filtered in along with the echo of voices—at times muted and distant and other times words rang out like a bell but in a language I did not understand.

A bucket stood in the far corner, and by its odour I could tell it was for relieving myself. Mr Chen had thought of everything, even if it was all strange and different to me. Nonetheless my mind was crowded with worries. How long could I stay there? What would people say if they knew I was under the protection of a Chinaman? They would assume all kinds of unsavoury things, even though he had been nothing but gentlemanly.

Struggling out of the bed, I checked my robe was tied and climbed to my feet, grunting and groaning with the movement. In the small space, I was able to take five steps and five back. There was a curtain, which I took for a doorway, but on the other side were more tea chests that partitioned off this area. If I wanted to, I could shift the boxes and leave. It was more to shelter me from any casual observers. I was safe, and, without money or acquaintances, I had nowhere else to go. Mr Chen had been extremely kind, and I was in no state to leave.

To ease the stiffness in my joints, I kept pacing backward and forward as best I could in the small space. The sounds of the street leaked into the room: carts trundling past, hawkers calling out in languages I did not understand. I tried to discern the Malay from the Chinese, but it was hard. The heat grew more difficult to deal with, so I lay down again and drowsed.

The smell of food woke me. This time there was a little bowl of rice, some meat and vegetables. Mr Chen must have left the food and drink so quietly that I never woke, even though he would have to have moved the boxes to get in.

I was hungry despite the heat, and I ate the food quickly. In another bowl was some clear broth. This I drank off. A jug of water and a small teacup had been provided to quench my thirst. I knew water could make me sick, but I was so hot and thirsty I drank several cups before I went to sleep again.

This situation continued for three days, until one evening, Mr Chen appeared while I was awake. The sound of tea chests sliding along the floor heralded his arrival, and then the curtain moved to reveal my rescuer and protector.

"Are you well?" he asked, bowing.

"Yes, much better. Please come in, take a seat."

There was nowhere for him to sit in the traditional sense, so he squatted down so that we faced each other as I sat on the bed with my back against the wall.

"Is anything you need?" he asked me in his accented English.

"My clothes?" I replied.

Mr Chen nodded. "They are cleaned and mended. However, you not be able to wear them. Too heavy. Too hot. I will bring more suitable clothes for you."

"More suitable clothes?" I drew my robe tighter.

"Different. Better for heat."

He drew a piece of paper and a pencil from his pockets. "Can you write your name? Where you staying before I found you?"

I took the paper and frowned at it, wondering why he wanted the information. "Very well. The innkeeper kept my possessions. He will not give them to me until the bill is paid." I wrote my name:

Mrs Charles Ingleford Leighton, and the address of the accommodation. I handed the paper back and Mr Chen studied it.

Lifting his eyes from the paper, he met my gaze. "It is hard for you to stay here. Very dangerous."

I studied him, saw the lines around his eyes which crinkled when he laughed. It was a nice face. "Why? Is someone looking for me?"

He nodded. "Yes. I hear talk. They think you lost in marsh. They think you dead. Best stay here." He went to continue speaking, then stopped.

"And?" I prompted, knowing there was more to it.

"British not like you here with me. Even in Chinatown not happy. Understand? Not good honour to find here. Also, friends of men who attack, look for you also."

"Oh dear," I said, and covered my mouth.

"You safe, if quiet and stay here. Later we make plan."

I sat back and closed my eyes, thinking through the situation. I had no money and no means of getting more at the moment. I had Charles' debts. Not only was the accommodation owed money, there were his gambling debts and no doubt I would be asked to defray them, too. I had nowhere to live, and to many of the British here, staying a night with a Chinese man would sink me. At present I could see no way out. "Yes. I agree. I am sorry to put you in this position. You have been so kind to me and you do not deserve ongoing complications."

He bowed his head. "I am good person. You hurt near my door. I not walk away. And you have this...Prudential Light."

Frowning, I considered his words. "I do not know what that light thing is. It has never happened to me before."

"Very interesting. I wish to learn more." There was a twinkle in his eyes and the ghost of a smile on his lips.

I leaned my head back against the wall and stared at the ceiling. "What about Mrs Li? Will she not tell people about me?"

"She like grandmother to me. Also, she saw your light and what it did. She says you special, good person. Only good people get inner power."

"What is this Prudential Light? It sounds strange."

"When men hurt you, the light come. It is power. Power from you."

I remembered that something unusual had happened, but was not prepared to admit that the light had come from within me. "Why do you call it that?"

"Some people have inner power. I call this Prudential Light because you tell me your name is Prudence. So I name your power after you..."

Ah, that was right, I had given my name to him.

"Well, Mr Chen, I am in a pickle. I have no money, no home, no way to get myself out of here, but I owe you my life. I am very grateful for your kindness."

He studied the piece of paper in his hand. "I will seek answer. Maybe later can fix."

I was quite astonished by the generosity of spirit I was being shown. I did not know much about the Chinese. Mr Chen was a merchant, that much was obvious, and given the way he spoke he clearly had some education, so he was a cut above the average labourer. However, I did not want to feel more indebted to him than I already was. "I will earn my keep."

Mr Chen blinked. "Earn?" His cheeks grew pink, and I frowned, wondering why this had embarrassed him. Then slowly it dawned on me that he had misconstrued my words. I realised that he must have thought I was offering my body, like some common street girl. I shook myself. I had not yet sunk so low, but I was a whisker away from being so.

"I mean help with your business."

"I have many business. Tea. Clothing. Import many things."

"I can sew, do embroidery," I said quickly. "I am also good with design."

Mr Chen swallowed and seemed relieved. "Not necessary."

"Yes, it is. If you can show me what you sell, I can see if I can improve it. Who do you sell to?"

Mr Chen stood up. "I cannot talk business with you."

"Why not?"

"It is private."

I laughed. "So is my predicament, but you helped me. I can teach you English."

"I already speak English." He stood taller, throwing out his chest with pride.

"I can teach you better English, and also writing."

"I can write."

"Can you read and write English?"

"Some."

I climbed to my feet and put out my hand. "Mr Chen, I will repay you through lessons in English elocution and reading and writing. Bring some contracts if you have them, and I will explain the fine print and stop you being cheated. Bring me a book and we shall read together. Show me a sample of the clothing you sell, and I will advise you on how to make it better and give you suggestions on what you can sell to the British. As I said, I can also sew. I have a good eye for women's fashion. I think I will be useful to you."

Mr Chen looked at my hand and then met my gaze, a glint in his dark eyes. "Very well, Miss Prudence, we have agreement." He shook my hand. And for the first time in years, I felt in some control of my life. I was indebted to a stranger but had the means to pay my way. I felt hope surge through me.

If only it was not so hot.

THAT NIGHT OUR LESSONS BEGAN. I HELPED MR CHEN WITH some sounds he had difficulty with and also some words in the contracts he did not understand. He had an agile mind. He showed me his writing both in Chinese characters and in English. He had a fair hand in English, but the Chinese characters were beautiful and flowed as if they had a life of their own.

"What do these mean?" I asked, pointing to some characters on the page. They appeared on the side of his paper.

With a smile, Mr Chen explained. "This is my family name, Chen. This is my first name, Yu Tang. It means jade flower...a white flower." He drew me a picture.

I studied his drawing, the rounded petals. "Magnolia?"

"Yes, ma-no-lia."

I repeated the correct pronunciation, and he followed along. It would take time, but I knew he could improve his pronunciation, fluency and comprehension. When I asked him about his education, he said he had been tutored and also attended school. "I learned official language, Mandarin, as I wish to be government official. I also speak my first language, Cantonese. I was not successful to be an official, so I came here to earn my fortune."

"Are you unhappy being in business?"

He glanced at me as he thought about his answer. "My life different than I want. I miss family. My mother. My country."

"Oh, I see." It was the first time I had thought about his family and connections. I blinked as I realised I had considered him in isolation, a loner with no one depending on him.

He drew more characters on the page with his brush and ink. "This is how to write 'Prudential Light'. It not perfect translation. In Chinese this mean 'soft light' or 'Róu Guang'."

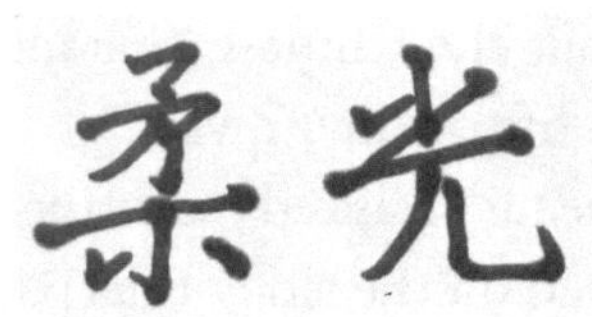

I STUDIED THE CHARACTERS BUT FELT THAT WRITING THEM WAS beyond me.

Mr Chen told me that many of the Chinese people in Singapore doing menial work were actually well educated. They came to look for opportunity, to seek a way to find prosperity in the world, often leaving behind their families and even abandoning opportunities for marriage. There were not many Chinese women here, he said, and I recalled that I had seen very few in the short time I had lived in the city.

After supplying me with his brush and paper, he asked for some ideas for women's clothing.

"You could aim for the Indian and local markets," I suggested. "It is hot in parts of India and here, and British women's clothing is heavy. Using lightweight materials, you could make dresses like this." I drew some pictures.

He showed me some simple blouses. I placed one on my lap. "I could embroider the cuffs and collars and make them more attractive to British women."

He pondered my drawings, tilting his head this way and that. "Singapore is a place where goods pass through on the way elsewhere. It is possible I could work something with this for the local market first. Then if sell well, send other places."

That is how we continued in the evenings. Every night Mr Chen and I ate a meal together, which he brought with him, along with other supplies for me. He saw to it that clean water for drinking and washing was left just outside my room every morning and my bucket was emptied. He brought me a new outfit of simple trousers and tunic. All my notions of being a lady were cast aside as I wore pants like a man. They were serviceable and cool, but nothing like as elegant as the clothes he wore. Sometimes he came in a simple satin tunic with trousers underneath; other times they were more elaborate.

The days were long for me, and incredibly lonely. I tried to sleep when it was hottest. Despite my very sedentary existence, I lost weight and felt weak most of the time. But my injuries were healing and I was slowly becoming used to the food. I passed the daylight hours embroidering some of Mr Chen's stock—cotton blouses made in China. Mr Chen was pleased because with the embroidery he could charge more for them, and they were selling quickly. He told me he had people in China who were copying my designs and that part of his business was going smashingly. His exact words!

One evening, Mr Chen returned to the subject that plagued me near constantly. "We must find way to return you to your people," he said. "The landlord not want release your possessions. Also, where you go? Will you follow your husband?"

"Do you know where he went?" I asked, unable to disguise the hope in my voice. I didn't want Charles, but I did want to find my son.

"No, he was tricky. He did not leave clear path. He did not use his name or your son's. If anyone saw him, they do not tell me."

My hopes were dashed. Charles was hiding from me as he was from his creditors, and I could not think of a way to trace him.

"Then I must return to England," I said with a sigh, "but that requires careful planning. I cannot just reappear without questions being asked. I need money for my passage and for essentials and I need my clothes."

Mr Chen nodded and slipped his hands into his sleeves as he thought. "You are best to wait for opportunity. I will bring British newspapers when I can. Perhaps you find what you need there."

I considered this. If I could travel as a companion to some

wealthy girl or an older woman, that would cover some of the costs. "That is a good idea, Mr Chen."

The next night, before we ate, Mr Chen asked me to summon my Prudential Light. It would not come.

I tried pulling strength out of me, using my mind. I tried to defend myself, but as there was no threat, nothing happened. Mr Chen taught me to meditate. He taught me to summon my centre and still nothing happened. We tried for a week or more and nothing happened.

"If you cannot summon light at will, you must learn other ways to protect yourself," Mr Chen said.

I bowed to him. "You are right. Will you teach me?"

And so, we changed our routine a little. After we'd worked on Mr Chen's reading and writing and before we ate each evening, Mr Chen taught me how to fend off attackers, using everyday things as weapons. In some ways those simple exercises transformed me, because they gave me the confidence to face the world of men. Often as I ruminated on my life during the day, I would picture myself throwing a letter opener at some prattling man of my acquaintance. It was a terrible thing to consider, of course. Most unladylike. I am not so bloodthirsty as that. However, there have been times when I have pictured what it would be like to shut someone up with a sharp object.

One day, I was excited because Mr Chen made a breakthrough in pronouncing the letter "r".

"Very good. Rabbits running around the room."

He repeated this creditably.

"You did it." I couldn't keep the smile from my face.

His cheeks flushed at my congratulations, and I was filled up with admiration. A gentle, kind man who was intelligent. I could not help but compare him to Charles, who had fixed notions, did nothing to improve himself, squandered money on gambling and was malicious to boot.

Something happened in that moment by candlelight. My heart

overflowed with warmth for Mr Chen. Before I knew what I was doing, I reached out and touched his cheek, and something flared in his eyes. I leaned in closer to him, and he to me. Soon our lips met, and instead of mere admiration, there was passion between us.

Mr Chen left me just before dawn, and I slept the day away.

You may utter all kinds of words about this, remonstrate with me, accuse me of heinous conduct. You need to understand the context, the way my life was at that time. Mr Chen was my lifeblood. He protected me, he was unfailingly kind, and he was attentive. While I tried to remain impassive, I could not fail to notice all of his good attributes. Yes, he was Chinese and different from me in so many ways: not only in the colour of our skin and the shape of our eyes, but in our customs and language. Yet there existed an understanding between us. Mr Chen never expressed any love for me, not in the way a British man might. It was dangerous for me to love him because I knew that there could be no future in it. But I could tell my feelings were reciprocated, and while I remained hidden, it was possible to dream.

I recalled what the priest had said to me in Calcutta. I thought he had been only trying to get money from me, but there were essential truths in what he told me. I had lost James, my everything, and I hoped desperately it would not be forever. And now, I did indeed love a man who was very different from me. The priest said he could see my inner light and that I was born with it. I thought it was something he must tell everyone, but that had turned out to be true, too.

THE LANTERN HAD BURNED LOW, AND I LIT A CANDLE TO LIGHT my way to bed. Everything ached after the hours spent at my desk. It was near three o'clock in the morning. The house was quiet as I slipped between the sheets. As I closed my eyes, I hoped that Milly did not go into labour that early morning, as I was so tired. Who knew writing about the past could be so exhausting?

# CHAPTER 11

While I was given a night's reprieve, Milly's labour commenced the next evening. When the maid came to inform me, I put away my pen and paper, drew my mind out of the past, and hurried to my niece's side.

"Tell me, Aunt," Milly asked as she walked around the room, rubbing her belly to ease a light contraction. "Tell me again about my parents and how much they loved each other."

"Of course, my dear. Faith was younger than me. I remember when she met the young curate, John Jones. He was clever and handsome and humble. Your mother practically fainted when he asked her to dance. There was never anyone else after that.

"My father was against the match because John Jones had very little money of his own. Your father despised money for money's sake. He wanted to help the poor, give to the poor. I believe if he had not met Faith, he would have given away his income entirely and lived cheek by jowl with the poor. His vision inspired Faith, who, it turned out, was aptly named. Our parents dabbled in Puritanism, I believe, for why else would they name us after Christian values? Edward's mother was called Charity."

"I am glad they chose Millicent for me," Milly said, and then gasped. "That one was stronger."

I checked my watch. "Closer in time as well. What good fortune that the midwife is still here with Jemima, helping her to tend Louis."

As the pain eased, Milly smiled. "'Tis lucky indeed. And I am blessed in Ambrose."

"You are. I am glad my opposition to the match did not deter you."

Milly laughed. "You were only thinking of my future. Fulton did pretend to be an employee of Edward. And you were not to know he had an estate and a substantial fortune. I did not know either. We hold no grudges against you. Things were not what they seemed." She walked a short way and then turned back to face me. "If your father was against the match, then how did they marry?"

I stood up and began to walk beside Milly as she paced the room, her arm resting in mine. "When Father realised the depth of their affection, he allowed the engagement, but he knew that all of Faith's dowry would be needed to keep them."

"Were they exceedingly happy? Like me and Ambrose?" Milly's dark eyes shone and a smile lit her face, until the next contraction began. "Ooh."

Rubbing Milly's back, I continued the story. "Indeed, they were exceedingly happy. Their life was full of love and contentment. Having you doubled their blessings; you would think they had been given an angel! Faith wrote to me about you. How pretty you were, how you had your father's eyes and hair but her chin and the Hardcastle stubbornness. You did not like gruel."

Milly laughed as her contraction eased. "I still do not like gruel. A most cruel concoction." She walked on, rubbing her belly as she went.

"Indeed, but very efficacious. Can I get you anything, my dear?"

Milly glanced sideways at me. "Ambrose?"

"I will fetch him and that snooty midwife."

"Oh yes, but I want you here with me too, Aunt. Jemima told me what you did for her. How you helped her. I want that too. Is that very demanding of me?"

Emotion threatened to undo me. I had raised Milly as my own. Her presence had helped me immensely, even as I mourned her mother, and my other loves. "Never, child. You shall always have my care."

Milly embraced me. "It is so good of you to be kind and caring towards Jemima, as you always have been for me. I have admired how your affection has grown to encompass us all. I feel that Jemima needs a mother figure. Have you noticed how nice she is being to you lately?"

Stepping away from Milly to the door, I paused. "Yes, now that I think of it, she has been more tolerant. Despite appearances, I do love her dearly, her and her rambunctious ways! Now, if you are fine for the moment I shall fetch Fulton and the midwife."

My heart soared early the next morning when Milly gave birth to a darling little girl. The birth was uncomplicated and soon she was holding her dear one, with Fulton gazing on adoringly at her side. It brought back so many memories. Thoughts of Singapore surged again, and the urge to write more pushed against my mind. For what came next ripped open my deepest secrets, my greatest heartbreak.

Fulton took the baby in his arms. "We are going to name her Arabella Faith," he said proudly.

"For my sister? How you honour her memory. I am sure she would have been pleased," I replied.

Fulton passed the baby to me to hold and went to dote on Milly, who by now was clean and comfortable in bed.

I gave the baby a final cuddle, feeling the tears surge forward. Arabella Faith looked up at me, and I felt a stirring of the elusive Prudential Light within me. Ah...Arabella had a gift too, I surmised, and I felt protective towards her, as just holding her brought my gift to life.

After placing the baby with Milly on the bed and bidding her and Fulton a good night, I returned to my room. I was extremely tired. However, the need to explain why holding Milly's baby meant so much to me overcame my fatigue. I had ample ink and paper, and I sat down to write.

### *Singapore, 1841*

For weeks, by the dim light through the window, with the smell of cooking filling the air, along with the voices of the people below, I scoured the newspapers for tidings and advertisements, seeking a way out of my situation. The seasons had changed, and now Singapore was often cloudy and rainy as well as hot. In this weather, too, mosquitoes were a plague, and Mrs Li had provided some incense and a smelly lotion to ward them off.

On one particular day, I was reading the paper as usual when I spotted something. Someone was advertising for a maid to accompany a young woman home to England. A small stipend and paid passage were offered. The sailing was one month away. This was exactly the sort of opportunity I had been waiting for. Excitedly I paced the room, waiting to share my ideas with Mr Chen that night.

Mr Chen took the paper when I handed it to him, after our meal. His eyebrows rose and he adjusted his legs to sit easier on the short stool he had recently taken to sitting on. "This does seem like a good way for you to return home. You would need your possessions, I expect. Some additional money for emergency. Yes?"

"Yes, getting my trunk back is going to be a problem. I cannot easily find clothes and things that I need for the English climate."

"We have time." He folded the paper carefully and set it aside. "I will speak again about your trunk."

"Thank you, Mr Chen,"

"Also, the dresses you draw are being made now."

"Are they selling?"

"Some sell, yes. Early time."

"Ah...you should say early days."

Mr Chen repeated the term correctly.

Over the next two weeks, I planned and imagined myself on that ship and how it would be, even being a maid to some girl I did not know. And then one day, with pent-up anxiety, I paced around and then, when I became too hot, I lay down on the bed, splashing water on my skin to cool down. Oh for a frosty morning, I lamented. I fell asleep dreaming of coolness, of damp grass, mist in the hills and the cold touch of rain. Dreaming of home. Not long now, I thought.

There had been no word on my possessions and that lack had been plaguing me. I had made up my mind to see if Mr Chen could see if there were second-hand clothes for purchase and I decided that would work, for if they were large I could alter them to fit.

When I woke toward evening, I felt strange and I tried to ignore the feeling. I had lost track of the weeks and surely it was time for my monthlies. My mouth filled with bile and I raced to the bucket to throw up. Feeling weak all of a sudden, I sprawled on the floor, feeling everything closing in on me. However, after night fall, I managed to climb to my feet, drink some water and keep it down.

Yes, I had been intimate with Mr Chen, but pregnancy was not possible, was it?

When I ate a meal with Mr Chen, I asked him about how many weeks I had been staying with him. He was quite precise about it. We ate outside my partitioned-off area. When Mr Chen was there, it was safe for me to come out. During the day, he would close off the space for me, although I was quite able to come out if I dared.

"Why do you ask?"

My face heated. "No reason in particular. I just wondered, that's all."

"I checked with the post office and there was no letter from the family who wanted a maid."

I sat there thoughtful. "There is still time for them to write." I had written my letter in a false name, Betsy Moore, just to be on the safe side.

He picked up the newspaper with the advertisement. "Another ten days before the proposed sailing."

"Mmm, I suppose that is cutting it a bit fine. Perhaps they had plenty of offers."

Mr Chen frowned. "Plenty of offers," he repeated carefully. "What does this mean?"

I smiled, as he had said the words perfectly. "It means that more than one person has applied for the position. Plenty means a lot. Offer means in this case to proffer or propose one's services.'

Mr Chen nodded. "Thank you for explaining. Shall we practise your fighting skills now?"

My body was feeling very strange and I did not want to think about why. Had the food been bad? "Perhaps you could read instead. I confess I am still rather hot."

The next morning, my illness was worse. I had a headache, I vomited and could barely keep down water. Mr Chen had already left on business so I had no idea if it was just me or if he was also sick.

I lay in the bed all day with a wet sheet over me, moaning and complaining to the ceiling that I felt so awful. I managed to make myself presentable by the time Mr Chen returned.

That evening, Mr Chen had a letter in hand and he bowed as he presented it to me. When he looked at me, he gasped. "What is wrong? You are so pale, even your lips are white."

"I have been indisposed today. Have you been well?"

"Yes, I am very well." The hope I had that my illness was due to bad food faded. I sat on the small stool and opened the letter. My application to accompany Miss Jane Potter was accepted. I was requested to confirm by next post.

"That is good news, yes?" Mr Chen said. He dished out the food but the smell made my head swirl.

"Just tea please, and some broth."

Again he narrowed his gaze. "What troubles you?"

My hope in being able to go home had blinded me to the obvious. My monthlies were late, I was feeling sick and I had been intimate with a man. It dawned on me that perhaps I had made a baby with Mr Chen. I glanced down at the letter, feeling my hope fade. Mr Chen's hopeful expression faded. "Prudence?"

"Perhaps you should call for Mrs Li."

Without hesitation he left, leaving his meal half eaten. Mrs Li came and took one look at me, and started to gesture for me to go back into my space. There she examined me and shook her head. After she left me there, I put my clothes back on.

They were talking. Mrs Li was angry, gesticulating wildly, and from the look on Mr Chen's face, he was upset too.

"What is it?" I said weakly from the curtained doorway, although by then I had figured it out.

Mr Chen shook his head.

"I am with child, aren't I?"

Mr Chen looked to the floor. "Yes. I did not think."

This was a blessing and a curse. I was carrying Mr Chen's child. What had I done? A Chinese-British baby in a world that would not accept such a thing, and us not even married. I was no better than a concubine.

Then it dawned on me. There was no way that I could leave in my condition, nor could I travel back to England and pass the child off as Charles' as the lie would be laid bare the moment the child was born. In any case, I don't think Mr Chen would have let me go, not carrying his child.

Mrs Li continued to upbraid Mr Chen, and I felt sorry for him. Finally, she left and I must have dozed off, because the next thing I knew, Mr Chen was kneeling by my side holding out a small bowl. It contained clear fluid through which the pretty blossoms painted on the bowl could be seen. "You must take this broth. Slowly." His voice was kind, his expression sad. "You have not eaten. Mrs Li left instructions."

I took small sips. "I am sorry, Mr Chen," I said. "It is my fault."

"No, not your fault. Our fault. And I think you should call me Yu Tang or Yu for short. 'Mr Chen' seems rather formal in our situation." He shared one of his rare smiles.

With a nod, I put my hand on his. "Yu Tang."

Something changed in our relationship. Mr Chen took tender care of me and when my morning sickness eased, we were intimate most nights and Yu Tang was so kind and gentle. He did not speak of love, but I could not stop myself. "I am in love with you," I said one evening. "I respect you, care for you, and I am so grateful for you."

He nodded, smiled and kissed my forehead, and then fell asleep. As my bed had proved too small for two, we shared a space on the floor. I studied his face as he slept, wanting to remember every detail. It was a surprise to me that I loved him and that I had not loved in that way before. It was more than gratitude. I desired him. I liked how he looked, the tone of his voice when he spoke to me, the way he held me in the night. His brilliant mind; his quaint ways. I loved that he was so different from me.

Over the next few months, I thought I might be too weak to carry the child. However, with Mrs Li's help, I soon regained my strength. She stopped haranguing me for being Yu Tang's concubine, although that is surely what she thought. My love and admiration for Yu Tang grew, for he was patient and studied hard every evening, and after many months his accent improved enough for him to speak with a British accent. Of course, he did not speak like a native, but he spoke correctly. His letter writing in English was faultless, and he was now able to challenge some of the contracts he entered into with the British, which often contained unfavourable terms. Not only that, he was able to change them and negotiate some of his own conditions.

Every day while I sat alone, embroidering the blouses for Yu Tang's business and feeling this new babe grow within me, I thought of James and wondered where he was, whether he was alive, whether he remembered me. I shed many a tear in my self-pity and grief.

One day late in the pregnancy, I was lying on my bed when a commotion began downstairs. It sounded like a number of people were approaching. Wary of being detected, I made sure my curtain was drawn and then barely breathed until the footsteps on the stairs receded and Yu Tang called to me.

When I left my room, my travelling trunk was sitting there. "My things!" Stumbling to my knees, I felt like kissing it. Instead, I ran my hands over the metal-clad wooden box as if I had been presented with a treasure chest.

Yu Tang stood with his hands in his side pockets, his traditional silk clothing a dark blue silk. He grinned and nodded as he watched me. "Yes, I waited until it came up for auction."

My heard jerked up at the word. "Auction? Why would my possessions be auctioned? I am not dead."

Yu Tang bowed his head. "You are presumed dead."

I gaped at him at first, but on reflection I supposed it was logical.

Yu Tang brought over a tea chest for me and helped me sit on it. He squatted beside me and spoke in a soft voice. "It is best, I think, that people assume that."

Our eyes met. "Why? I do not understand."

Yu Tang looked into my eyes. "I am afraid your husband left more than just the bill for your accommodation. There are many debts, so perhaps it is best if people think you are gone."

There was sense in that, I saw. Also, it occurred to me that if everyone in Singapore thought me dead, I could reinvent myself, escape the shame until I returned home. What I really wanted was my family, and I had not been able even to write to them. "Yes, I see what you mean. Did it not seem odd that you purchased this chest? Will people gossip?"

Yu Tang smiled at me and there was a hint of merriment in his eye. "And even if they do, what of it? But there was someone bidding against me. They may, perhaps, wonder."

I rolled my eyes. "Someone wanted my trunk? Whatever for?"

"My thought exactly. However, there are those who look for opportunity and buy regularly at these auctions."

I put my hand in his and squeezed. "I owe you so much. Tell me, was it expensive?"

Putting his other hand over mine, he replied, "Not too expensive. I fear that the landlord might have taken items from your chest. I hope you will not be disappointed. When I won the bid, there was much laughter because I had purchased women's clothes. Some of the other bidders thought I was too stupid to know what I was doing, that I did not understand English. You should have seen their expressions when I told them one of my many wives wants to wear Western clothing!"

With a chuckle, he stood to make tea. I let out a little laugh, but his words sobered me. "I see," I said, and swallowed back the questions I wanted to ask. The question of family and wives and children had not arisen between us. Maybe I was deceiving myself because I was caught in this fantasy, living in hiding, learning to protect myself, while teaching and loving a Chinese man in an unsanctioned union. I was as far from my middle-class upbringing as I could get. Every few days, I would try touch my Prudential Light, but it remained elusive.

"That was clever. They were wrong to underestimate you."

Yu Tang studied me. "You have helped me in so many ways, Prudence. Because of you, people may underestimate me, but they will be wrong, and then I will have the upper hand."

"I might have helped, but you were born clever."

"Now who is flattering me?"

I smiled, but my gaze was fixed on the trunk. I wanted to kneel down and open it to see if my things were undisturbed. I was about to waddle over and do just that when Yu Tang raised his hand and stopped me. "Best not look now."

"Why not?" I knew there were no valuables in there. Everything had been sold. My good winter clothes were in England and my most valuable items in the trunk were a warm jacket and my boots.

Yu Tang inclined his head. "You are full with child now. Your time will come soon. You must rest. No unpacking now. It is not good."

"I am perfectly capable of looking in my chest," I retorted.

"Capable, yes, of course. But I ask this because of my beliefs, my customs. Unpacking this will cause unrest in the house. Please leave the chest alone. Now you must think about the baby and your health."

I sat back, idly rubbing my distended abdomen, trying to penetrate Yu Tang's meaning. It made no sense to me, but if he felt strongly about it, I was willing to indulge him. The Chinese had a whole raft of customs and beliefs around everything. I knew only what I had observed, and at times Yu Tang would instruct me. As I had not been out of doors for at least ten months, I had not tested my understanding of any of it.

As for the health of myself and my baby, Mrs Li came every day to check on me—at least, I think that is what she was doing. She had also set up a shrine of sorts and prayed and burned incense. Her chief gods appeared to be Buddha and also Quan Yin an androgynous god, worshipped by many Chinese. I had by now learned a few words in Cantonese, the language spoken by Yu Tang and Mrs Li, but not enough to have a conversation, so I could not ask her what it all meant. Yu Tang explained that she was burning sacrifices to idols and to her ancestors and praying for my health.

As if reading my thoughts, Yu Tang said now, "Before, Mrs Li was coming to check on you every day, but now she will come every few hours."

"Why?" I tried not to sound petulant, but this did sound a little excessive.

"She will look after you. When the baby is born you must rest. Mrs Li will look after you for thirty days."

"Thirty days? Oh, that is similar to what happens in Britain. We have a confinement period where the mother rests and someone helps with the baby. So that is fine and if it makes you happy."

Yu Tang sighed and then smiled a little. "I am grateful you want me happy. By contrast, I want you and the child safe. Your wellbeing is important to me."

I got up and waddled over to squeeze his hand. "Thank you for your care, Yu Tang. I am grateful." And I was: when we discovered the pregnancy, he could have thrown me out on the street, or pretended he did not know me. I realised with fresh eyes that he had taken a great risk in sheltering me.

My predicament was as intractable as ever it had been. If my condition were known, I would have to stay away from British people forever and would never be able to bring the shame home to my family's door. It was bad enough that they might know by now that my feckless husband had left Singapore with a string of debts in his wake, and worse that they might well think me dead. And my poor son! Was James being cared for, fed, educated? I turned my head away, because this line of thinking made my eyes prickle with tears.

Some days when I pondered my fate, I felt as if a veil had been lifted from my eyes. At home, I'd thought I knew how the world worked, but bit by bit my travels had made me see how wrong I was. My husband's behaviour was appalling, but it was nothing new;

newspapers and novels alike spoke of the ills of rascal husbands depleting all their funds and those of their wives, which became theirs upon marriage. I was beginning to see how unjust this system was for the wives of such men.

Travelling to Calcutta had shaken me too. To see so many people, so much poverty, and yet beauty, too. And now I'd seen Singapore with its mesh of cultures, fostered by the British for trade. The world revolved around money and status. We British thought we knew best, but now I thought differently. The world was so much bigger than I had imagined. Cultures older than ours existed, and they had the accumulated wisdom of ages. Mrs Li's remedies worked, no matter that they seemed strange to me.

But the thing that had changed me most profoundly was meeting Yu Tang. He was the most intelligent and talented man I had ever known. Unlike most Englishmen, who might perhaps have a smattering of French—and Latin if they were well educated—in addition to their mother tongue, Yu Tang could make himself understood in Hakka, Hokkien and other dialects as well as his native Cantonese. But as the language of commerce was English, it was this language he had sought to master—and master it he had. I had no doubt he would do well in business as a result. A British man would take notice when Yu Tang spoke and hopefully would be honest in his dealings with him because of his fluency.

Yes, my views on life had changed so much. I was no longer the Miss Hardcastle-Smythe of old, but nor was I Mrs Leighton. It was time for me to be someone new.

One night close to when the baby was due, Yu Tang was sitting with me as usual, reading a newspaper, and a companionable silence had fallen between us. Yu passed me a small cup of green tea, and I thanked him and took a sip. I had grown accustomed to the taste and now looked forward to it. This thought made me look back on my time in this upstairs hideout, surrounded by tea chests and humidity. It was a coolish night. A breeze blew in from my small window and for once I did not feel like an oversized, sweating frog.

"What are we going to do, Yu?" I asked quietly.

He looked up from his paper, sipped his tea and responded, "Do?"

I was forever rubbing my stomach, feeling the baby move and kick. It comforted me. "After the baby is born. What is going to happen?"

Yu Tang blinked at me, his expression quite neutral. "What do you want to happen?"

All of a sudden, I could not speak. My eyes filled with tears and my throat closed. "I...I..." As much as I loved this man, I knew I could not live like this in a small room, hiding from my own people and from his, any longer. I would perhaps be forever separated from my home and family if I stayed, and my status would be no better than a concubine or whore. I could not marry him as I was already married, and to pretend otherwise was beneath us both. It was impossible.

He folded his paper and placed it on the ground next to him. "Let us get through the birth first." His voice was soft and calm. I knew him quite well now and I thought his emotions and thoughts were not far from mine. He had still not professed love for me; I did not think it was his way. But he had been quite charming when I confessed my love and admiration for him. More than all of that though was trust. I trusted him. Trusted him with my life.

"But..."

He shook his head. "We will discuss this after the child is born. It is bad luck to talk beforehand of plans, to talk of things that will cause distress, emotion and tears. All your energy should be on your health and the baby's. Understand?"

I nodded. At that moment, a sharp pain made me gasp. "Oh!"

Yu Tang bolted upright, knocking his cup of tea and spilling it on the newspaper. "It has begun?"

"I am not sure." I rubbed my belly. "We will need to wait and see."

The baby was low in my belly, and even passing water was hard.

I stood and walked back and forth, Yu Tang watching me like a hawk all the while. Another pain some ten minutes later had me gasping. It was stronger, like a band across my middle. It confirmed the start of my labour.

"It is time," I said, reaching out to Yu Tang. He took my hand.

"I will fetch Mrs Li."

Yu Tang hurried away, leaving me to pace up and down by lantern light and soothe my pains.

By the time the old woman arrived, my labour was well under way. Very soon those ten-minute pains became five-minute pains. Mrs Li encouraged me to walk back and forth and squat to help the baby move into the correct position. As well as lighting candles, incense and praying a lot, she comforted me and encouraged me, and even though I could not comprehend most of her words, we understood each other.

Giving birth in Singapore was different from my first experience of motherhood. With the assistance of Mrs Li, I was supported to stand and use the wall to lean on. This allowed the baby to come more quickly, I believe, and with less pain. Of course, I did cry out, and it did hurt, but not as much as I remembered from James' birth.

The emotional pain was worse, if anything. I thought constantly of my son, how much I loved him and missed him, and how much he must have grown. However, Mrs Li did not let me dwell on this. She made me look at her and she breathed with me and soothed me. My perfect daughter arrived sometime before dawn. The picture of her small face still lives in my memory, so much like Yu Tang.

Mrs Li was excited by the birth. She smiled and nodded, and after cleaning me up and helping me to bed, she called to Yu Tang, who'd been pacing beyond the curtain in some distress. He hurried in, face pale, and his eyes met mine. I nodded to assure him I was well. Then Mrs Li passed over the wrapped bundle that was his daughter. Tears glistened in his eyes when he held her and rubbed his face against her head. The moment was full of tenderness, and I knew then that no matter what happened, my daughter would be loved and cared for.

"What will you call her?" he asked me.

"You want me to give her a name?" I replied automatically, not realising he would defer to me.

"Yes, tell me what you would like, and I will give her a Chinese name to match."

I thought about it for a little while. "What about Lily? A white lily. She is a gift from her father."

Yu Tang bowed his head, and I could see he liked my choice. "Lily. In my tongue she is to be called Baahow, which means White Lily." Baahow was close to what I heard.

He handed Lily back to me and wrote her name on a piece of paper he pulled from his sleeve. He showed it to me.

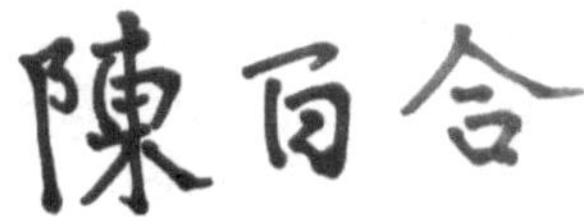

I still have that piece of paper with her name on it to this day.

I closed my eyes, trying hard not to ruin the moment by bursting into tears. I had to be brave. I had to have faith. "Chen Baahow," I said experimentally.

I looked down at my sleeping daughter. "Hello, Lily."

That was when the wave I had been trying to hold back hit me. To love and to hold and to know you had to part ways. When I started to cry, Yu took the baby from me while Mrs Li fussed over me and made me drink broth and eat stew. After I had calmed, I fed my daughter, Lily Chen, and we both slept.

AFTER THE BIRTH, I WAS MADE TO REST—AND I MEAN REALLY rest. I was forbidden to get up and do anything other than take care of my toilette. Yu Tang and Mrs Li brought me food and drink, and Mrs Li stayed with me and took care of the baby, bringing her to me only to nurse.

"It is the tradition," Yu Tang told me when I asked him about it.

In the second week, I felt strong enough to talk to Yu Tang about what we should do. Previously reluctant, he folded himself onto the floor, crossed his legs and drew out a newspaper from his wide sleeve. He held it while studying me, nostrils flaring and lips pursed as if silently making a decision, then he handed it to me.

When I took the paper, he began to talk. "You cannot stay here much longer. When Lily turns one month, it is time for you to return home." He had circled an advertisement which he now pointed to. My heart pounded, and fear, loss and love combined in my chest. I had to force myself to concentrate on the words of the advertisement.

A Miss Maria Lindsay was in need of a chaperone on her return journey to England. A first-class ticket was included, with a poop cabin and fine furnishings. The young woman's father had passed away, and it was her intention to return to her family in her homeland. Barely seventeen, the charge of Miss Lindsay should not be too hard.

The ship was to sail after the full moon, which was a few days after Lily turned one month. I knew an opportunity to travel in comfort like this was rare, and my current situation untenable. I stared at the advertisement unseeingly for a few minutes, then, drawing in a few breaths, I lifted my gaze to meet Yu Tang's. I could barely see him for the tears in my eyes. He came to sit by me on the bed and just held me. What was there for him to say? We both knew this was the best solution: a paid passage back to England, respectability maintained, and my baby girl left behind with Yu Tang, a man who pleased me on so many levels, and who I knew would cherish our daughter.

Eventually, Yu Tang rubbed my shoulder. "It is not good for your spirit to stay hidden here forever." He pointed to the advertisement. "This is an opportunity for you to return to your home. You have a life and a future with your family there. I have responsibilities."

"Yes, I know." I barely got the words past my lips.

"A Chinese man has many dependants, and even though his heart may want it, he cannot abandon them to pursue a dream. There is nowhere we can be together openly, nowhere where it would be acceptable for a white woman to be with a Chinese man as man and wife, particularly when that woman has a husband living. We know this."

I nodded, because although I had been trying desperately to think of a solution to our dilemma, deep inside me I knew there wasn't one. It was time for me to go back to where I came from. But I had not anticipated I would have another child to consider. My daughter's dark eyes regarded me, and I cried wholeheartedly for a few minutes.

"I will care for our daughter, protect her, and I will tell her about you," said Yu Tang tenderly. "You will be forever in our memory. Will you write to this Miss Lindsay?"

I nodded, and after that, Yu took our daughter and cuddled her while I cried myself to sleep.

By and by, I wrote to Miss Lindsay and offered my services. I signed my name Mrs Wainwright, a name I made up, and purported to be a widow. As there was no Mr Wainwright, no man could have a say in my life from that day forward.

The acceptance of my offer came quickly. Apparently, an older widow was just the type of person they were looking for, even though I had no real references. They must have been keen to make the sailing.

Planning for my departure took time. I had lost weight despite my pregnancy, and I needed to adjust all my clothing, including those in my trunk. Yu Tang brought me three new dresses and a blouse in the designs I had given him. They were finely made and fit me perfectly. One was a light cotton, one was an evening dress in silk, perfectly suited for being in company on board the ship, and the third was made from fine sprigged muslin.

"Thank you, Yu Tang. Are they selling well?"

One of his rare smiles graced his features. "Sales are improving. I have not had the latest report from India yet."

As Lily approached one month of age, I was able to get up and busy myself with preparations, both for my journey and for Lily. At my request, Yu Tang brought me some fine cotton to make some dresses for my daughter, which I enhanced with embroidered pink roses and some lovely, embroidered edging. I tried not to think about the time when she would fit into these, and I would not be there to see it.

One afternoon, Mrs Li came in, carrying something. This she presented to me with a spate of words, most of which I couldn't follow. I opened the cloth and found there a number of red eggs and a gift for the baby, a lovely silk wrap. The precious cloth would be a treasured heirloom for my child.

"Thank you!" I said in Cantonese.

When Yu returned, he also had gifts: some sweets of Chinese make, and money for Lily. Gifts for the baby were traditional and the money and items would be kept for her. He had also procured a roll of red embroidery silk and notions for me, so I did not have to be idle on my sea voyage. He knew me well, and I was grateful.

After Mrs Li left for the evening, Yu Tang sat with me for our meal, while Lily slept on a rug on the floor. He presented me with an envelope.

"This is to assist with your expenses on the trip."

In a daze I took it. "Thank you. I shall repay you."

"No need. This is a gift. You have helped me, and you are the mother of my first child and, therefore, you will always hold a special place in my heart." He placed his hand on his chest and bowed his head. Then, regarding me again, he continued. "Also, I give you this so you can remember your time here affectionately." He passed over a box, and when I lifted the lid, there was the lovely little bowl he had brought for me to eat out of. It was indeed something I would cherish, being so fine and pretty. Then he reached behind him and drew out another box. This one contained a tiny teapot, enamelled in green with white magnolias. It was a beautiful thing and significant: a gift to remember him by. This time I managed to keep my emotions in check. "Thank you, Yu. I will cherish these gifts always, and remember you with fondness. Thank you again for your kindness."

He bowed his head and then nodded when he met my eye again. "You learned a lot here, but not how to use your Prudential Light. I think that is because of your upbringing. I will do my best to make sure Lily can use any gift you have passed on to her."

I blinked. He thought Lily would have some talent? I was heartened to know it. For while I was much better now at defending myself, using everyday items and physical skill, my inner power would still not come when I tried to command it.

On the day of my departure, after celebrating Lily's first month, an important milestone in Chinese culture, Mrs Li gave me herbs to take with me to dry up my milk, and she showed me how to bind my chest to assist the process.

I tried to delay the moment I said goodbye to my daughter. I held her, rubbed my face on her head, sang to her and inhaled her scent. I wanted to keep the moment forever. I had written her a letter, although all my excuses for leaving seemed so thin. A mother's love should endure all obstacles. Yet, I did not belong in my daughter's life.

Mrs Li talked to me and I tried to ignore her pleas, until I relented and let her take Lily from me. A huge push of emotion nearly brought me to my knees. When I saw the look of pity in Mrs Li's eyes, I was nearly undone. She dashed away with Lily before I could change my mind.

While Mrs Li took Lily to a wet nurse, I felt utterly bereft. My two children were both lost to me. One I could openly discuss and pursue, the other I must forever keep hidden in my heart. I did not think I could bear it.

It was nearing time for me to leave. Yu came to help me dress. He placed a jade shard on a leather thong around my neck. "Please wear for good health."

I touched the cool stone and my eyes burned with unshed tears. "Thank you. I have nothing to give you in return."

"You have given me many things."

Then, with my wooden chest secured to a cart in the street below, it was time to leave. I could say that I did not weep over Yu Tang, that I did not stain his robes with my tears, that I did not express my heartbreak or my wish for the world to be a different place. However, I set out to be truthful, and so I cannot.

Yu Tang stayed behind out the front of his shophouse as the men he had hired wheeled my chest along the street. I walked behind them, wiping my eyes and not looking over my shoulder. I knew that if I did, I would have run back and be damned, all our plans torn to shreds.

I had to face forward, go forward, and not look to the past.

The heat was unbearable that day because I was wearing my English clothes. Months of being inside wearing the far more suitable thin trousers and top had not prepared me for such heavy garments, despite them being light by English standards. I wore a lavender skirt and white blouse with a black jacket from my travelling trunk. My black bonnet finished off my attire. While not full mourning, it was appropriate attire for the widow I had told Miss Lindsay I was.

Arriving at the port without incident, I met with Miss Lindsay and her Singapore-based guardian. Miss Lindsay was dressed in mourning, too, a black crepe dress with matching gloves and hat. Her veil was rolled up out of the way so I could see her face.

"Good morning, I am Mrs Wainwright. We corresponded."

Standing by her side was her guardian, Mrs Clunes, a hard-faced woman who lacked any warmth. She was at least twenty years older than me and dressed in a pale green muslin dress, remarkably in the style I had designed for Yu Tang. Lifting her nose in the air, Mrs Clunes said, "I see you have arrived promptly. I do not think we have met, and I know most of the English families here."

"That is because I have only just arrived from Penang and am keen to get home." My prepared lies slid easily from my lips.

"As you said in your letter." The woman appeared dubious, and studied me closely. I returned her gaze coolly and tried not to fidget.

Mrs Clunes turned to her ward. "Very well, Miss Lindsay, the ship sails on the tide. Is this woman acceptable to you? We have no references as to her character, but she seems decent enough, if a tad sallow. Her accent is refined, so she must be of good breeding."

My breeding was exceptionally superior to that of Mrs Clunes, if her manners were any indication. To speak so of me in my presence was the height of bad manners. Although I was affronted, I kept a neutral expression and a firm grip on my tongue. "Ah yes, the heat does not agree with me, ma'am. I have suffered terribly and have not been able to socialise. My husband passed away in Penang and, well, with no family and only passing friends to ease my burden, I desire to return home with all haste—as I am sure do you."

Miss Lindsay met my gaze. She had hazel eyes and reddish, curly hair that frizzed in the humidity. There was sweat on her upper lip, and her eyes were red and puffy. I could see she still mourned her father and my heart softened towards her.

"Would you like to do some needlework on the journey, Miss Lindsay? It is my greatest passion—that, and sewing in general."

The girl nodded, her expression lightening. "Yes, please. I like to read as well, when I can," she replied in a quiet, low voice. "I can also play and sing, but my heart is not in it at the moment."

"I am sure we shall be able to keep ourselves entertained." I knew our poop cabin would likely have a porthole, which would allow in light for us to read and sew by on fine days, and which could be opened to let in fresh sea air.

Mrs Clunes passed me an envelope. "For your trouble and additional expenses. You should be met at the port when you arrive. If something goes awry and there is no one to meet you, I have provided sufficient funds to transport you both to Miss Lindsay's address on arrival. Then a little more for you to fund your way home from there."

I did my best to mask my surprise. Mrs Clunes had been most thoughtful and generous. This, together with the money Yu Tang had given me, meant I knew I could see myself to rights. "Thank you, Mrs Clunes. Come, Miss Lindsay, let us make our way on board and find our cabin."

Miss Lindsay dashed forward and hugged Mrs Clunes. The woman appeared unmoved by this display of affection, but she patted the girl stiffly on the back. "Be a good girl and listen to Mrs Wainwright. Remember what I told you. Do not talk to strangers. There are scoundrels out there who will steal your money along with your heart."

I looked about me one last time, wishing to see my daughter and Yu Tang, wanting with all my heart to be able to throw myself into his arms and somehow discover a miracle that would allow me to stay. But alas, he was not there to see me off, and I knew I would never see Lily again. I turned away to hide my emotion and forced my thoughts away from Lily, and James, and the heartbreak I would carry with me forever. I could not risk everything by being seen bawling in public. Taking Miss Lindsay's arm, we said a final farewell to Mrs Clunes and I guided my charge up the gangway and onto the ship.

OUR CABIN CONTAINED TWO COTS, A COUCH WITH DRAWERS underneath to store our things, a worktable in the corner that appeared roped to the bulkhead, and two chairs. The cuddy, where we could eat, was on the same level. The noise of the crew above our heads permeated everything. Luckily I knew from experience I would get used to it.

I opened my travelling trunk and sucked in a breath. Nestled beside the rice bowl that Yu had gifted me was a small bundle of cloth. I picked it up and untied it. Inside was a small statue of Quan Yin, the famous god of the Chinese that Mrs Li burned incense for everyday. It had to be from her. I knew she had never approved of me and my relationship with Yu Tang, so I was touched she thought well enough of me to present me with such a particular gift.

Upon lifting out some items, the lovely, decorated teapot Yu Tang had given me clinked. It was small, just enough for one cup of black tea in the English style and several small cups of Chinese green tea. Memories flashed across my mind: the white teapot and matching cups I had always used with Yu Tang; a spoon that might have been silver; beautiful, patterned chopsticks that I had mastered after a time. For my own sanity, I knew I had to set these memories aside lest they undo me completely. So I packed the teapot and bowl carefully down in the bottom of my trunk.

As Mrs Wainwright, I was alone. No children, no husband. But I had a chance at a future if I was careful to keep my dignity, even amongst my own family. I began to ponder what I should tell them. In the end, my sisters Charity and Faith would be the only ones who would know some of the truth. I did not know it at the time, but my father had passed away, and Mother followed soon after. They were spared my shame.

It was not long before the motion of the ship made Miss Lindsay and I unwell. The amenities were satisfactory, but both Miss Lindsay and myself were laid low for many days with seasickness. This allowed me to weep silently in my bed, to grieve for my child— my children—and imagine Yu Tang's smiling and intelligent face, now lost to me.

By and by, we recovered, and Miss Lindsay and I began to sew, embroider and read in the afternoons when the light through the porthole was bright enough. The deck was busy with the crew and other passengers, mostly the men who spent their days and nights up there when the weather permitted. We took what we could of the air through the porthole, and when we went through to take our meals. In good weather and with a calm sea, we could spend a half an hour in the open air. The food was ample if dull. In the evenings we retired early, neither of us keen to socialise. Miss Lindsay wore black, and we worked on some grey linen she had brought to make her another dress for her arrival in England, when she would enter a period of half-mourning. She was young, and black did not suit her wan complexion.

With a groan, I stood up and eased the crick in my neck. I had written quickly, without discernment, and as I picked up the last page, I wondered if any of it made sense.

Before I retired to my bed, I crept around the house to check that all was well. Milly was asleep but the midwife was awake, tending to the baby. Fulton lay on top of Milly's bed, holding her hand. Such comforting affection brought tears to my eyes. I was so relieved that Milly had found love and affection with an excellent man. How had I ever thought him common? It was rather awful of me, I own. However, a lot had happened at the time, and the thought of having what I thought was a good-for-nothing upstart steal my Milly's heart could not be borne. I am not a snob, but over the years I had let my situation override the good intentions and broad understanding that I gained in Calcutta and Singapore. It had all worked out well in the end, though, for Fulton was a decent man in every respect, a well-bred gentleman with adequate funds to provide for my Milly in a fitting manner. In addition, he had been nothing but tolerant and kind to me—except if I upset Milly, when, quite rightly, he took her side. Now we were all travelling well together, even with Jemima and my nephew in residence.

As I watched the sleeping pair, it occurred to me that perhaps I was a tad envious of their love. For love each other they did, in the way I would hope to have loved Yu Tang, had our match been permissible. Having loved and lost, I understood how lucky they were to be together in happiness, even if it was born of terrible circumstances. Having one's house torn down by a giant machine and one's arm ripped off, leaving one's life in the balance, was not conducive to felicity, to be sure. As Edward had replaced the arm, with even a better model, Fulton was hale and hearty. However, they and their love have endured and indeed, thrived. With a small smile, I closed the door behind me and set off along the hall.

Before I'd gone three paces, Jemima appeared out of the dimness, walking towards me, candle in hand. "How now, Aunt?" she asked quietly.

"What are you doing up?" I asked rather sharply. She was meant to be recuperating after the birth. Jemima staying in one place and resting appeared to be impossible.

"I was restless, Aunt. I am worried about Uncle Ferdy. I expected him to visit before now."

I blinked in surprise. I too would have thought that he would have come to see Jemima's son. "No. It is rather odd. I haven't seen him since you were hexed. Have you tried calling out to him? That usually works."

"Yes, of course. But he has not shown up."

"Well, there is nothing to lose sleep over I'm sure. You should be resting, and concentrating on recovering."

Jemima heaved a great sigh. "Very well. But I am worried.

Something bad has happened to him, I am sure. If all was well, he would not stay away, even if we had argued."

Together we walked towards Jemima's room. "It will be all right, Jemima. Let us think more on it tomorrow. Good night."

As I headed back to my room, I felt a chill of apprehension. It was strange indeed for Mr White not to call in.

# CHAPTER 12

I arose late the next morning and stood at my desk, gathering the pages of my memoir together and tying them with string. Was there more to my story? Had I emptied myself out? Despite my late night, I felt remarkably refreshed. Perhaps a weight had lifted, or by writing down my story I had set down burdens long carried. Certainly, I had delved deep into my past and unearthed my darkest secrets. It must have been more liberating than I had ever expected.

My stomach rumbled, so I left my room and went to check on my newly extended family before heading downstairs to have breakfast.

Sunlight slanted through the windows in the morning room. On taking my seat at table, I greeted my nephew Edward, who was diligently writing in his journal at a small desk against the wall. I also bid a good day to Fulton, who had come in to see if there were any special orders for breakfast.

"Yes, please. Are there any kippers this morning?"

"I believe so, Aunt Prudence," Fulton replied in his polished tones, and hurried out again.

I picked up one of the morning papers and began to read the news.

In due course a plate of kippers arrived, along with some hot muffins. Fulton returned and busied himself filling his plate. I poured tea while Edward got up from the desk and came and took half of the muffins, with butter and jam, some on a plate, some in his hand and one in his mouth. I wanted to slap his fingers, the greedy lamb. However, he was always so busy with his writing and mumbling and spending time with Jemima and the baby that he probably worked up an appetite. His engine, as they say, was always running hot.

I took my time to enjoy the kippers and finished off with a hot buttered muffin and tea. While I was not as plump as I had been when I first went to Willow Park to take over supervision of Jemima, I was still amply supplied with curves. Worry will deplete one's appetite, I suppose and Jemima certainly got on my nerves. Overall, the move to Willow Park had been a welcome change to the humdrum of my life in the cottage. Milly and I were close and we kept ourselves busy, but since that time life has been a swirl of action and adventure.

I looked back on those years in Kingsfold, looking after Milly who had come to me as a baby. We lived cheaply, not being well off. Not a lot of money for beef. We ate far too many scones. Only the really rich could afford good meat and a healthy diet. What good food I did manage to obtain, I fed to Milly to help her grow strong and healthy. We were not so poor as to be destitue, but we were never flush with cash, dependent as we were on my small stipend and what Edward's mother and then Edward himself gave us. If not for their generosity, I would have been living in the workhouse, or as a poor relation of my sister's and excess to requirements.

I was just refilling my teacup when the doorbell sounded.

"Were you expecting a visitor, Fulton?" I asked, but given that our household included two new mothers, it seemed somewhat unlikely.

Fulton was drinking tea and staring out the window. "Not I. You, Huntington?"

Edward shook his head.

Discombe came to the door with a platter in hand, on which lay a visitor's card. Fulton stood, picked up the card and frowned. "Miss Lily Chen, from Chen's Emporium International." He turned the card over. "For Mrs Wainwright."

My cup slipped from my hand and smashed against the table, followed swiftly by my plate. I must have fainted or had a turn, because next I knew, Edward was patting my cheeks and Fulton shaking my shoulder and calling my name. "Aunt Prudence?"

With their assistance I sat forward and tried to get my bearings. The footman had come in and was bent over, trying to pick up pieces of broken crockery. I could not draw breath, let alone speak.

"Heavens, who is this Miss Chen to send Aunt Prudence into such a spin?" Fulton said to Edward.

I saw a look pass between them. "I have no idea, but we are going to find out." Fulton turned his head. "Fetch Miss Chen in, please, Discombe."

"No, wait," I said faintly, but if the menfolk heard me, they simply ignored me. My heart was beating so hard I thought I was going to die. I could not quite believe what was happening; it was as if reliving those months in Singapore through my writing had conjured my daughter back into being. All these years I had wanted to see her, know about her, but we had agreed that I would not contact Yu Tang more than once: after I'd written to tell him I was home and safe. I had kept this promise.

A sniff of smelling salts roused me, and I took as deep a breath as I could manage.

"Are you well, Aunt?" Edward asked with concern.

Still unable to reply, I merely squeezed his hand.

At that moment, a slim girl in a pale blue dress, wearing a white chemisette adorned with a frugal neck frill, stepped into the room. I had tried to picture her over the years. As a baby she had seemed all Yu Tang and only a little like me. Now I could see myself in the shape of her brow and the curve of her chin. Paler than Yu Tang, she had his dark eyes and jet-black hair. Flawless skin, cheeks a peach colour and lips full and pink. A stunning beauty, she was a sight to behold. This was what I had made with Yu Tang.

Our eyes met and she lowered the carpet bag she was carrying to the floor. "You are Mrs Wainwright?" Her accent was flawless. You could scarce tell she was born in Singapore. Yu Tang must have paid dear to have her taught so well.

With Edward's assistance I climbed from the chair. I gazed at her wonderingly, lovingly, taking in her beauty. "Yes, I am Mrs Wainwright," I managed to say.

The girl hesitated and I could see she wanted to come and embrace me. Her gaze shifted to Edward and Fulton, a look of confusion of her face. The two men looked as astonished as I felt.

My mind was oppressed. How was I to explain her? It was one thing to write about her in my memoir, but to be presented with the real person, in my family circle, right now before they had read it. I felt my world crumbling down.

"How did you find me?" I asked stupidly.

"I went to the Kingsfold address, and the tenant told me you were established at Hatfield. I knew from the papers that Hatfield had been destroyed. I was able to make enquires in the village. I have now come here. I hope you do not mind."

I shook my head, my throat now thick with emotion. "No, I do not mind."

Fulton cleared his throat. "You two have met before?"

"Yes," I said, just as Lily said, "No."

My legs were steadier now, and despite the rapid and painful beating of my heart I took a step towards her and she to me. I lifted my hands out in supplication, and she grasped them.

"I never thought I would see you again," I said, tears spilling down my face. I saw Edward shoot a perplexed look at Fulton out of the corner of my eye.

Lily had tears too. "I also longed to meet you."

With those words, I tugged my daughter into an embrace. I cared not what Fulton thought, or Edward. A part of me wondered if they would cast me out when the truth became known, but I found it no longer mattered to me. I had been beastly to them in the past, but I thought those past sins had been forgiven and that we had settled into a family situation of mutual affection. As I held my daughter, I realised that I had been through a great deal, and I could endure what life threw at me next, whatever it was to be.

Lily sank into my arms and sobbed into my shoulder. I rubbed my hand along her back.

"Oh, Mother!"

There were two intakes of breath.

"Mother?" Fulton repeated, the surprise evident in his voice. "Aunt Prudence, is there something we should know?" His tone was mild when he asked this. Ever the gentleman.

Easing Lily from my embrace, I turned to them. "Obviously there is, and I will explain everything shortly. However, for now, could you gentlemen please give us some privacy?"

Fulton flushed. "Of course." He nodded curtly to Edward. "The library, old chap."

From the desk where he had been seated, Edward swiped up his journals and bolted to the door. The two of them turned back before exiting, the curiosity in their expressions plain as day. It was as if I had transformed into a gargoyle.

The door closed behind them.

And then we were alone. I led Lily to the settee and sat down next to her.

Emotions roiled inside me, but nothing except love filled my breast for this beautiful woman. I took in every feature, every movement she made. The tilt of her head as she wiped tears from her eyes, the way her tongue slipped along her lips before she spoke. I was bursting with questions, but sensing that she would tell me all I wanted to know and more, I held my tongue.

"My father has sent me to England to manage his business concerns here. He felt I was the most appropriate choice, given my connection to you. He also knew I wanted to meet you."

"Ah, he has prospered then. I always wondered how he was doing."

With a nod and a shy smile, Lily said, "He is a respected man. He has a big company now with offices in China, Singapore, Hong Kong and London. He has worked tirelessly to improve our family's fortune."

I nodded, remembering how intelligent and hardworking Yu was. It was no accident that he had done well. I could see from Lily's clothing and deportment that no expense had been spared on her upbringing, either, and I was glad.

I blurted out, "I am not sure what your father has told you about me. I have wanted for so long now to apologise to you for leaving you. Please know, I did not want to. I hope the shame of your birth did not touch you overmuch."

Lily blinked at me, obviously surprised. "I had no shame. Father married a woman from Canton when I was about two years old. The story he told everyone was that he had married a white woman and she had died after my birth. I never had any problems. Father told me the truth when I was old enough to understand and also to keep a secret. I have wanted to meet you ever since. It was a relief to learn that you had not died while bringing me into the world." She reached out and laid her hand on mine. "I am grateful to you and my father for what I am, who I am, and all that I have achieved. You will hear no recriminations from me. Besides, my father gave me the letter you left for me when I turned sixteen. He thought I was old enough then to understand it." With a squeeze on my hand, she added, "It was a beautiful letter. I could feel your heart break and my yearning to meet you only increased since then."

More tears trickled down my cheeks. Lily handed me a delicate handkerchief and patted my shoulder. When I could speak again, I said, "I am so happy your life turned out so well. I did not know your father for very long, yet I trusted him with my life and yours. He was kind to me and helped me when no one else would."

Lily nodded her understanding. Then, patting my hand, she stood up and fetched her carpet bag. "Father has asked me to present this token to you."

My daughter knelt in front of me, the bag by her side. From inside she drew out a lacquered box, the kind associated with the Orient, and lifted it to my lap. It appeared quite heavy, and it felt so as it rested on my knee. "That is kind of him. It is beautiful."

Lily frowned at me. "You must open it. That is not the gift, only the wrapping."

"Oh, I see." With a glance at Lily, I lifted the lid, and there, nestled in a compartment with red silk lining, were three gold ingots. "Oh my..." I gasped. No wonder it was heavy. Each bar must have been worth at least £1000. In another compartment was a jade figurine, and I thought that was rather special, too. I opened the flap of a third compartment, and found a string of pearls. Lily then showed me a drawer at the base of the box, in which contained a wrapped, solid round of Pu-er tea. This type of tea could be aged for years, growing in flavour and fetch a tidy sum. We had often sipped it after our evening meal, Yu and I. The scent washed over me, bringing back such rich memories.

I was speechless. On top of the tea, I could see a letter poking out and glimpsed some of Yu Tang's beautiful handwriting, familiar in spite of the passage of time.

I covered my mouth. Distressed, I met Lily's gaze. "He should not...I cannot..." I sucked in a breath. "You should have these." I lifted the box to hand it back.

Shaking her head, Lily put her hand on mine once again. "He was adamant that you accept these gifts. He said that if not for you, he would not have been so successful in business, and this is but a small token from him, a share of his success."

Gold bars? Pearls, jade? These were all things of high value. It was not their worth that was important to me, though. It was what they represented. Chen Yu Tang valued me, even after all this time. I closed my eyes, breathing slowly so as to not dissolve into tears yet again.

I was tempted to read the letter, but as Lily was still with me, I decided to wait until I was alone. The most immediate problem was how to introduce her to my family. Until now, only Charity had known of Lily's existence and the circumstances of her birth. Those secrets had died with my sister, I was certain. Edward had never hinted that his mother had said anything to him, and his reaction of utter surprise today supported that. My nephew and Milly did not know I had been married or that I had had a son all those years ago. With such a negative experience, I did not want it known. Perhaps it was wrong of me to feel shame for being duped by Charles and having my son abducted.

These days I trusted this household with my life. I had to trust that they would accept Lily's origins and keep the truth about my story to themselves. It would do Lily no good to be considered illegitimate and tarnished by the shame our society at large would probably apply to me. I had been willing for them to read my story in my memoir. That was now pre-empted by the arrival of my past.

Shutting the box, I put it beside me on the settee and drew her closer to me. "We have so much to discuss, of course. But first, what are your plans? What do you hope to do in England?"

Lily smiled lightly and looked down as if abashed. "I have been in London these six months. I have been waiting for the right time to find you. Running Father's business takes a lot of time and planning. The brother nearest me in age is in control of our Singapore businesses, and my next youngest brother is managing the Canton warehouses. The youngest brother runs our Hong Kong offices. Although I employ an Englishman as a manager, I make the important decisions for our English dealings. However, I have learned that English society is sometimes less flexible than Chinese when it comes to women and business."

Lily was twenty-three years old.

I nodded sadly. "From what I can recall from my time there, that is true."

Her shoulders dropped and she let out a slow sigh. "There is more. My brothers are traditional. They desire me to marry in order to firm up connections to other merchant families. We did not separate on the best of terms."

"You do not wish to marry?"

Lily lifted her chin, and I detected steel in her. "If I did marry one day, it would be a man of my choosing. I do not wish to marry for money or connections. My younger sisters do not object to my brothers' wishes and so they are preparing for these arranged marriages. Father says it is tradition, except he has told my sisters privately to choose their own happiness and that they need not agree to it if they do not like their prospective husbands."

From the little I knew of her father's culture, it seemed it was quite unusual for Lily to have been given so much responsibility and freedom. It was no wonder she desired more than a traditional arranged marriage.

"How many brothers and sisters do you have?" I asked.

"I am the eldest of ten children living. Two died as infants. My next brother is twenty-one years of age, the next nineteen and the other is eighteen and was a twin with my sister. The other two marriageable sisters are seventeen and sixteen. My...um...my Chinese mother died last year."

"And your father?"

"My father lives, but he is old now."

I tried to calculate his age. He was perhaps a bit older than me, but surely he was no more than fifty.

"I see."

Seeing my puzzlement, she added, "He is fifty-five years old. He is clear of mind, but he suffers from arthritis and is not as lively as he once was."

Acknowledging her words with a nod, I recalled he looked a lot younger than he was. I then asked, "And how have you found London?"

Lily met my eye. "It is cold, and the food is very dull."

I chuckled. I liked her frank reply. "Indeed. Having been warm all your life, it cannot be easy being in England."

Lily nodded and continued, "Also, the people are not always kind. Sometimes it has been dangerous."

My heart sank. "I am afraid my fellow countrymen are not as used to the variety of people in the world as those who have travelled abroad. I am sorry you were troubled by their ignorance."

"Yes, an Oriental lady has not the same standing as an English one," agreed Lily. "Also, I dare say some people do not like to see a woman in trade." Her smile was bright, and I was glad to see that she did not seem cowed by the situation.

"However do you manage? Surely you are not in real danger?"

Lily nodded. "At times, yes. I have had to use my gift."

My ears pricked up. "Gift?"

Lily frowned. "Surely you know about it. Is it not from you? Father always said so."

A nervous tremble overcame me, but I ventured, "Do you mean the Prudential Light?"

Lily frowned. "Yes, Father said he called it that in you *Róu Guang*. He said its related to your name, Prudence, and that it means 'soft light'. He said that in your life you had to hide your gift, and by the time he met you, it was extremely hard for you to use it. Father said I was able to use mine early because we nurtured it. He also trained me to fight, to look after myself. He said my gift is more resolute spirit, *Bu Qu Xin Hun*—and he encouraged me to use it when I needed to."

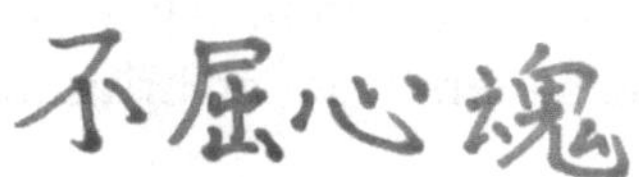

. . .

I BLINKED, THINKING THAT WOULD HAVE MADE THEIR HOME LIFE interesting. "What can you do with your gift?" I asked, fascinated. I was thinking how astute it was of Yu Tang to understand my plight. I had gifts, that much was clear; I had seen my brother's spirit and talked with him as a child, and in that alley in Singapore, I had been able to repel my attackers. Perhaps I could yet awaken the gift within me.

"Well," she replied, "I can fight, including fending off attackers. Father said you could do this when threatened, too, but that you couldn't control it. He trained me from a young age, so now I can refine the gift to suit the situation. I can also move fast and leap high. Combined with some defensive techniques Father showed me, I am able to look after myself. I try not to kill anyone, but when my life or someone else's is at risk, I do not hold back."

I was stunned. There was so much more to my daughter than met the eye. Also, Lily sounded like Jemima: brave, strong and indestructible. Could the family cope with two such extraordinary women? I supposed it would have to.

Just then there was a commotion in the hall, and as if thinking about her had conjured her up, I heard Jemima's voice. Sighing, I patted Lily's hand and stood. "You are about to meet the family. Are you ready?"

"You will introduce me?" She looked hopeful and yet anxious. "Surely you need not. Call me a friend, perhaps."

"I'm afraid my nephew and Mr Fulton already know of our relationship," I replied.

"Oh yes, that was my fault. I am sorry. Could we not say you cared for me when I was a baby and that the title 'Mother' is an honorific?"

"Only if you wish it; I am not sure they would believe me. But be assured, my family will keep our secret, for they are your family too. Do you not wish to be known to them? With your gift I think you will fit right in." I feared her response, as I knew the lie would not wash with my family and would only undermine the trust that had grown between us all. Besides, I had written it in my memoir, so they were going to read the circumstances of her birth.

Lily stared at her hands and then looked up, meeting my gaze. "All right. Let us tell them, if you would not find it too distressing."

I exhaled with relief. "Pfah! I never thought I would see you again in my life. Now that you are here, I want them to know you too."

Lily stood and embraced me again, and I hugged her back, cherishing the feel of her in my arms. As we pulled apart, Jemima bustled in, dressed in a pink robe with a chintz overlay, an elaborate outfit that could pass for afternoon tea apparel. Milly was behind her, looking wan in a pale blue robe with a darker blue trim.

"Milly! You should not be out of bed!" I exclaimed as Fulton hurried in behind her and guided her to a chair.

"I am not missing this," Milly said, a militant glare in her eye. Her gaze flicked between me and Lily. Obviously, the gentlemen had not taken refuge in the library but had dashed upstairs to gossip with their wives! I shot them both a castigating look, but there was nothing to be done about it now.

Jemima's eyes flashed as she assessed the scene, then she nodded once and sat down, Edward standing sentinel behind her. I was grateful she held her tongue—a difficult task for her, to be certain.

"Well, I see you have all come to stickybeak," I said with a sigh.

"Aunt Prudence, what is going on?" Jemima said, acknowledging the visitor with a nod. Her gaze then switched back to me. I knew it was too good to be true that Jemima would keep quiet for long.

"Impertinent girl, I will explain everything if you would only let me get a word in edgeways."

Jemima lifted her shoulders and then sighed. "She is back to her old self after the fainting spell you told me about, Edward. That is a relief," she said to the rest of the room.

There was nothing for it. I garnered my resolve and reached out to take Lily's hand, pulling her gently to my side. Lily, I noticed, was not quite as tall as me, and slighter of figure.

"This is Miss Lily Chen. Lily, may I present my nephew, Mr Edward Huntington, and his wife Jemima, who I now know since recently completing my family tree is also a blood relative. This other young lady is my niece, Milly, who I raised like a daughter after her parents died, and her husband and my benefactor, Mr Ambrose Fulton."

Lily curtseyed creditably.

My four young relatives nodded at her politely, but continued staring at us with an expectant air. I drew in a breath. It was now or never. "Lily is my natural daughter," I said finally. "She was born in Singapore and her father is Chinese."

Jemima's mouth dropped open, but she shut it with a snap and covered it with a hand. "Oh, Aunt. But I said terrible things to you about never having had a child. How horrid of me. I am so sorry."

I smiled beatifically at her. "Your insult did not touch me, Jemima. Think nothing of it. You were in pain at the time, and I know you did not mean it, so all is forgiven. Also, Lily's birth is not something I could ever talk about freely, so your misconception is understandable." As the focus was on Lily at this time, I did not wish to bring up the existence of James, if he was even still alive.

Jemima sat back and allowed herself to relax. "Thank you, Aunt. Hello, Cousin Lily. I am delighted to meet you."

Lily inclined her head.

Milly smiled and wiped her eyes, which had started to leak tears. "I am pleased to meet you, Lily. Please excuse me, I am only happy to have a new cousin." My niece then proceeded to cry into her handkerchief.

Lily nodded in acknowledgement. "I am delighted to meet you, Milly."

Edward came forward, offering his hand to shake. "How do you do?"

"Well, thank you. I am pleased to meet you, sir."

"Edward will do," he said, grinning. "Family and all that."

Fulton approached last and bowed over Lily's hand. "Welcome to the family, Lily."

My daughter cleared her throat, clearly moved by their welcome. My chest filled with pride when I saw that my family had accepted Lily as I had hoped they would. They were shocked and perhaps bewildered, not yet knowing all my history, but they accepted the truth of my words and, for now, asked no further questions.

Lily faced them and folded her hands in front of her. In her excellent English, she said, "Thank you for the welcome. I must confess I was a little anxious about it; I did not know what to expect, so it was a risk. I did not wish to ruin my mother's reputation or presume on her good nature. But I was charged by my father with an errand, and I have had a lifelong wish to meet her, you understand. I would ask that you be discreet and not spread word abroad of our relationship, for her sake. I do not know all your ways, but I am aware that your society does not smile on such situations."

"It does if you are a duke and have lots of money," quipped Jemima.

Lily turned to her. "I understand that is so. Women have a more difficult time, it seems."

"It is not fair, though," Jemima said, and folded her arms. "Sauce for the goose should be sauce for the gander."

Lily frowned, glancing at me.

"She means that there is a double standard at play: men should have the same restrictions, face the same repercussions, as do women," I explained.

Lily nodded. "Oh, I see. My father said there is nothing fair in life. That we must make the most of the situations we find ourselves in and pray for good fortune and health."

"He sounds like a logical man," Fulton said.

"Secrets are tricky things," Lily continued. "I grew up knowing about my mother and why she had to leave. My father explained these things to me, even at the risk that I might inadvertently speak of them, which would have pained his wife, whom he married after I was born. She always knew that I was special to my father, but she thought my mother had died. She was not unkind to me, and then she was too busy when she had nine children of her own to care for. I realise knowledge of me is new to you, and I am sure it will take some time for you to adjust."

Conversation erupted then. The others peppered Lily with questions about her home, what it was like there and what she was doing in England. My secret was out. They only needed my memoir for the details.

After an hour or so of intense conversation, Lily glanced at her pocket watch and rose to take her leave.

"Oh, but you must stay," Jemima insisted. She turned to her host. "Do invite her to stay, Fulton."

Fulton, God bless him, was as patient as a saint with her. "Indeed, it was on the tip of my tongue to do so, Jemima."

Lily broke in to protest, "Oh, I could not possibly impose."

Milly, who now looked rather tired, said, "You came a long way, Cousin. Surely you do not mean to return to London this evening. You must stay here with us."

To my delight, Lily was swiftly offered a room, and a footman was sent to collect her things from the inn where she was staying.

Dinner that night was an interesting affair, as Lily entertained us with tales of Singapore, her family, her voyage and interesting perspectives on life in London.

"You are so beautiful," Jemima said in her blunt way. "I can see you slaying gentlemen with one look, with one flick of your fan."

Lily blushed and inclined her head. "You are kind to say so, but I am not ready for marriage just yet."

"Why? You are older than both Milly and I, if the year of your birth is correct."

Lily smiled and looked between us all. "I am a businesswoman. A gentleman would not like that. And I learned at a young age that English law would grant my husband all my money upon marriage, and the right to rule over me. I do not wish that."

"Is it not the same in China?" Milly asked wonderingly.

"Not exactly the same. The female head of the household wields a lot of power, through influence over her husband and her sons."

"Interesting," Jemima commented. "Influence, is it?" She glanced wickedly at Edward.

"Do not get ideas, love," Edward said mildly. "You already do too much manipulating as it is."

An expression of mock outrage came over Jemima's face. "It is not manipulation if you are clever and know what to do."

Fulton cleared his throat. "Let us perhaps have less talk in general of men having an advantage over women. In this house, the women rule; is that not so?" He lifted an eyebrow at Edward. "You know this to be true, old friend." A footman finished filling their glasses with champagne, and Fulton lifted his in a toast. "To new beginnings. To a son, Louis, for Edward and Jemima, a daughter, Arabella, to Milly and myself, and to Aunt Prudence reuniting with her daughter, Lily, who we welcome to the family. Health and happiness to us all."

⚜

LATER THAT NIGHT WHEN EVERYONE WAS ABED, I WAS ABLE TO draw out Yu Tang's letter. Lily was asleep in the room next to mine, and I felt great comfort in knowing she was there. I was still in a state of bewilderment, and I knew that it would take time for us all to adjust. I never thought I would have my daughter so close to me, and I was so proud of how she'd turned out, so grateful to Yu Tang for doing right by her.

From my dressing table, I took down the small rice bowl that Yu Tang had gifted me when I left him all those years ago. It was white with green-stemmed orange and pink flowers spread out over its surface, and they were just as bright as ever. It was the miracle of Chinese kilns and a skill much envied in Britain. As well I drew out the jade necklace he'd given me the day I left. The leather cord had long since disintegrated so it now sat on a fine chain, one that my sister, Charity, had bequeathed to me. It had brought me good fortune and good health, I thought. I was rarely ill and, given all the activity in my life these past two years, remarkably resilient.

When we battled that monster's minions, I had used the skills that Yu Tang had taught me to apply everyday things in my defence. Umbrellas and hatpins thrown with deadly accuracy, for example. Milly learned too, and we had helped Jemima and the others prevail.

For the first time, I was able to reflect on how fortunate I had been in many ways. And now I had met my daughter, who I'd never thought I would see again. My mind turned inevitably to my son, James, and I pondered whether he was alive or dead, happy or sad, and whether he remembered me.

Letting go a long sigh, I unfolded the letter and read.

*Dearest Prudence,*

*I hope this letter finds you well. If you are reading it, then you have met our daughter Lily, who has been a joy in my heart. No daughter could be as good in spirit or as strong in mind as she. I hope you are pleased with her, as I am, and that you know I have been faithful to my promise to you all those years ago.*

Please accept this humble missive from one who honours you and offers prayers daily for your good health and fortune. Not a day has gone by when I do not think of you and our time together. Your beauty and your grace remain in my memory, and your tender heart so true, even when you were in the direst of straits. It was my honour to assist you and keep you safe. It was a gift to love you and hold you close to my heart. I fear I did not know what you were to me until you were gone from my sight. My spirit was very low for months after you left. Only your letter telling me you had arrived safely lifted my mood.

I kept my promise about our daughter. I have cared for her, loved her and protected her. Lily learned of you from my lips. Even though now she has many brothers and sisters, and her life has been good, I send her to England to discover a future for herself, one not dictated by tradition. There is a strong part of her that is from you. I saw it from her earliest days. I like to think that she is the best of two worlds, united in strength.

We have prospered and prospered well thanks to your guidance. The gift of language you taught me proved invaluable. Your creativity in design and advice on the fashion market paid great dividends. Please accept this token from me as a return on your investment in a humble merchant to whom you gave many things.

As surely as you emit the magical and potent Prudential Light when your life is threatened, your inner light burns brightly in those you love. Lily has inherited your gift and with guidance can use it at will. Guide her to use this power for good in your country. I dry my tears now as Lily leaves me to travel across the sea. I feel in some way what it must have been like for you to part from her. It wounds me to the heart to say goodbye to her, knowing this is the last time I may see her. Why is the world a cruel place that separates those we love and cherish from us?

I have lived many years now and the year I spent with you was the most significant, because you opened my mind to possibilities, to differences, to love. It is always my regret that I did not find a way for us to be together. However, I know that I did the right thing to send you back to your home, for eventually your light would have faded, living in seclusion and away from the world as you were. To be shunned by your people and mine would have wounded your spirit greatly. I hope that you have found fulfillment in this life.

My soul hopes that you have been happy and that you think well of me, if you think of me at all.

Your dearest friend
12 December 1863

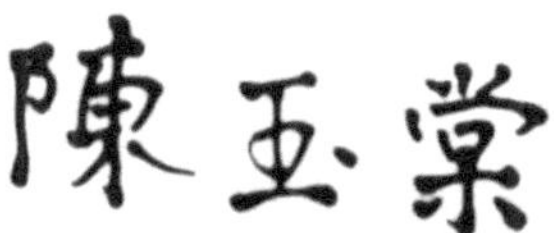

Oh, Yu Tang, you did the right thing!

I'd had to leave. I could not regret that decision, except—it left so many 'what ifs' in its wake.

While I no longer loved Yu Tang with the passion I once had, I looked upon his memory fondly. I didn't believe I would have survived that night on the streets without his help, Prudential Light or no. Now I felt dismayed that I had never really learned how to use it. It thrilled me that Lily had this power and could wield it. I came from a special family, and I had passed on membership in that family to Lily. After glimpsing the power in Louis and Arabella, I had to ensure that the talent was fostered and they learned to use it. I thought of Milly and wondered if she too had a talent that we had not recognised.

I prepared for bed and then lay down and read the letter twice more. I tried to connect to my Prudential Light and while I thought I had failed, my dreams were rich and strangely lifelike.

I saw a large house in my mind's eye. The air was thick with heat, but a breeze swayed the leaves of the palm trees that grew around it. I floated into the building through a window. A plume of incense rose from a stick in a holder on a side table. In a chair sat a man. He was dressed in a red silk robe, and he had slippers on his feet. He was smaller than I remembered, thinner, more hunched, with fine lines around his mouth and eyes. His hair was cut short and had grown grey. He looked up as I approached. Eyes wide, he exclaimed, "Prudence?"

I put out my hands to him, and we touched. It felt so real. "Yu?"

"Yes, it is me." He smiled, a look of fondness in his features. "I would know you anywhere."

I sat up suddenly, the scent of perfumed incense in the air. It was as if I had actually been there. Yet, how could that be? Perhaps, it was a strong dream, because I had read Yu's letter a few times before falling asleep. And yet, it had seemed so real, and he had spoken to me. It felt similar to the times I had seen my brother, Brandon—he had seemed so real to me then, too. And the time I visited Wilbur, but I do not think I actually went to his house by conventional means. It was part of my gift. Mr White asked me if I spoke to the dead and I admitted that I did, and the living. It was so frustrating though not to be able to direct my talent at will. It was hard to take credit for something I had no control over.

Disturbed, I tried to go back to sleep but eventually gave up. The house was cold, and I pulled on a robe and slippers. Perhaps I could heat some milk in the kitchen to help me go back to sleep.

# CHAPTER 13

In the dim light of the hall lantern, I crept slowly towards the stairs, hoping to stop my pot of hot chocolate spilling over the tray.

"Can I have some of that too, Aunt?" Jemima whisper-shouted from her bedroom door. There were two cups on the tray already, possibly foresight on my part.

"Of course," I replied, and changed direction. I could hear baby Louis gurgling and cooing as I approached. Jemima had decided to feed the baby herself, which meant she was up at all hours. Luckily, she had a night nurse to help out.

I entered the room. Edward lay sprawled on top of the bed in his nightshirt, his curls standing up. It looked as if he had been supervising and had fallen asleep.

The baby kicked in the cradle. I put down the tray of hot chocolate, poured Jemima a cup and handed it to her. "May I?" I asked, indicating with my chin to baby Louis. "Where is the nurse?"

"Gone to fetch some more linens for Louis," she replied, taking a sip. "He is lively and finding it hard to settle. He cannot possibly be hungry. He has been feeding this last hour at least."

I picked him up and placed him on my shoulder. "There, there, young man. What is the problem?"

I could feel that he had a lot of wind in his tummy. Jemima would not listen to advice about diet and would eat the peas at dinner, whereas Milly avoided them because she was compliant. Arabella did not have as much wind. I soothed the baby, holding him upright and rubbing his back until all that nasty wind came out. Louis was a strong baby, able to lift his head a little and look at me. "How do you do, young sir. Are you ready to sleep now?"

As I put him back in his cradle and swaddled him, Louis relaxed and soon closed his eyes. I smoothed his hair with a forefinger and sighed.

I grew conscious of Jemima staring at me, and went to the tray to pour myself some hot chocolate. As we were both awake, it did not hurt to chat.

When I took my seat, Jemima began. "How is the memoir going, Aunt?"

"Very well, considering. I am not sure how much more there is to the story. As you know, some of it is catching up with me now."

"It is indeed. How does that feel?"

I took a sip and met Jemima's frank gaze. We had not always been friends. But we had the measure of each other and had resolved our differences. Lowering my cup, I considered my niece. Cousin Wilbur had been preternaturally young. Only murder had removed him from this life. Why I thought of him just then I did not know.

As I relaxed back into the chair, I responded, "It is hard to articulate. Part of me feels like I am in a dream. Happy to see Lily, of course. It's like a part of me that broke off years ago has come back to make me whole again." Tears sprang to my eyes and I searched for a handkerchief in my robe pocket. "I hope that my friends will understand the circumstances."

"Are there any more surprises?" she asked, her gaze keen, as if she craved more excitement.

"Possibly," I said cautiously.

"Why did you not marry Lily's father? Was it because he was Chinese?"

"No. I would have married him if I could, although, of course, our society would have looked at both of us askance. Yu Tang was a lovely man, educated and clever. I could not marry him for the simple reason that I was already married."

"What?" Jemima's head tilted to the side.

"I had married in England back in 1836."

"Oh, that was to Charles Leighton."

I blinked, surprised.

"I confess, I read some of your memoir. Just flicked through a few sections."

Appalled, I rounded on her. "Jemima!"

Her cheeks grew pink, and Edward twitched as if my voice had cut into his slumber.

"All right!" she began, flapping a hand as if putting out my fire. "I am not proud of myself. And it was only a few pages...here and there. It is a bit of a jumble, if you must know."

"It is not finished yet. It is not orderly. I have not decided what I will share, yet, if any of it. Memories are like threads. You pull one and a whole section of the past comes undone. The final copy will have the parts I want to share."

Jemima waved a hand. "Aunt Prudence, you should publish all of it. You will make a fortune. Anonymously, of course. It has scandal, intrigue, love, betrayal...secret babies!"

I near choked on my hot chocolate. "You read the whole thing!"

Jemma blushed. "Did I? But it is not finished. Did you ever find James?"

The cup clattered on the saucer as I tried to draw breath. "No, I never found my son."

Jemima covered her mouth. "Oh, Aunt. That is terrible. Now that I have a child, I understand that bond. How could you bear it?"

Sagging into the chair, I replied, "I did not bear it well." I blinked hard against fresh tears then turned to her, feigning outrage in every pore. "Really, Jemima, you should not have read my memoir, or any part of it. Why did you?"

Jemima pouted. "If you must know, I wanted to get an understanding of you, about why you act the way you do. Why you hated me so at first."

I gave a tight-lipped smile. "I have alluded to that in part. But foremost I have not had a moment to reflect on any of my writings. It is just a raw, unfinished remembrance of past happenings at the moment."

"Cannot you just tell me now?"

I sighed and threw up my hands. "I am fairly certain you have worked it out already, and I have apologised in my way. It was mostly to do with Milly. I had hoped that Edward would choose her for a wife. His mother put the idea in my head, actually. 'How lovely would it be if Edward married Milly,' she said. At that time, Edward was at school and not yet sixteen. I will not say it was her dearest wish, because it was only a passing mention, but that had my mind going in a particular way. Milly, as you know, is a remarkable woman, and I raised her and loved her as my own. Then you arrived and tore all my plans to shreds. A charming, beautiful, elegant, rich, clever young woman with claims on Edward's affection." I shrugged. "You definitely had his attention. My vision of Milly's marital bliss was shattered as soon as I looked at you. Of course, as time has gone on, we have all been shown that things turned out the way they were meant to." I met her stare. "Does that accord with what you have discerned, Jemima?"

Jemima wiggled in her chair, making herself more comfortable. "Well, yes, if you must know, it does. However, you put a certain slant on the situation that softens it somewhat for me, knowing all the parties as I do now."

We smiled at each other. If we had been at war, I would say we'd reached a truce, but we were not, and I saw that Jemima's affection was genuine. Then a certain circumstance flashed in my memory. I refilled my cup and took another sip.

"You thought you could outsmart me by buying fabric and giving Milly dresses and exposing her to Fulton." As I sat back in my chair, I sniffed a little. "That did work out well, I grant you, but you could not have known it would, and thus cannot take the credit."

Jemma sat up straight, as if I had shot an arrow at her. "Of course I cannot take credit. I did not make them fall in love. I do not control their hearts, but I confess I did encourage them when I saw which way the wind was blowing."

I smiled and drained the last of my hot chocolate. Then I yawned and tried to smother it with a hand. It was as if Jemima's vociferous energy had exhausted us both.

"Do I still annoy you, Aunt?" she said gently.

Given what I had just been thinking, my face grew hot. I put my empty cup back on the tray. "To be honest, my dear, you do rub me the wrong way at times. Mostly deliberately, I believe. However, I confess I have an affection and a respect for you that endures."

Jemima smiled, her blue eyes sparkling. "I love you also, Aunt Prudence." Then she yawned too, picked up her cup and drank off the last of her own chocolate. "The nurse is back so I really must go to bed. Louis will wake again soon to feed and I really must rest."

"Oh yes, I as well." We both stood, and Jemima reached for my hand and squeezed it gently. "I will not tell a soul about what I read. I promise. I beg you, though, to keep in the part about the Prudential Light. That is fascinating. We are a special family."

My cheeks heated. "Yes," I replied, "I have decided to keep that part, even though I do not understand it as I should." I was tempted to tell her about my dream visit to Yu Tang, but decided to keep it to myself.

I headed to the door and paused as I turned back. "Sleep well, my dear. Shall I assist you in the morning with the baby?"

Jemima yawned again. "Oh yes, please do. Edward is useless. He just falls asleep all the time. He sings a lullaby and then drifts off himself in a moment, leaving Louis awake. And I dare say he cannot tell one end of the baby from the other. Luckily, the day nurse is as competent as the night nurse. If you come around nine, the nurse can take a break, and I shall get up and dressed."

"So early? Should you not be resting?"

"I *am* resting. I am not hunting down the murderers of my father, am I? Come to think of it, I still haven't had any word from Uncle Ferdy. I need information from him before I can start looking. I must own that I am seriously concerned about him. He is still not answering me when I call. If I could spare Edward, I would send him searching."

"Perhaps, if Mr White does not respond tomorrow, you should discuss it with Edward. He may have a solution."

Jemima yawned. "Yes, I will do that."

I left the room, nonplussed. Jemima was still keen to find those who murdered her father. Motherhood had not lessened her ability to tread where others feared to go. While it was quite shocking that Cousin Wilbur had been murdered, I did not think hunting down those responsible was a ladylike activity for a married woman and mother, even one like Jemima.

I found that I was asleep as soon as my head hit the pillow. Perhaps because of my interaction with Louis, my dreams turned to the birth of my son and the joy I had in him before he was taken from me so cruelly.

It was early when I awoke. The sun had not yet risen, but the birds were twittering in anticipation of a new day. I sat up but I felt as if I had not slept, so full of the past had my night been. A strange feeling came over me. It was as if I was not alone any longer. A coppery, metallic smell reached my nostrils; was that *blood?* Turning quickly, I saw a shadow move, and a moan filled the space. "Who is there?" I hissed.

With my heart hammering, I stood up and went to look, throwing open the curtains to bring in some early light, but there was no one there. Yet, there had been, I was sure. I feared there was danger looming, only I did not know what. What could I say to the others, in any case? I checked the room again and my heart rate settled. There was no one there, yet I could not shake the sense of foreboding. As it was still early, I took my time with my toilette, dressing carefully and then went downstairs. I hoped Lily was there and I was keen to see her once more, even it if was just to gaze at her and admire her beauty.

# CHAPTER 14

Downstairs with a rug over my lap, with only the crackle and pop of the fire to disturb the whispers of the house as it slumbered. It reminded me of how houses breathe and wheeze and nothing is ever truly quiet. At night, throw up the window and hear the animals— the fox cries, the frogs croaking in the pond— the rustle of the leaves and the trickle of a stream.

I was the first one up, besides the servants. I was eager to see Lily again but had to be patient for she was not yet up.

My conversation with Jemima had me thinking about how those past happenings had shaped me and my views on the world. I was often hard on the younger people around me; I seemed to swing between outrage at all they got away with and envy, laced with respect.

The quiet snick of the door closing alerted me to company. It was Jemima, dressed in her flamboyant pink robe, her hair half in rags as if she were planning to go to a ball. "Jemima? I thought you would be sleeping in."

She sat down with a *flomp*, yawned loudly, and met my gaze. "I have just finished feeding Louis and he is tucked up asleep with Edward, and I thought to see if you were up."

"Have you been reading my memoir again?"

Jemima stretched languidly. "Yes, of course I have. But it was your letter from Sir Giles that you had tucked in there that has me curious."

"Really! You are impossible." I snorted in mock outrage.

"He proposed to you, did he not?"

My cheeks grew hot and I shook my head. "You are the most impertinent..." I sighed. "Yes."

"And you told him you were already married?"

"Yes, he took it well."

"He wrote you lines of a sonnet so I think he did. But why on earth did you not tell any of us you were married? Why pass yourself off as a spinster?"

"It is complicated."

Jemima shook her head. "No. It is not."

I frowned as I tried to reconstruct my thinking at the time. "I was angry. I was ashamed. I had been deserted, my son stolen. I wanted no man to have control over me again. By taking the name Wainwright, I thought there was no way a man could hurt me so deeply again. When my sisters died, the truth of my marriage died with them. My parents died before I returned to England. You see, I kept the name, I called myself a spinster and left my fake widow status in the past."

Jemima shook herself. "You think you know someone and then all these secrets come out. I pity Sir Giles. I suspected he admired you."

"You did? Did you not think I was too old and decrepit for such amours?"

"Absolutely. I thought Sir Giles was too, but that goes to show you that I do not know much. You are not as old as I once thought."

"I think that is a compliment."

Jemima yawned. "It is definitely a compliment. But I am tired now and I shall go back to bed."

⚜

NOT LONG AFTER, FULTON TURNED UP. "GOOD MORNING, AUNT Prudence. I hope you slept well."

I was going to reply in the affirmative but instead told Fulton of my strange moment. "Fulton, I have a sense of foreboding."

"Indeed, most disturbing. I shall have the groundsman search around the house and have the footmen check all the rooms. I have learned not to ignore feelings."

"Thank you, Fulton, for taking me seriously."

"Breakfast is being set up in the morning room. Shall you take my arm and accompany me there? Milly and Edward are asleep. Jemima, I passed in the hallway. I believe Lily should be down soon for I heard her moving about in her room."

Putting my rug aside, I took Fulton's proffered arm and went with him into breakfast. Not long after, Lily joined us. She was shy at first, but with encouragement from Fulton was soon filling her plate and chatting amiably.

Later, Lily and I walked into the village and explored. It was lovely to see things from Lily's perspective. "It is so different to home and to London. So quiet, so peaceful, so empty."

"Let's take a look in the drapers. They have some interesting things on display. And please tell me what it is that you import."

While Lily told me of the different goods she imported, we admired the gloves, the bonnet trimmings, and I ordered a small amount of linen for a project I wanted to work on.

By the afternoon, the household was awake, and we all talked, played cards and read.

Fulton dropped me a note to let me know that nothing had been found by the servants but that he was on the alert and assured me not to worry.

That night at dinner, I enjoyed spending time with Lily, who sparkled with liveliness and intelligence. It warmed my heart to see my family accept her and truly like her. There was no time for wondering what life would have been. Lily exclaimed over the food we ate, so different from her home or what she prepared herself. "So much meat," she said. "I do not think I could get used to it."

Desserts were also something to be talked over. "Do you not like rice pudding?" Jemima asked. "It is a favourite of mine."

"We do not eat the rice in this way. Although I have had it with coconut milk, but the rice is a different variety to this."

"There is more than one variety of rice?" Milly asked. "I did not know that."

THE NEXT DAY PASSED OFF IN A SIMILAR MANNER, RELAXED AND full of laughter. I felt so blessed to have had this time with my daughter, time I never imagined having.

Lily returned to London on the Monday, but not without promising to return on the weekend next.

The morning after Lily left, I went downstairs for morning tea, where I found Edward, Fulton, and Jemima, who refused to stay abed.

"Did you find any other skeletons in your closet, Aunt?" Jemima said by way of greeting.

"Enough to keep you entertained, dear girl," I joked in return.

Jemima smiled and sipped her tea. "I cannot wait."

"Indeed, so it would seem." Unbeknownst to her, I had found a new hiding place for my scribblings and locked the manuscript away.

"I say," Edward said. "I will be pleased to see our cousin Lily again. Such an unusual and interesting young woman."

Fulton leaned back into the settee and stirred his tea. "Indeed.

A woman of business. I would wager she must be quite capable if her father entrusted her with his concerns."

Of Lily's other skills, they had not been apprised. Although I itched to tell them, I foresaw that they would probably like to see rather than hear about these particular talents, and I wanted Milly to be present, in any case.

Jemima had replaced her elaborate pink robe with a demure gown of navy blue, adorned with small delicate silver buttons in a double row down the bodice and a thin line of embroidered silver vines along the hem and sleeve edges. She had at last adopted a crinoline, even though I did not particularly agree with that innovation. In the winter I preferred layers of warm petticoats. This made me ponder whether I was too set in my ways.

"So, Aunt Prudence, have you had any news from Sir Giles?" Jemima said before biting into a small round piece of shortbread.

As I was mid-sip, I choked on my tea.

Edward passed me a serviette to mop up the mess. "Jemima!" Edward said in reproving tones.

Fulton rolled his eyes. "Is nothing sacred to you, Jemima?" he added.

"Must you pry into all my concerns and advertise them to everyone?" I responded.

Jemima swallowed a mouthful. "But Aunt, there have been times when you have pried into mine." She looked at the plate of sweetmeats and selected a macaroon. "Besides, I am dying to know what the next instalment of your life will be."

It was my turn to roll my eyes and shake my head. "I have not heard from Sir Giles, if you must know. Does that satisfy your curiosity?"

"But then I will have nothing to gossip about."

I smiled. "We all have our cross to bear, Jemima."

Fulton lowered his cup and looked between Jemima and me. "Then it is true?" Fulton appeared eager.

Edward coughed. "Yes, indeed it is so. Sir Giles is a good sort of man."

My heart sank. "Surely you did not tell them, Jemima!"

Jemima looked to the ceiling and pretended not to hear me. She had told them about the proposal. Why is it that the people you love and respect can so easily drive you to distraction?

"Thank you for your comment, Nephew. However, the matter is private and I do not wish to discuss it."

"She cannot accept him because she is already married," Jemima added smoothly, as if she hadn't just added coal to the fire.

Fulton's cup jiggled and he put it back on the tea tray. "Married? Have I missed something?"

"It is in her memoir. She kept her marriage secret for reasons. Actually, I can understand why."

The daggers I glared at Jemima slid right by her. I really wanted to do her some violence. Unfortunately, all my hatpins were upstairs, and I only wore a lace-trimmed cap. I pictured ramming it down her throat. "Jemima, please. Have a care for my—"

"We are family, are we not?" Jemima said. "Edward and Ambrose deserve to know, and besides, at the rate you are writing this thing, they may not live to see all your truths revealed."

"But I had always assumed you were the maiden aunt. Mother never said you had been married." Edward seemed genuinely grieved.

"I asked her not to. Charity understood why."

Despite her insensitivity to my feelings, I found Jemima's openness somewhat refreshing. It would, I realised, be a relief to lay these secrets before my family.

"Yes. I was married long ago," I said to Fulton. To the rest of the table, I said, "The whole of the story you will have to wait for. Jemima has been sneaking a peek at the memoir I have been penning." I knew she had read the whole of what I had written, but there was more.

Fulton nodded politely. "You will have a ready audience, let me assure you." He poured another cup of tea and took a sandwich. Then, meeting Jemima's eye, he said, "Please refrain from ruining the surprise for us."

Edward blushed. "Yes, Jemima, you ought not upset Aunt Prudence. As she has undertaken to write a memoir, we should at least wait until she gives it to us to read."

Jemima inclined her head. "Very well, I shall reveal nothing more. Forgive my impertinence, Aunt."

"I will try, Jemima, but at this moment it is difficult." I could not help but let some of my irritation show.

I was about to say more when the footman let the nurse in. "I am sorry, Mrs Huntington," she said. "Young Louis is unsettled."

Jemima put down her plate and stood up. "It appears that Master Huntington wants his morning tea as well. If you will excuse me."

As she left the room, I took stock. Jemima's pointed comments had me wondering. I really had to start thinking about Sir Giles' offer. It had already been established that I could not accept him as I was already married, but how would we go on? Were we never to see or speak to one another again? The lines of the sonnet led me to suspect that was not the case. Yet would I have accepted him if I were free to do so? Would I be able to remain his friend now that I had declined his proposal? Would he care to be acquainted with me, knowing my reasons? How would he fit into my life? I was content right now, and felt almost complete, too, now that Lily had found me again. What would Sir Giles make of her? With all these considerations in mind, I went back upstairs to my scribblings.

After flicking through a few pages I had already written, I saw that Jemima had left some comments here and there.

Publish this, Aunt! Secret babies! Foreign adventures. You shall make a fortune!!

Further on, I found more. And scribbles. The woman had no sense of decorum.

Thinking of Jemima and her father sparked a memory.

**England, date unknown**

Once I thought I had met Wilbur Hardcastle, Jemima's father. Now I began to ponder that meeting. Did I meet him in the flesh, or had it been that other kind of meeting, in spirit, like I had with Brandon when I was young or like recently when I dream-visited Yu Tang?

In that meeting, which seemed to be in the drawing room at Willow Park, Wilbur seemed young and fit—although not exactly charming.

"What are you doing here, madam?" he asked me, quite rudely.

"Visiting you, obviously," I replied. How I knew who he was I cannot recall. I just knew he was my cousin Wilbur. "Although why I bothered I will never know." There was no sign of the staff or of tea things. Now that I think about it, I had no recollection of travelling there.

"Did you come to see my daughter?" he asked me. "She needs friends."

"Everyone needs friends. Is your wife at home?" I asked.

"Been dead these ten years. Poor lamb. Poor me, too—I miss her so."

"I am sorry to hear that."

"Who are you again?" he asked, forehead creased but eyes watchful. "You look like one of my Hardcastle relatives."

"Really, Cousin Wilbur, you must pay attention when your guests are announced. I am Prudence of the Hardcastle-Smythes."

"Oh, that lot. Dunderheads the lot of them. Except maybe my great-nephew Theo."

That was all that I recollected of the encounter.

It may seem odd for me to have stopped my writing there. But I had to, because Wilbur Hardcastle was suddenly sitting in my room, in the only remaining chair, and glaring at me. Not that he looked like the Wilbur I had met all those years ago. This Wilbur was skin and bone, and quite a sight to see. If anyone heard me cry out, they did not come to investigate. When I realised he meant me no harm, I found I could speak.

"Wilbur?" I ventured.

"Of course, who else would it be?" he replied grouchily.

I tried to respond to this but could not find a polite way to do so. "To what do I owe the pleasure of this visit, Cousin Wilbur?"

"I am uneasy. Jemima is in danger."

My eyes widened. "In danger? She has given birth to a healthy boy and is up and around. I assure you she is quite well and back to her normal self." God help me.

"A boy?" He frowned. "That was quick." He rubbed his chin.

"Congratulations, you are a grandfather."

He glowered at me. "While that is nice to know, it is not why I am here. Huntington told her how I died."

"Yes, not the particulars, mind, only that you were murdered. I believe Jemima wants to ask Mr White about it."

"Ferdinand?"

"Yes."

Wilbur fell silent.

"Is that a problem?"

Wilbur looked up from his contemplation. "No. Ferdinand might help her find those responsible. The problem is that they are coming for her."

"What? Now?"

"At my execution, they thought she was powerless and thus not worth killing—and besides, she was family and protected. But now it seems she has something they want..."

I blinked. Wilbur was serious. I was not imagining this meeting. "One lot already tried to take her ruby heart. She defeated them. Why are you telling me this?"

"No one else can hear me."

I nodded slowly. "And?"

"You can."

"Why can I see you though? Is it my Prudential Light?"

Wilbur growled and shook his head. "No. You have a natural ability to see through the veil. Not well developed, I admit. I have been trying to get your attention for a while."

"Did I meet you in spirit when Jemima was young?"

"Indeed, you did. Very curious and unsettling that meeting was. Trust the Hardcastle blood to throw out the strangeness."

"Will my Prudential Light be useful in assisting Jemima?"

Wilbur looked aghast. "How should I know that? Your talent is stunted, turned in on itself. If you can call on it at the precise moment it is needed, then certainly. As it is..."

Wilbur was not into flattery, it seemed. "Do you know when this will occur?" I wanted to ask how he knew, but the day-to-day activities of ghosts—if that is what he was—were not something I wanted to be familiar with.

His head jerked up. "No. I have no concept of time. Not really. It seemed like yesterday when they drained me of my life force with their damned extractor machine. It is fortunate I have enough left to be able to talk to you. It has taken a while to build up the strength." As he spoke his body began to fade, losing integrity with each word. "Be her friend, Prudence. Protect her, will you?"

"I will," I said, and then he was gone.

Protect Jemima? When she was so powerful herself? Yes, she was only learning to use it. But she was impervious to harm. Surely, he was mistaken. However, according to Edward, Wilbur had been a great magician, and he had been murdered, his attackers leaving no clues of their deed.

Prompted by Wilbur's warning, I went to check on Jemima. The night nurse was just exiting the room, a loaded basket of laundry on her hip, when I tip-toed down the hall. "Is Mrs Huntington asleep?" I whispered.

"Yes, ma'am. They are all abed. I am taking this bundle down to be laundered."

Still anxious, I walked through the house and nothing was untoward. The night nurse returned to her trundle bed and all the other servants were asleep. On returning to my room, I dropped onto the bed, breathing hard as I tried to calm my nerves. I think I must have slept eventually. Waking late, I tidied my hair and dress and joined the family. The babies were asleep in their nurseries, watched over by their nurses. Ally was in attendance though, being bounced on Fulton's knee.

"How is the bonny lad today?" I asked.

Ally turned at the sound of my voice, and lifted his arms to me. Fulton paused and handed him over.

"Now young man, do not pull the ribbons on my cap."

Of course, Ally gave them a tug and my cap went awry. I played with Ally for a time. Milly sewed quietly in the corner, a healthy glow in her cheeks. She was recovering from the birth nicely. Jemima frowned into a book.

Milly looked up. "It is time for Ally to have a snack before his afternoon nap." She rang the bell and John came. He left to fetch the nurse.

I snuck a hug with Ally before I had to let him go. He waved to me at the door. Such a gorgeous young man.

"You missed the scones and cream, Aunt," Milly said in a soft voice. "The kitchen are sending in some soup and fresh baked bread. There is also leftover rice pudding. Do you wish anything else?"

"I assure you, my dear, what you have outlined is ample to my needs. May I say how well you are looking?"

Milly chuckled. "I am still rather tired, but as the rain has stopped, I hope to take a walk in the garden this afternoon." She lifted a hand to forestall my protests. "I know that tradition would have me still in a darkened room, but I would feel so much better out of doors. Would you care to join us?"

"No, thank you, dear, you should enjoy some quiet time with your husband."

Edward came in and went to talk quietly to Jemima.

"Has anyone heard from Mr White?" I enquired of the room.

"No," Jemima said. "I am concerned. He has not responded to my repeated calls."

Edward swallowed the last piece of sweet bun. Sweet bun? Where had he got that? "If we do not hear from him by the end of the day, I shall go in search of him tomorrow."

"Tell me, Nephew, have you officially joined that brotherhood?"

"Technically, I have been invited, and have made positive overtures in response, but I have not yet been initiated or bound by oaths. They are still in sad disarray after Geneck's attack. I am finding it hard to commit because I cannot tell if they are good or bad. At this stage some are good and some are bad. I think Cousin Wilbur was right not to trust them."

Their depleted numbers was the one reason they were keen for Edward to join—that and finding out all his secrets. My nephew was not slow on the uptake. He also had some forbidden texts that Wilbur had stolen from the *Societas Magicae* and given to him. I had seen them once or twice before he covered them with one of his spells. I do not miss much.

\#

A few nights later, I was sitting in my room at my desk, thinking on my memoir, when I heard raised voices.

Getting up, I opened the door and the voices became clearer. Jemima, Edward and someone else were talking. I crept into the hall and quietly stepped further down, certain that the third speaker was Mr White.

Their door was ajar and the three were inside. It was a small sitting room that adjoined Edward and Jemima's bedroom.

"I am telling you, Huntington. You must give them up."

"Nothing I have seen convinces me I should."

"Do you mean I cannot convince you?" Mr White's back was stiff with outrage. I had not seen him so overcome by his feelings before.

"Not all of that bad lot were caught up in Geneck's attack." Edward remained firm.

Mr White shifted his stance, placing more weight on his right leg. It looked to me as if he were in pain. "We find new brethren emerging every week. There have been some twenty at least in the last six months."

"Then tell me who killed Wilbur. Jemima wants to know."

Mr White fell back as if stunned. "But Jemima cannot know who carried out the execution of her father. It is forbidden."

Edward leaned in, as fierce as I had ever seen him. "But not forbidden to me."

Mr White stood his ground, lifted his shoulders and angled his chin. "Actually, you need to be inducted before you are granted any privileges. Your membership is associate only, and on my recommendation. Until you undertake the trials and make the oaths, you cannot delve into *Societas* business. It is in the bylaws."

"What tosh!"

Mr White put his hand on Edward's arm and leaned in close. "I have come to warn you that you are in danger. Word has got around that you are searching for the executioner. I warn you that this individual loves his work, and you don't want him looking for you."

Edward's eyes widened. I saw fear and calculation there. "Jemima is protected, though. She is my wife."

"Indeed, she should be protected. But they also know she has great power, and you know what greed can do. She was not protected previously. Those renegades took her."

"What has that got to do with anything? If they were renegades then they do not care about the rules," Edward said.

"Yes," put in Jemima. "What does my power have to do with anything? It is mine, not theirs."

By this time, I had stepped through the open doorway, and I could see Mr White lit by candle glow. He was wearing robes like a monk, a dark brown cassock with a loose light brown robe over it. "You...I cannot...You do not know what they can do. The executioner has a machine, Jemima. It drains the victim's magical power until they expire."

"You mean until they are dead?" Jemima said, voice rising.

Edward's head jerked up. "What do they do with that power once they have it in the machine?"

"It is available for the brotherhood to use at will. In my experience, they use it in their spells."

Edward's fists balled and his cheeks grew red with fury. "That is outrageous. I do not want to be part of a brotherhood that kills its members and thinks it is right to steal their powers."

"Steal is such a strong word," Mr White argued.

"Really?" Jemima blurted hotly. "Is that what happened to my father? They drained him until there was nothing left, stole his life force?"

Mr White deflated. His shoulders slouched forward and he hung his head. "Yes. It is what they did."

Jemima stood up and paced the room. Anger radiated from her.

She flung herself around, her nightgown and robe swishing around her body. "Have you used my father's power, Uncle Ferdy?"

"No, no." Mr White was much like his name, white, even to the lips. "I stayed away. I could not."

Some of Jemima's ire lessened. She turned her back on him and wiped her eyes.

Mr White turned to Edward. "If you return the sacred texts, it might be enough to satisfy them. Maybe then they will not focus on Jemima."

Edward huffed. "I doubt that. Cousin Wilbur left them to me. Besides, the texts will only give them more power. I would rather use them to protect her."

Mr White bowed in acknowledgement. "I see that I cannot reason with you. I have done my best to support you both. In my way, I have tried to defend you against those that mean you harm. Please stay safe. I must leave now and allow you to rest."

I was not fast enough to back away and Mr White near collided with me as he strode to the door. He took me by surprise, as I had expected he would simply vanish.

"Mrs Wainwright?" Mr White could not have looked more appalled.

"I am sorry. I heard raised voices and came to investigate. Is everything all right with baby Louis? With Jemima?" I asked.

By then, Jemima and Edward had turned and were gaping at me. "What do you do here, Aunt?" Jemima asked.

"I was working on my memoir when I heard voices. I have only just walked up to the door as Mr White was leaving."

"Is that so?" Jemima replied, her eyes narrowing. "Very good timing. Uncle Ferdy was indeed just leaving."

Recovering himself, Mr White bowed and walked past me heading to the top of the stairs. Left alone in the corridor, I blushed and pointed over my shoulder. "I best return to my room. Have a good night's rest."

Edward glowered at me but Jemima smiled as she slipped her

arm into the crook of her husband's elbow. "Good night, Aunt Prudence."

I returned to my room, leaned my back against the door and sighed. Wilbur was right. Jemima was in danger. I had heard the real urging in Mr White's tone, the genuine fear. Did I think him complicit? No, because I'd also seen the faded bruises on his face. He had been beaten and I imagined that was because he was either protecting Jemima or fighting those who were after her.

I had not mentioned Wilbur's visitation to the others. It was best that I speak to my nephew as he would be more likely to believe my story. Opening my drawer, I began to count how many hatpins were in there. I had been building up my supply. I had some extraordinarily long ones, weighted too for greater accuracy. They might be required.

# CHAPTER 15

The day I had been waiting for dawned bright and clear. Lily was returning to join us for the weekend. Travelling on the afternoon train, she arrived in time for dinner. We talked into the evening and had a late supper. I was working on a lovely baby bonnet for Arabella, sewing some pink flowers around the brim. Lily admired my work and was delightfully sociable with the family.

Next morning, she presented me with a bolt of some lovely pale green silk. To Jemima and Milly, she gave a generous bolt of cream silk, embroidered with gold thread. My young relatives were thrilled.

"Would you like a tour of the house?" Milly asked. "It is not as big as Hatfield, which is currently being rebuilt, but the garden is lovely. I have not been much out of doors for weeks and as the weather is fine today, I would like to view it."

"Yes, let's," added Jemima, who hated being cooped up. "I wonder how different the gardens are from what you know, Cousin Lily."

Lily bowed her head. "I would like that. Will you join us, Mo—Mrs Wainwright?"

"No, thank you, dear. I will see to morning tea. I think we should have something special to celebrate your visit." The cook had assured me that she would have a sponge cake ready.

I took up station in the drawing room, making sure all the cushions were arranged as I awaited the return of Lily and the others. Then there was a commotion at the front door and shortly afterwards, the door to the drawing room opened.

The footman bowed. "Sir Giles to see you, ma'am."

My head shot up in surprise. At that moment, Edward and Fulton entered from the other door.

Sir Giles walked in, but before we could speak, he was waylaid by Edward and Fulton, who greeted him. That was when I noticed that there was another person with Sir Giles. I tried to catch a glimpse of him, but the young men were in the way.

Edward and Fulton eventually stepped back. Sir Giles came forward, the young gentleman behind him. "Mrs Wainwright." He bowed briskly and then stepped aside. "Let me present someone I think you will be glad to see. This is Mr James Leighton."

I felt as though all the blood had drained from my body, and I could scarce draw breath. My heart suddenly pounded so hard I could hear it in my ears. "James!" I managed to gasp.

My son looked like his father, but I could see a likeness to me around his eyes and in the shape of his ears. He stepped forward, smiling wonderingly.

"Mother! Sir Giles told me it was you, but I can scarce believe it to be true."

Edward gasped and Fulton made an oath. It was definitely a time of surprises. Shakily I reached up to touch his hair, and my son hugged me, placing his head on my shoulder. "Mother!" he said again.

The room fell quiet as we embraced. Tears spilled down my cheeks. "James, my boy. How good it is to see you."

"And I you. I never thought to find you again."

"I did not abandon you. Please know that. Whatever your father told you, I did not willingly separate from you. Your father took you, and I did not know where you had gone."

Soothingly he whispered, "I know. Sir Giles explained some of it to me."

Just then the ladies arrived at the door. James stepped back and stood beside me. Just as I was thinking about how to introduce the half-siblings to one another, Lily spotted my son.

"Mr Leighton? What do you do here?"

James jolted as if shot. "Miss Chen?"

Then, to my astonishment, the two started speaking in Chinese. I glanced between them, my mind simply unable to put the pieces of this puzzle together. Then it came to an awful conclusion. After that it appears I fainted, for I woke up on the settee with all these faces hovering over me.

Lily was the first to speak. "Mother?" she said softly. "Are you well?"

James' eyes widened. "Mother?" He looked between Lily and me.

I wanted to sit up, explain, but my overwhelm held me frozen. I studied James' expression and then Lily's. Their expressions both held surprise but not horror. As far as I could tell, they were not romantically involved, and the relief of this helped me get a grip on myself.

Jemima and Edward helped me to sit up. Sir Giles was regarding Lily with surprised interest. Fulton passed me a snifter of brandy, and I tossed it off, wishing for a full bottle. Dutch courage was what I needed. How was I going to explain this situation to the people who meant the most to me, including Sir Giles? I looked at him afresh: he had brought my son back to me. I could not be more grateful.

Morning tea was announced and brought in. I tried to adjust my clothing and slid my lace cap into place while I looked up at the expectant gazes. First things first.

"How do you know Lily, James, and why do you speak Chinese?"

"Well, actually, I work for Miss Chen," James replied.

"He is the manager I told you about," said Lily. "He speaks Cantonese well, and understands my culture, so he was a good fit for my business."

My gaze returned to my son.

"Father took us to China," James explained. "I grew up there, and I learned the language from my nurse. Father got into trade and did well in China. He took risks, but they paid off. We returned to England some five years ago as Father's health deteriorated. He died not long after."

I let out a shaky breath. So Charles Leighton was dead.

Sir Giles pulled out a piece of paper and gave it to me. Upon unfolding it I discovered it was Leighton's death certificate. I stared at it, not quite taking it all in. I was a free woman.

Lily was looking at James with a strange expression.

"James is your elder brother, Lily," I said quietly. "I am not sure if your father told you all of my story: just before I met Mr Chen, I was abandoned by my husband, who took my son, James, with him. I did not know if he went to Australia or China. I tried everything I could, but I was never able to find them."

Eyes wide, Lily straightened her shoulders. "You are my brother?"

James met her gaze. "It appears so. I did not know about you before today."

"Nor I you." She chuckled and shook her head. "Life is strange. Perhaps you were a part of the tale I did not fully understand. So I have another brother." She laughed out loud, as if having another brother was the icing on the cake. We stared at her, and she stopped. "I have an excess of brothers," she supplied by way of explanation.

"This is all so strange," Jemima said. "Can the timing of these revelations be a mere coincidence? I think not. There is some force at work to bring these two together from different parts of the world."

I was beyond trying to make sense of anything. James and Lily were here and they knew each other—I had simply never imagined such a scenario. "A cup of tea, if you please, Jemima," I said. "And a large slice of cake."

"Yes, Aunt. Coming up."

I looked at them all in turn as they separated and began to partake of the tea. There was cause for celebration, certainly, but I also felt as if someone had let off a bomb and blown my life apart.

After I had fortified myself, James came up to me. "May we speak in private?"

"Indeed. I must hear your story. Fulton, may we repair to your library?"

"Of course," replied Fulton. "As long as you need."

James and I sat side by side on the dark brown chesterfield in Fulton's library.

"Mother, it is so good to see you. This is a moment I have longed for most of my life," said James earnestly.

I patted his hand, trying to sort through my emotions. "Do you even remember me?"

"A little. I remember your smiling face. I remember playing outside with a ball and you laughing as you tried to kick it, but your feet became tangled in your skirts."

"Ah, that was in Calcutta."

"Father told me you were too sick to join us. I remember crying for you on the ship. Seasickness plagued me, even though the seas were fairly calm. When we got to Canton, I did not see Father much. He gave me to my amah, and she cared for me and taught me Cantonese because she did not speak much English. Our fortunes waxed and waned depending on Father's fortunes, but eventually, some of his trade deals made money.

"Father never spoke of you willingly. When pressed he told me you had died in Singapore. When I was older, I made enquiries, and it seemed that a Mrs Leighton did disappear in Singapore after we had left, and was presumed dead."

I nodded. "I arrived as Mrs Leighton and departed as Mrs Wainwright. Your father had left debts I was simply unable to pay. The debtors would have been after me, and I had no money."

"Did he leave you with anything at all?" James asked.

I met his brown eyes, so similar to mine. "No, nothing more than a few pennies. I had nowhere to live, and he had left my possessions with the landlord as a surety. I had nothing. Not even my clothes."

James looked stricken. "But what did you do?"

"It is funny to think back on it now, for in a way, the desperation I felt that day led me to the one thing that saved my life: Lily's father. After I had been down to the docks to try to trace you, I was walking the streets in utter despair. Somehow, I crossed the bridge to the southern side of the river. There were warehouses and shophouses along the shore, ramshackle buildings, alleys. It was there that Yu Tang—Mr Chen—saved me. Or, actually, I saved myself, but Mr Chen took me to his shophouse and kept me safe."

"I see," James said softly. His hands clenched and he shook his head.

I put my hand on his. "It is not what you think. Mr Chen did not take advantage of me. I do not know how to explain myself to you. Your father had taken everything from me, squandered my dowry, sold all my jewellery and then abandoned me, taking you, my precious boy. Yet, in that dire situation I found tenderness, kindness and eventually love with Mr Chen. Much as I wished to, I could not stay with him as I was still married to your father. Because of my actions—our actions—I had to leave Lily behind me." I blinked back tears once again, but I knew there was more to say, so I wrangled my emotions back into check. "Enough about me, though. Tell me about your life."

James nodded, his lips quivering as if on the verge of some deep emotion. "Father eventually struck it rich. He hired a tutor for me in preparation for our return to England. Once here, I went to school for a bit. However, after he passed, I found that his affairs were in disorder. After selling his possessions and clearing his debts, I knew I needed to find employment, which is how I met Miss Chen. I mean, Lily."

There was more to his story, just as there was to mine, but this was all we could manage at the moment. A soft knock at the door interrupted us. "I am sorry to disturb you both. We are to dine soon." This was Milly, who offered a shy smile.

"Thank you, dearest. We will join you presently."

We stood and made for the door. But I had to be sure, so I asked, "Just how well do you know Miss Chen?"

James' cheeks grew pink. "Miss Chen employed me some three months ago. She is precise in her instructions, and we have been getting on famously. Our relationship is entirely professional."

Studying his face, I watched for pretence but saw none. I felt relief flow through me. "Who would have thought that fate would bring you together? I am so glad."

"It is the Chinese connection that brought us together. Father's actions, though deplorable, created all of these circumstances."

"Indeed, that is so."

Arm in arm, we went out into the hall.

After the meal, we retired once more to the drawing room. After keeping his distance, Sir Giles sat on the settee with me. "Perhaps I should have asked to hear more of your story when we met in the garden that day," he said. "There is obviously more to tell."

I looked at him carefully. There was no rancour in his expression, no angst evident.

"I would have told you if you had stayed to listen," I replied.

He inclined his head. "I believe you would have. You have had an interesting life, Prudence."

"Only parts of it were interesting, Sir Giles. There were many years when I lived quietly, away from society."

"Mmm..."

"Are you scandalised? I will understand if you no longer wish to associate with me; if you wish to end our acquaintance." I found I felt very anxious about his response to this. I looked down into my lap.

But Sir Giles smiled, really smiled, so that his dark eyes twinkled. "After all the trouble I went to to discover whether your husband was alive or dead? You mistake me, my dear. That effort will not be in vain. I wish to be better acquainted with you and your past. You are a much more interesting subject than I imagined. Have you thought more on my offer?"

I felt my cheeks warm. Our voices were low, and it appeared that no one was taking note of our conversation, but I would have bet my best bonnet that they were all listening and waiting with bated breath for my response.

Our eyes met. "To be honest, I had not given it much consideration because I thought it impossible. However, now that the situation has changed dramatically, I can say that I look favourably on the renewal of that offer," I said.

Sir Giles smiled even more broadly, and that expression softened his features. I could see the handsome man that he had been, and in many ways still was. He took my hand and we sat comfortably together in companionable silence, watching my young family in action.

⚘

AFTER STAYING UP LATE UPDATING MY MEMOIR WITH THE current happenings and trying to think of ways to tie it all out, I yawned heavily and decided to go to bed. I wrapped my hair in rags and put on my night bonnet, then donned my favourite frilly nightdress. My son had gone to stay with Sir Giles at his invitation and would visit again on the morrow before returning to his work in London. Lily was due to travel on the same train, and I was pleased to see that an easy camaraderie had sprung up between them. It gladdened my heart to see what pleasure each took in their new sibling.

Not more than a few minutes after I finally laid my head down, I dropped into a deep sleep. Thus I had no idea what time it was when I heard my name called urgently.

"Prudence! Prudence, wake up!"

I opened my eyes and a ghastly, ghostly apparition, glowing in blue-white light, loomed over me. I was about to scream but Wilbur's shade cut me off. "Quickly. They are killing Jemima."

"What? Who?"

His face loomed large in mine, losing coherence as if he had used all his energy to appear before me. "They have the baby..."

I threw off my covers and raced to the door illuminated by the residual light of Wilbur's ghost.

My heart raced and my breath hitched as I reached the door. Then I heard sounds: a thump. A cry. The rumble of voices too low to discern the words.

Once I opened the door, Wilbur faded. A full moon helped light my way, its silver beams showing me the corridor. I crept along, not certain Wilbur had the right of it, but afraid he had.

The door to Jemima's room was ajar and light flickered within. The baby was crying, and something snapped in me. I pushed the door open. A man stood there wearing a dark brown cassock. One of the brotherhood. He was dangling the baby by its feet.

Without a thought, I stepped in. "Give that baby to me!" I cried.

The man turned and then I saw what lay beyond. Jemima was trussed up in some machine, a large, framed thing, with pulleys and cogs and wheels. A large rubber cup adhered to her belly. Her mouth was stretched in a silent scream. I closed my eyes and saw her as a bright light, so white and hot she reminded me of a star.

Blood was smeared on the wall next to the bed, and there lay Edward, crumpled and senseless.

"Get out, you stupid old woman!" hissed another of the brotherhood, who strode forward, hand raised as if to strike me.

The first one, with the baby, cringed as Louis screamed. "Let's give her the noisy brat. We can deal with them after we are done here."

The second intruder sneered, his hand up in the air, fingers curling. "I'll turn her into a toad or a toad's breakfast."

"I've had enough of this." The first one tossed the baby at me. My heart seemed to stop as I reached for him, catching him in my arms as gently as I could. I could scarce believe my outrage at the careless treatment of an innocent baby. The men turned away from me as if I were nothing.

Then there was a noise in the hall behind me, and I thought there must be more of them. Inside my breast anger burned, and something else had ignited there. Jemima was hurting. They were using that machine to drain her power. Not because she had done anything wrong, just because she had something they wanted. Stealing her power was their object, just as Wilbur had said.

The magician who had thrown Louis to me turned to the machine. "Do it faster. Let's finish it. The house is waking up."

The second one, tugged on the lever. The wheels and gears started to turn faster. Jemima writhed, jaw clenched, hands fisted in the restraints they had tied her with. I could feel the machine. I could feel Jemima waning. I could not let this happen

Cradling the crying baby to my breast, I reached inward for my Prudential Light, and to my surprise I found it was there, just under the surface of my outrage. Hardly knowing what I was doing, I directed it towards the men, and it spat out of me. The brother who had his hand on the lever noticed my light. His brow furrowed. "What the devil is that?" he shouted.

The first magician who had been holding Louis turned just as my power washed over him and through him. His eyes rolled up and his legs buckled as if he were a puppet whose strings were cut. Then the light hit the machine and it flew apart. The other man stood solid for a moment, but then he, too, began to crumple, his arms falling to his sides, his head lolling back and his legs folding. His body thumped as it hit the floor.

The sound of someone approaching made me spin around. From the dark hallway, another magician surged forward, hands raised as if to hurl a spell at me. But then Lily appeared above him, her leg connecting with his upper body, and then she kicked him in the head. The intruder fell forward, face hitting the floor with a *thwump*. Lily descended slowly, her yellow silk sleeping suit barely rippling.

"Are you all right, Mother?" she asked.

Baby Louis whimpered in my arms. I could barely speak as the light was still with me, still pulsing through my senses. Then I noticed that Louis' light had responded to mine, and for an instant he glowed white, too.

"Yes...I think so," I stammered.

Lily went to free Jemima from the wreckage of the machine. I frowned at it, realising that my Prudential Light had laid it to waste, though it had left Jemima completely unharmed. Lily spoke again. "Mr Fulton is tackling the other two below. Is everyone all right?"

Louis was gazing up at me as if he had seen a great marvel.

Lily helped Jemima climb free of the machine, and she stood rubbing her wrists where she had been bound to it. "Edward?" she said hoarsely.

Lily raced over and shook Edward's shoulder, trying to wake him. She peered closer. "A head wound, but it doesn't seem too bad." She held his wrist for a minute. "His pulse is strong. He will hopefully regain his senses momentarily." She looked at me. "And you, Mother? You appeared dazed. But I saw your Prudential Light."

I nodded. "They threw Louis. I caught him. I was so outraged, so scared for him and Jemima. The light just came when I called it."

Lily came up to me, drew me into her embrace. "You can let it go now, Mother. Just relax your mind, let go your fright. You have saved them all."

Following Lily's advice, I made a conscious effort to let go of my fear and outrage and the light faded. Then I burst into tears, sobbing like a lost thing into the arms of my daughter, with baby Louis wiggling and gurgling between us.

Then Fulton came running in and Lily guided me out of the way. Together he and Lily lifted Edward to the bed. Jemima wiped the tears from her face and stood by her husband's side.

"Edward?" She sobbed and wrung her hands. "I was asleep. So tired I could not wake. And by the time I did, they had me trussed up, and I could not stop them."

I handed Louis to Lily, who took him tenderly, then I went to Jemima. She grabbed hold of me fiercely and cried on my shoulder. "They hurt me. They hurt Edward and Louis."

"It will be well now. You will see," I replied soothingly. "Louis is good, you see."

Fulton growled as he checked Edward for other injuries. "I hope he has not been hexed again. I am loath to call on Mr White for assistance."

Jemima wiped her eyes and pulled away, a little calmer now. "Thank you for saving us, Aunt. How did you know we were in trouble?"

I met her gaze. "Your father warned me."

Jemima's mouth fell open. "My father? But..."

"Yes, I know. His ghost came to me." At the look on her face, I added, "It is part of my talent, only lately understood. In rare circumstances, I can talk to spirits, even live ones."

Jemima's eyebrows furrowed. "You talked to my father?"

"Yes. He woke me up and screamed at me to help you."

Jemima looked at me as if she was only seeing me for the first time. "You talked to my father?" she said again. "Next time please come and get me. I want to talk to him too."

Jemima had been weakened by the attack, so I led her to a chair and eased her onto it. She reached immediately for Louis, and Lily passed him into his mother's arms.

"Edward must have sensed something. He came in, but they held poor Louis up by the feet and threatened to dash his head against the wall. Edward just froze, but I could see him working a spell. Before he could release it, the other one bashed him across the skull. It happened so quickly, Aunt. We could not even shout for help."

"It must have been frightful, love. Are you hurt?"

Jemima shook her head. "I do not think so. They had just started their dreadful process, so I do not think they got much power out of me before you interrupted them. But tell me, what was that you did? What was that light? Was it the Prudential Light you wrote about in your memoir?"

It was Lily who replied. "Yes, that was the Prudential Light," she said. "My father told me of it. He saw my mother use it when she was attacked in Singapore. She has a gift, you see. But I did not know she could talk to ghosts."

"I visited Yu Tang the other day," I confessed. "I didn't mean to; it was in a dream."

Lily froze, her face dropping. Then I realised what she must be thinking. "He is not dead," I reassured her. "He was alive. I did not know I could travel like that, you see. He recognised me and called my name. I will tell you every detail later."

Lily relaxed, an expression of relief replacing her look of horror.

With my arm around Jemima, I met Fulton's eyes. "There were more of them, I presume?"

"Yes, five in all. Two in here. One in the hall, two downstairs. I heard them moving around. I thought we had burglars but did not suspect evil magicians."

I frowned. "But Edward placed wards around the house. How did they get in?"

Fulton's eyes widened. "Ah well, from what I can tell they came through the roof. I believe the wards were not placed there. An oversight I am sure."

Just then, Edward moaned and lifted a hand to his head. Slowly, he sat up, looking stricken. "Jemima! The baby!" He blinked a few times and looked around, seeming to take everyone in. "Oh." And then he lay back down and started to snore.

I frowned, perplexed. "What has got into him?"

"Head wounds can be tricky," Fulton supplied. He leaned over to check Edward's eyelids. He tilted his head and grimaced. "I think he is merely asleep now and not unconscious." He slapped Edward's cheeks gently. "Come on, wake up."

Edward moaned and spoke low. "Headache!"

Satisfied, Fulton left him alone and then startled when Milly ran into the room.

"Oh, heavens," she cried. In her hand were a number of hatpins. "I am too late to help, and I have been practising so hard."

Lily smiled at the sight of the domestic weapons. "Oh, I see. Did you teach Milly this, Mother? I recognise Father's 'use what you have available to fight back' routine."

"Yes," I replied. "I believe that is where Milly gets it from. A little trick I taught her."

"Is Arabella all right, love?" Fulton asked.

"Yes, the nurse is with her in our room and I bade her stay there. With all these bodies, we will have some explaining to do. I do not believe the nurses will cope well with them."

Jemima closed her eyes and breathed out slowly. "There are no more of those renegade magicians in the house. For now." She opened her eyes and there was a malicious glint in them. "Uncle Ferdy has some explaining to do, too, if he wants to maintain visiting rights," she said grimly.

Fulton drew Milly into his embrace. "Thank heavens you're safe.

I am glad you know how to use your weapons, but I wish you did not need to."

Milly rolled her eyes. "But I want to be useful too. I want to be a fighter like Jemima and Aunt Prudence." She paused. "And Cousin Lily."

Fulton kissed her full on the mouth. "You are a strong woman already. Stay safe, please."

Milly shifted her head from side to side and then smiled, love lighting up her eyes. "I will try, Ambrose. Hard as it is in this family."

"Indeed," he replied, and gave us all a look that spelled love and reproach in equal proportions.

Lily stood up. "I have some incense in my room that should help repel these uncomfortable vibrations. Violence and evil magic leave a nasty aftertaste." She bustled out.

The others all turned when they heard alarmed voices coming from downstairs. "I fear some of the servants are awake. We need to act quickly to keep a lid on this." Milly's gaze shifted to Fulton, and the pair quickly headed for the stairs.

Lily returned a short time later and lit some incense, which filled the room with perfumed smoke. It drew me back to the incense Yu Tang had burned to repel mosquitoes and other types Mrs Li had used in offerings at her shrine. It hit me then what an extraordinary life I had led.

Milly came back some ten minutes later. "We have contrived to boil the kettle in the morning-room fire." There was always a kettle there to keep the water warm and to make fresh tea. "Discombe had sent most of the servants back to bed but John has agreed to serve us fruitcake. That is all we can manage. If that is agreeable, perhaps we can go down. The doctor has been sent for. He shall be along shortly so that Edward can have his injury seen to."

Before we had all stood up, the front door knocker sounded, and Fulton went down to bring up the doctor.

"Come along, Jemima. Edward is in good hands, and you need something to calm your nerves. Perhaps some brandy?"

Jemima nodded, still clinging to me. "I feel very strange, Aunt."

Concerned by this sudden admission of weakness, I closed my eyes, and in my mind's eyes she still burned as bright as she had in the machine. However, now her glow was outside of her as well as in, like a thick mist. It was puzzling. Some of the drawn off power still clung to her, it seemed. No wonder she felt strange.

"Come with me and we shall see what we can do." I had no idea how to fix the problem, but I thought perhaps the power those renegade magicians had drained from Jemima remained behind when the machine had been destroyed. Perhaps if she was happy and calm, she might reabsorb it in time. More likely, Edward or Mr White could deal with it.

With Louis moved in with Arabella, we put him down, as he was fast asleep. Jemima stuck close to me as we made our way downstairs to the morning room, where she sat on the settee next to me. This passivity was so unlike her, but she had had a massive shock. A renegade magician had dangled her baby son by his feet and threatened his life. Indeed, I still felt the outrage at that man's actions. I wanted to find the rest of them and rend them limb from limb. How dare they attack a child!

❧

"We have dead bodies and we need a magistrate to deal with them. There is nothing for it," Fulton said. "I had best fetch Sir Giles." We were gathered in the morning room after taking about half an hour to settle babies, night nurses and put some things to rights.

"Oh, I suppose you are right," I replied. "Are they really all dead?" I was strangely unaffected by their deaths. I had not meant to kill anyone but they were harming those I loved and cared for.

"The two in the bedroom are. Lily knocked out a third one who had been lurking in the hall, and appeared to be attacking you. He broke both his arms after she dented his skull. He fell badly and is the one moaning loudly. The doctor is seeing to him now. The one I punched is a bit of a mess so he is beyond saving. It appears Milly spiked the other one in the neck." Fulton smiled at his wife.

"I thought you missed the action, Milly," I commented as I rubbed Jemima's shoulder.

"So did I. It was dark. I thought I had missed and Ambrose got him. I am glad I did, even though it is quite shocking that he is injured."

I shook my head. "It is inconvenient, having to clear away the bodies," I replied. "You'd think these fellows would have a spell that snatched away their remains once they were terminated."

"That is very businesslike of you, Aunt. Are you not upset? Do you need your smelling salts?" Fulton asked.

Milly sighed. "Do not tease her, Ambrose. I told you she is more than she seems."

"More than she seems?" Fulton laughed uproariously, whether in amusement or shock, I could not tell. "That is an understatement." He flung out his arm, indicating the upper floor. "She just killed two magicians single-handedly."

I turned in my chair and glared at him. "I was saving the baby and Jemima. What did you expect me to do, hide under my eiderdown?"

"Of course not! You could have yelled for me." He thumped his chest. "I am the destroyer of evil in this house. I feel superfluous."

My mouth formed an "oh" of surprise. "Well, yes, I could have if I'd had the presence of mind, Fulton dear. You could have dispatched them quickly and saved me a lot of trouble and bother."

Fulton relaxed. "Yes, well, I did not mean that to sound so boorish. Of course, I appreciate all you have done. I merely wish I could have helped more."

"Where is Uncle Ferdy?" Jemima said sleepily at my side.

Come to think of it, it was odd that Mr White had not come,

considering he had warned of this very attack. He was always listening for Jemima, watching over her like a guardian angel.

With a nod to Jemima, I said, "I will try to reach him."

"You?" Jemima replied, brow furrowed.

"He is always listening, is he not?"

"Well, yes." Jemima laid her head against my shoulder as if speaking was too much for her.

I closed my eyes and called to Mr White. *Oh, Mr White, are you there?*

There was no response. Not that I had ever called upon the magician before. However, I was about to open my eyes when suddenly I was somewhere else. Mr White was there, bloody and torn and tied to a chair. "Mr White?" I said, and I could hear the shock in my voice.

He did not speak to me—could not speak to me—but I understood it all in a moment. He had gone to fight them, but they had captured and abused him unto death. "Oh, Mr White, I am so sorry."

A hand gripped my shoulder, and I was back in the morning room. "Aunt Prudence?" It was Fulton. "Are you all right? We seemed to have lost you there for a moment."

I shook myself. "I am quite well." I did not know how to convey the news or whether they would believe me.

"You do not look it," Fulton said. "You look like you have seen a ghost."

"A drink of brandy will set me to rights."

I could not tell Jemima about Mr White in her current state. Tomorrow or the day after, perhaps. Not with Edward being tended to by a doctor and her power in disarray.

Fulton handed me and Jemima a snifter of brandy each. I inhaled the fumes and relaxed. "I have sent Harry to fetch Sir Giles. As John is tending us, I thought the other footman could be useful, given he was awake. I suggest we touch nothing, except to tend to the wounded. How we will explain all this is troubling me greatly. Sir Giles is such a practical man."

"Indeed, he is," I replied. "I suggest the truth."

Fulton whirled and faced me, his face a study in horror. "How can I tell him that dear old Aunt Prudence killed two men on her own?"

"If it is too much for you, then do not. I can certainly elucidate him."

Lily stepped forward. "My mother used the Prudential Light. I felt it in my own skin."

Fulton flashed a small smile at Lily. "I understand what she did, but will the magistrate? I have three dead bodies in my house."

Milly reached up and touched Fulton's elbow. "It is all right, my dear. This time, you did not kill all of them."

Then in the flicker of candlelight I saw Mr White. "Oh hello, Mr White," I responded without thinking, as though he were actually there. He looked as beaten and torn as when I'd reached out previously. I looked around at the others, and they were gaping at me. "Oh? Forgive me." They must think me quite strange, talking to an empty space.

Jemima sat up and looked around, realisation dawning on her features.

"Tell her I am sorry," the ghost of Mr White said. "I tried to stop them, but they were too strong for me."

I swallowed and relayed Mr White's words.

Jemima clutched at my hand, her eyes still darting here and there, but it seemed she could not see her Uncle Ferdy. "Aunt?"

I pointed to where his ghost stood. "He is over there. I am sorry to tell you, but he has passed away. He has died of the injuries he sustained in trying to stop them coming for you."

"Goodbye," Mr White whispered, and slowly faded from view.

Jemima let out a wail. "Uncle Ferdy?"

I embraced her. "If you ever doubted him, now you know that he valued you and tried to stop those who would harm you."

Jemima began to sob. Milly came over and sat on the other side, patting her on the back.

Milly met my gaze. "Have you always been able to see ghosts?"

I glanced sideways at my beloved Milly. "When I was a child, I had conversations with my brother who died when I was a baby. My parents were scandalised when I told them I was talking to him and they thought I was being disrespectful. Not much between then and now. As I started my memoirs, the gift returned to me, and I recognised it for what it was. It was the ghost of Wilbur that woke me in time to save Jemima."

Milly's eyes sparkled. "I am so proud of you, Aunt. You should never hide your talents, but I can see that you needed to for a while at least."

With tears in my lashes, I replied, "Thank you for understanding."

Discombe arrived with a tray of brandies. With urging, Jemima took another snifter and I finished mine. I could see I was not going to be able to return to my bed anytime soon. I had to face Sir Giles' questions.

Lily entered the room, wearing a wrap over her silk sleeping suit. I had not seen her leave. She picked up the snifter of brandy and downed it. I was waiting for her to choke on it, but she calmly put the glass back and took a seat in an armchair. I could tell by the shape of her brow that she had news. "What is it, Lily dear?"

Lily met my gaze. "The man with the neck wound has died of his injuries."

Milly sucked in a breath and her gaze sought Fulton's. He immediately went to comfort her. "You were fighting in self-defence," he said to her.

"But I killed someone," she replied, as if only half believing it.

Fulton held her close, and over his head, I saw his fierce expression.

"Fulton, what is the problem?" I asked.

He flashed me an angry look and I blinked at the ferocity of it. "*I* am meant to keep my family safe."

"Oh, Ambrose," Milly said softly. "You were asleep, and I was awake with baby Arabella. I had to act immediately."

"But I should not have been sleeping. I should have been protecting."

"Protecting what?" Edward said, stumbling through the door. He was clutching his bandaged head with his hand. "My, the room is spinning?"

Jemima leaped up, miraculously recovered, it seemed. "Edward! Come and sit down. You have suffered a nasty blow. You should really be in bed."

Blood stained the collar of Edward's robe, and the curls poking out from the bandage on one side of his head were stiff and black with dried blood. "I recollect intruders."

"Yes, we were attacked, love. It is over now."

He sought Fulton's gaze. "Is that why there are dead magicians in our room?"

"Mmm, yes," Fulton replied.

Edward turned and faced Jemima, having the wherewithal to check her over. "You are unharmed?"

"Mostly."

He frowned as if he was trying to pull the memories forward. "And Louis?"

"Safe," I said. "Asleep in his crib with Arabella in the nursery, being watched over by both nurses."

"And where was the nurse when the attack occurred?" Fulton asked.

Jemima lifted her chin. "Yes. What a fright she must have got."

"Tending Louis in her room, next to ours. She fainted," I supplied.

"At least they did not harm her." Fulton crossed his arms.

"The doctor could not tell me what had happened. I thought

the worst when he woke me." Edward leaned over and drew Jemima into an embrace.

By the shake of his shoulders, I saw that he was weeping, and turned my head away. Poor man, I thought to myself. Both husbands were frustrated that they had not saved the day.

I yawned loudly. "I beg your pardon. I fear the night's events are catching up with me." I had been burning the midnight oil a lot recently, trying to make sense of my memoir. I feared that I would have to supply a copy to Sir Giles sooner than expected, given what had occurred.

Lily came up to me and knelt by my knee. "Do you wish to return to your bed, Mother?"

I reached out and squeezed her hand. "I am afraid we will all have to answer to the magistrate before we can take to our beds."

# CHAPTER 16

The house began to awaken around us. Footsteps coming from the attic, a low rumble of voices, signalling the servants getting up to prepare for the day. I checked the clock, and it was now four fifteen in the morning.

It was dark outside, and on this day in particular, that made me think of the blackness of men's hearts. Our attackers had lacked genuine human feeling. They had killed a brother magician, one who had previously been known to them. I did not know all the ins and outs of the *Societas Magicae*, who had become renegade and who had not. However, I did know it was appalling to break into a house and intimidate its inhabitants, threaten a newborn babe and attack a young mother in her bed. Edward was in the way, so they attacked him and could have killed him. All because of a desire for the power that Jemima had drawn from Geneck when she killed him. Apparently, it was a potent mix of magic and vampiric life force that had adhered to her own talent. That she was a woman and not welcome among them was not the greatest of their follies. Not all magicians are created equal. Some have power and intelligence, others less of both. My gentleman magician nephew had power and intelligence and the renegades had hounded him, Fulton and Jemima to steal the knowledge of his devices. It seriously eroded my trust in the magical fraternity. No wonder Edward held back from joining them formally. He had better become their leader and reform them all.

I had killed two men with my Prudential Light, a power I could clearly only call up defensively to protect myself and others who were dear to me. I closed my eyes and considered that this would be important to Sir Giles. However, I knew that this revelation would change how he viewed me, even felt about me, and that made me sad.

A thump on the front door made us all jump. The butler, Discombe, opened the door and soon Sir Giles was ushered in.

Fulton stood and greeted him. "Thank you for coming. I am sorry to have inconvenienced you at this hour."

Sir Giles swept the room with his gaze and acknowledged us with a nod. "Your man tells me there is death in the house. Death is a great inconvenience to all those concerned. I have yet to summon my deputies. Perhaps you can show me first."

"Of course."

Sir Giles nodded and then turned to us gathered there. "Please remain here until I give you leave to retire."

"We shall begin upstairs." Fulton led the way.

While Sir Giles inspected upstairs, I found it difficult to sit still. What was the man going to think of me, killing people and leaving them lying about on the floor in people's bedrooms? If I was an assassin, I was a poor one. Still, lives had been lost because of my actions.

Jemima still sniffled now and then as she pressed into Edward. The poor young woman had been brought so low by this attack. I closed my eyes and could still see the aura of her power dispersed around her. Recently, I had detected a vibration from Jemima but it was only after this attack that her power had become visible to me.

"Jemima, dear. You are safe now. The baby is safe, and we are all safe," I tried to reassure her.

Jemima shook her head. "I should have stopped them."

Edward had regained most of his senses. "You were asleep, love. So exhausted. I thought I had taken steps to protect us. I did not expect attackers to climb in through the roof or that they would dangle our newborn son in front of me before they tried to dash my brains out. It was most unconscionable conduct, completely outside the *Societas Magicae's* rules. These attackers were renegades. Had to be."

"But the machine...what was that?"

Edward met his wife's gaze. "I believe it is a replica of the extractor they used to drain your father and kill him."

"How do you know about this machine?" she asked.

"Brother Ferdinand told me of the machine and showed me a drawing. This one was empty of power and the wood was new; there were no magical leftovers from previous extractions."

"Oh?"

"Is Brother Ferdinand still here?" Edward said to me. "What does he say?"

I hastily looked around. I had thought Mr White's shade was gone for good, but there he was, still bloodied, disfigured and bruised. Edward could sense him, I was sure, for how could he know to ask me?

"Mr White, were these attackers from the *Societas Magicae?*"

Mr White lowered his head. "Formerly," he replied, his voice raspy, as if from too much screaming. "Not all the brotherhood came back into the fold after Geneck's attack."

A frown deepened on Edward's forehead. "Just how many members does this brotherhood have? Geneck killed so many, but they seem to be everywhere, and no longer abiding by their own rules of conduct. It is disgusting. If I was running this brotherhood, I would make them swear binding oaths to do no harm."

I cast a glance at Mr White's shade. He nodded as if agreeing.

"It is a good idea. Reform the *Societas Magicae*, if you can." Then his shade faded once more.

"Mr White agrees that reform is best for this brotherhood, and he asks you to undertake it, if you can. He has left us now," I said.

Edward met my eye and nodded, understanding.

Just then heavy footsteps announced the arrival of Fulton and Sir Giles. The latter announced to the room, "Mr Fulton has offered his library to me to carry out interviews. If Mrs Huntington is well enough, I would like to start with her."

Edward whispered to Jemima, who nodded.

"I will speak to you now," she said.

Sir Giles inclined his head. "If the rest of you would be so good as to return to your rooms and not converse about the matter until after I speak to you, that would be most appreciated. Mrs Wainwright, you may stay here until I call you."

Lily stood up. "Must she stay alone?" she asked Sir Giles.

He met my gaze. "She will be all right."

Milly got up and with the assistance of Fulton made her way out of the room, with Lily behind them. Edward stood with arms crossed.

"You may wait in the hall for your wife, Mr Huntington. I will speak to you next. Mr Fulton advises me that a doctor has tended to your injury," Sir Giles said.

Edward followed Sir Giles and Jemima out and I was left alone in the morning room. It was not possible to sit still and contemplate my fate, so I climbed to my feet and paced before the fireplace. I was not sure how much time passed; the fire needed more coals, so I threw in a shovelful. The tea things needed gathering, so I put them on the tray. I was restless, anxious, and—I had to admit—scared. I took the kettle off the fire as it needed refilling.

"Mrs Wainwright?" the butler said, appearing at the door and breaking me from my reverie. "Sir Giles will see you now."

"Thank you, Discombe," I replied wearily. In a daze, I made my way to the library to be interrogated.

"Prudence, do take a seat."

I sat but I did not look up. How could I look at him, knowing I had taken a life—two lives?

I felt Sir Giles lean over and press my hand. "You saved them. You saved the baby and his mother. He is unharmed, except for some bruising on the foot and lower legs. I do not think there will be any lasting damage."

A sob may have escaped me.

"Prudence, look at me."

His voice was soft, considerate, and I turned my head and looked into his dark eyes, which glittered like jet in the candlelight. "There, that was not too bad, was it?" He patted my hand. "I know there is a lot about this strange family I have yet to discover. You must finish that memoir soon or I shall go mad with waiting." He chuckled, then continued. "This is what I do know. Five men broke into the house this night. Three of them were upstairs, two particularly targeted Mr and Mrs Huntington. Mr Huntington was struck unconscious, but not before his child was dangled before him to subdue his actions. Mrs Huntington was trussed to a machine and unable to move or assist in the defence of her child or her husband. The assailants did not ask her for anything or demand money or goods. Mrs Huntington said she did not know why they attacked her and said that they were unknown to her personally. She expressed the view that these same assailants had murdered her father some time previously."

A nod was all I could give to this.

Sir Giles smiled at me, just a small smile, but it was enough to counter the flutter in my heart. "Can you tell me what happened next?"

I swallowed. "I was up late, and I was trying to go to sleep when I heard voices and a thump. As that was strange, I went to investigate." Should I mention that Jemima's father woke me and sent me to render aid? I peered at Sir Giles. He knew our family was extraordinary. If he truly wanted to belong to it, then he must face the truth. Should I consider taking a man as a husband who I could not be myself with? Definitely not. "Actually, if you want the pertinent details, the ghost of Cousin Wilbur, Jemima's father, woke me and demanded that I save his daughter. I then heard the voices and the thump."

Sir Giles blinked slowly. "A ghost woke you up?"

I studied his face and the changing emotions on his face. "It is the truth," I said simply.

Sir Giles shook his head slightly. "I think you believe you are telling the truth, but if I wrote that in my report, then I might be locked up in an asylum. Could I please record that you heard voices and a thump?"

I nodded. "As you wish."

"And you went to Mrs Huntington's room?"

"Yes," I replied, and I explained what happened there, leaving no detail unsaid.

Mr Giles was quiet a few moments, and I could see he was thinking hard. "So, in your own words: one of the assailants tossed the infant to you, Jemima was screaming and Mr Huntington was unconscious with a head wound. Then the two assailants suddenly became lifeless for no apparent reason."

I blinked at him in confusion and was about to call him impertinent when I realised what he was doing. He lifted his eyebrows, and I could see he was begging me in his way to accede to this version of events. "Well, I did not touch them," I confirmed.

Sir Giles smiled. "I have examined their remains and there are no apparent injuries."

I nodded and began to fidget. It was most uncomfortable, but I could see where Sir Giles was coming from. I could be honest with him, and this was a relief. But in his role as magistrate, he had to record the facts, and as he did not witness the Prudential Light and there was no evidence of it, then he had to write plainly.

"Did you witness Miss Chen engage with one of the attackers?"

"Oh yes. It was magnificent. I believe she kicked him in the head."

He scribbled. "You saw her hit the man in the head," he confirmed.

Frowning at him, I said quickly, "He was coming for me and he meant to kill me. She saved my life with her actions. Sir Giles, what are you doing?"

He looked up at me, and I saw the strain on his face. "I am writing a report, as I will have to refer this case to another magistrate, and the coroner will need to decide the cause of death in all these deaths. Given my close association with this family, I cannot sweep it all under the table."

"Oh, I see. That is most annoying. If only the intruders had all disappeared instead of lying around dead or injured."

I recalled that Milly had stabbed one with a hatpin, and that Lily had told us he had perished. I hoped fervently that Milly would not face a charge of murder.

"Indeed. Most annoying and unfortunate."

I snuck a quick look at him. "To be attacked by unknown assassins in one's home. 'Tis mysterious in the extreme."

"Indeed. Now, if you will excuse me, I must interview Mr and Mrs Fulton."

Standing up, I nodded stiffly and left the room. Edward was in the drawing room with a cloth tied around his head, and I was glad to see him, as I had had a thought. "Nephew, may I have a word?"

"Certainly." He gestured to an armchair next to him.

"I mean, in private. There is a closet just in the hallway."

"A closet?" His eyes widened, and no wonder, because I sounded more like Jemima with her scheming ways than my usual self. I looked behind me, and saw that Jemima lay dozing on the settee. Why had she not gone to bed? I shook myself. I had more important things to think about than Jemima's sleeping habits.

I led Edward to the closet, and we stepped inside. With a great shove, Edward pushed the odd bits and bobs stored there to the back to make room for us. "What do you want to say, Aunt?" he whispered.

I lowered my voice. "It would be most convenient if the bodies of our attackers were not here."

Edward blinked. It was not easy to read his expression in the dark closet. "You want me to remove the bodies?" he asked finally. "What about the injured man?"

"Him too. By magical means, if you please. So they won't be found. I think Sir Giles would find the situation easier to deal with if they were simply...not here."

"And the servants, the doctor? They have seen and know things..."

"Can you not make a spell to make them forget?"

Edward shifted position and I think he was rubbing his jaw. "What about Sir Giles? Do you mean for me to erase his memory as well? Because if so, I have a few qualms about that, particularly if he is going to be a member of the family."

I had not thought that far ahead. "You may not need to do that. I have high hopes of him accepting this family for what it is. But if he raises a fuss, then we may need to reconsider."

"He knows about us?" my nephew enquired. "I hadn't realised you knew so much."

I *tsked* at him. "I am no fool, Nephew."

"I can see that," he replied, rubbing the side of his head, just below the bandage.

"Sir Giles has a fair idea that we are not an ordinary set of people. He is an intelligent man and not overly superstitious. But he is also a man of morals and cannot accommodate all of this in the usual way. He intends to refer the case to another magistrate because of his connection to me, to us. He cannot write what actually happened because he knows that he would appear ridiculous. However, he does have four dead and one injured man on his hands."

"How do you know he has this moral dilemma?"

I let out a frustrated gasp. "Because I told him the truth, but he has written it without the truth. I fear that if this gets out, we cannot rely on his discretion—or protection. His role as magistrate requires him to follow certain protocols, particularly to refer it to another magistrate and the coroner. Do we really want a coronial inquest?"

Edward sighed. "I see what you mean. Let me see what I can do. It may take a while. Can you distract Sir Giles?"

"Distract him in what way?"

"I have no idea. You are clever, Aunt, so I am sure you can think of something. I need him occupied so I can do the rest."

I nodded. Edward was the spell caster around here; I would have to do whatever I could to help. "All right. Let us get out of this ridiculous closet."

Cautiously re-entering the hall, I brushed dust from my sleeves. Edward slipped upstairs and, with an idea in mind, I headed to the kitchen to request a special breakfast and a tankard of Fulton's best ale for the magistrate.

The sun was not quite up but dawn was leaking into the sky, which was patched with clouds. When I had readied what I needed, I grabbed the tray and headed to the library.

As I approached, the door opened and Milly came out, rubbing tired eyes. "Aunt Prudence, I did not see you." She held the door for me as I brushed past. I still had not dressed, so I hoped Sir Giles would forgive my informal attire.

"Mrs Wainwright?" Sir Giles said and stood up from the desk. "I thought you had gone to bed after our interview."

"How can I sleep with the house in uproar?" I put down the tray in front of him.

"I thought you might be in need of some refreshment, so I have brought a little something."

Sir Giles gaped at the tray. "A little something?"

On the tray were three pork pies, four scotch eggs, a large slice of a raised mutton pie, a wedge of old cheddar, slices of bread, pickled onions and some mustard pickles. Tucked in on one side were five thick slices of ham. The foam from the ale slowly slid down the side of the tankard.

"I best get you a plate."

Sir Giles lifted a hand. "Prudence, there is no need—"

"Oh yes, there is. I realise you cannot enjoy this repast without one."

A grin changed his features. "Why do I get the feeling you are trying to bamboozle me, like your niece?"

I blinked and put my hands on my hips. "Bamboozle you, pray? I am merely being attentive to an officer of the law in pursuit of his duty at an inhospitable time of the day."

Sir Giles relaxed a little, shaking his head. "Tell me."

I did not know where to look. "Am I that transparent?"

"More so than your niece. What are you up to?" He gestured to the tray. "Not that I am averse to your offerings."

We shared a look, and I broke eye contact. "I thought it might be easier all round if this event had simply not occurred."

His brow furrowed. "Whatever do you mean? What's done is done."

There was a knock at the door and the butler entered, ushering in the footman, who was bearing a tray with a teapot, cups, a plate and cutlery. "The housekeeper thought you might need these." Tea was always on my agenda.

"Thank you, Discombe." The footman put down the tray. "Thank you, John."

There was a low table in front of the sofa, so I placed the second tray there and arranged the cups and plates while Sir Giles glowered at me. "Prudence?"

His voice was low and a trifle serious. Here was the first test of our relationship. Here was the moment when I took a step that might dissolve our liaison before it began.

"Take a seat, please, and help yourself," I said. "We might as well partake of this meal while we talk. I find myself rather hungry after all that has happened." I sat down, gestured to the other settee and then began serving food onto my plate.

Sir Giles hesitated for a moment then took a seat. He cut a pork pie in half and slid one piece onto my plate and the remainder onto his own.

I shot him a look under my eyelashes. "Sir Giles, I fear I have inconvenienced you."

He flashed me a look and then picked up his pie. "Not at all. You did not instigate the attack."

"I know, but something you said made me realise the awful position I have placed you in."

Sir Giles swallowed a mouthful of pie. "What have you done, Prudence?"

"Well, I know the events you have heard about tonight are not at all easily explained. So I thought it best if there were no bodies, nor an injured man to bother with—and thus, there'd be very little explaining to do."

"What?!" Sir Giles sat stock-still, staring at me. "I cannot think what you mean."

"Edward has sent the unfortunate victims away, you see. And he is in the process of making the servants and the doctor forget what happened."

"What?" said Sir Giles again. "Are you out of your mind?"

"No, of course I am not out of my mind. However, I saw the predicament you were in. You could not tell the truth, and if you had to pass any information on to another magistrate and a coroner...well, it would cast undue suspicion on various members of my family and stir up even more trouble. I can't allow that."

"You can't just make the evidence disappear."

"Why ever not?"

Sir Giles threw his hands in the air. "You are very impertinent, Mrs Wainwright!"

I tried to keep a serious face, but I found him calling me impertinent rather funny. I smiled.

"We will see about this." Sir Giles stood up and marched out of the room.

I poured myself a cup of tea and tried to relax into the settee. If Edward's actions had been successful, there would be nothing for Sir Giles to investigate. Some ten minutes later, he returned.

"Prudence, you have gone too far."

"Tea?"

He spluttered. "Tea? What kind of farce is this?"

I chuckled. "The everyday kind in this family. Do calm yourself, and sit. You will see by and by that this is the best course of action."

He sat down as if he was suddenly made of lead. I passed him a cup of tea, which he took unthinkingly. He put the cup down and picked up the ale and drank deeply. Then he lowered the tankard, frowning like a thunder cloud.

"Are there any bodies in the house?" I asked, and sipped my tea.

He shook his head. "No, not anymore."

"Did you ask the servants what happened here tonight?"

He narrowed his gaze at me. "Yes. They said the house was in an uproar because Mr Huntington fell and hit his head and there was a big commotion about it."

"And did they wonder why you were here?" I asked.

"No. They seemed to think I was a guest."

I nodded and tried not to smile. Even addled, Edward was an excellent magician.

"Then your job is done. Or rather, there is no job to do."

Sir Giles' eyes narrowed. "You should never do such a thing again. I won't stand for it."

"Well, if you insist."

Sir Giles looked utterly nonplussed. "And you expect me to be grateful for this highly unorthodox state of affairs?"

I bent over and lifted a slice of raised mutton pie in his direction. "I do, actually, because you have yet to realise that

Edward could have altered your memory, too. I asked him not to. I did not think you would appreciate it."

He blinked rapidly at me, trying to take this in. A vein throbbed in his temple and I feared he might have a stroke. "You mean, *I* could have forgotten the night's events?"

I arched an eyebrow, and decided to let him answer that himself.

"Well, I...well..." He glared at me and then the angry lines softened and he hung his head. "You trust me. I'll be damned, you trust me."

"Yes, I do—we do. I had an inkling you would be understanding of the unusual nature of my family, given your feelings for me, and mine for you. However, if you really cannot stand to recall tonight's events, we can remedy that, and you will be none the wiser."

He lifted a hand. "No. No interfering with my mind, if you please. I like it just as it is."

"But your principles — will they not be compromised?"

He sat back. "You are intolerable. You try to bamboozle me with your shenanigans and then change things and expect me to accept things as you present them."

"Not all the time. Just certain times, in particular situations. And in fact, only this once, thus far."

"Mmmm," he said, and looked back down at his plate. He took a bite and inclined his head in appreciation. "This is extremely good pie. And did you just mention your feelings for me—?"

Edward came in. "The doctor is finishing up; he thinks Louis should be all right."

"That is good news," I said. "How is Jemima?"

"I have taken her upstairs and she is going to feed Louis. The baby is quite upset after the doctor's examination. Jemima has recovered her 'can do anything' demeanour." Edward's gaze fell on the tray. "I say, is that pork pie?"

For a moment, I thought Sir Giles was going to remonstrate with my nephew. "Why, yes," Sir Giles replied.

Edward came over and squeezed in next to Sir Giles. "Don't mind if I do. I'm totally famished."

Sir Giles might have gaped, but then shook his head slightly as if amazed.

"Where did you put those renegades, Nephew?" I asked.

Edward swallowed a mouthful. "Sent them to the priory. It is their mess so they can deal with them."

Sir Giles's mouth dropped open and then he gave a shake of his head. A sliver of sunlight peeked through a gap in the curtains. Sir Giles' gaze met mine. "Would you care for a stroll, Mrs Wainwright?" he asked.

"Indeed, I would. However, I fear I must beg you to await me downstairs as I am not dressed." While I had managed to put on a robe over my nightdress and slippers on my feet, I was not fit to be seen out of doors.

Sir Giles had the audacity to blush. "Truly, I did not notice."

"Enjoy what you can of the food. Best be quick as my nephew has an insatiable appetite."

I went upstairs and dressed as quickly as I could. It took me a bit longer than I expected because I was caught up in a thought. If we had been required to blank Sir Giles' memory, would he have remembered asking me to marry him? I had no idea of the long-term consequences of Edward's finagling with people's memories. I was pretty sure he had not changed mine at any point, but I had no way of knowing. When it came to it, could I really have countenanced doing such a thing to Sir Giles?

I knew I could not live with a man I had to hide my life from, so I was relieved at Sir Giles' reaction to the true situation. I also knew I was free to make this decision entirely in accordance with my own wishes; if I married Sir Giles it would not need to be for money, or for my social standing, but because I liked him, admired him and found him good company. I was no longer a young woman who had to toe the line for her parents, or marry to oblige her family, or even comply with community expectations. It was a rather freeing thought.

The footman informed me that Sir Giles awaited me outside. I wore a soft bonnet over my lace cap as it toned nicely with my maroon gown, trimmed with ecru Chantilly lace. My gloves were hand knitted, and my new leather boots were snug. I had finished off my ensemble with a pelerine that was once my mother's.

Sir Giles bowed as I approached and then turned, offering me his arm. We made our way down the winding path to the street.

"Now, I want to thank you," he began, a slight smile tilting his mouth as he looked at me, "for not interfering with my memory, but more importantly, for trusting me. If you are agreeable, I think we should speak to the vicar and get the banns read."

I chuckled. "What, no special license?" He was still keen to marry me, then. It was time to ask myself: did I want to marry him? Did I love him? Rather than being his appendage, as I had been for Mr Leighton, I rather felt that Sir Giles was mine. A smile I tried to fight won out. I did like his turn of mind. I liked him and could possibly be in love with him.

"If you are that keen, I can certainly be off to see the archbishop," said Sir Giles with a chuckle. "However, I would much prefer to remain at your side and make plans for our future. What say you?"

I replied without hesitation. "I like your idea immensely. There is much to settle and see to."

He turned me to face him. "You do not want to leave the babies, do you?"

"No, I do not, not yet. And Lily is here to stay for a few weeks, as well. Perhaps James can visit again. Now that this present danger is passed, we can enjoy some normal family life."

He frowned. "Present danger?" His voice had dropped low, wary.

"Yes. You never know what is going to happen next when you associate with magicians and women of power like Jemima."

He inclined his head. "And you."

With a hand to my chest, I exclaimed. "Why, yes." He was right. I was a woman of power too, like Jemima and my daughter, Lily.

"Tell me, do you often talk to ghosts?" I felt a shiver pass through his body.

"I can go several years without seeing nary a one. I must say, though, that my talent also includes travelling to visit the living."

He stopped and faced me. "Who did you visit?"

I confess I blushed. "Accidentally I called on Mr Chen, Lily's father. I hope he did not have a bad turn afterwards."

"Prudence, you are amazing. If I can survive you then I am a worthy man."

I pursed my lips. "Is that a compliment?"

"It is meant to be. Thank you again for trusting me."

I had brought along my memoir and pulled it out from the bag I was carrying. "As you acknowledge, I trust you. Now you can read my memoir. It is still a bit of a mess, but I want you to know everything that's in my past. After reading that, if you are still keen to marry me, then we can request the banns. If, however, you change your mind, then I will understand."

He took my missive, tied up with string, and held it in both hands. A long sigh escaped him, and he looked at me with tears in his eyes. "I know you have told me part of your story. I feel very moved that you trust me with the whole of it."

For some strange reason I needed a handkerchief, which Sir Giles supplied. "Thank you. I am touched by your sentiment and general acceptance of my rather unusual history."

By and by, we returned to the house.

Sir Giles bowed and tucked the manuscript under his arm. I waved the handkerchief at him.

"Oh, and ignore the notes from Jemima. She has added commentary in places, and I have yet to revise it to a final version."

He bowed. "Understood. We shall speak again soon."

I stood at the door as Sir Giles rode away. It had been such a long day already. As I entered the house, I smelt delicious baking. "Are those scones?" I asked John, the footman.

"Indeed, ma'am. There are breakfast makings in the morning room. You will have it all to yourself as everyone else is upstairs abed."

I made a beeline for the morning room. Despite having had a small portion of pork pie, I was hungry. "Thank you, John. Please ask Cook to send me double of everything. I have a remarkable appetite this morning."

# EPILOGUE

After the banns had been read sufficient times, we were able to be married. Jemima was her old self again within a week. She did, however, seek me out and let me put my arm around her several times. Motherhood had changed her, I think, and the attack had certainly given her a deep fright. I think it was the contents of my memoir that really softened her towards me, though.

When I pondered it, I realised that my recent shenanigans had all the hallmarks of Jemima's own behaviour. I was more like her than I had thought: incorrigible and impertinent traits must run in the family. Milly must have taken after her father's side, for she was mild and amiable, but no less brave and intelligent than Jemima.

Fulton gifted me a lace pelerine to wear with my wedding gown. Jemima gave me beautifully delicate lace gloves that had been her mother's. Milly gifted me a blue topaz necklace. Edward offered me a small vial of potion. "In case of emergencies."

"Whatever is it for?"

"It is a potent rescue remedy. An ancient potion that I gleaned from Cousin Wilbur's journals."

"Dear Nephew, why would I need this?"

"I hope you never do. But I am sure something that can revive the nearly dead is a worthy gift and useful in a time of crisis."

I suspected that he was needling me about my age, but his bright blue eyes were innocent looking and happy and, indeed, proud.

Taking the gift as intended, I gave Edward an embrace and a kiss on the cheek. "You are a remarkable young man and I suspect a very talented gentleman magician."

Edward blushed and looked to the floor. I tucked the vial into my reticule, hoping I never needed such a thing. But in this family, you could not take normality for granted.

❧

My son, James, walked me down the aisle and Lily was there, dressed elegantly in a pale green dress and doting on Arabella, who was six weeks old by then and had blossomed into a bonny, contented baby.

Milly and Fulton stood by the aisle, Milly all smiles and blushes. Fulton just beamed as if he were a proud parent, Ally resting on his hip. Ally blew me a raspberry as I glided past. Next to them stood Edward, the Jemima, with a sleepy Louis in her arms. The baby's face was chubby and his dark hair streaked with blond tips.

I had a moment of doubt before the wedding service, but it was fleeting. The sure feeling that I was doing the right thing stayed with me. Did I think I was too old to be married again? Well, only time would tell.

It was a wrench to leave everyone after the lovely wedding breakfast. Sir Giles had suggested that we spend our honeymoon at his house in the country, and I had agreed. It was not too far by carriage to the village and, if I wanted, I could see my family every day.

What went on during my honeymoon is between us. I can say,

though, that I fell asleep in church on Sunday and also nodded off when the family came to visit on the Friday. My nights had turned into a bit of an adventure.

Before long, Sir Giles and I settled into a life that we both enjoyed. There was the occasional adventure. How could it be avoided, when a Hardcastle was involved? There was much joy and love and respect between us. I had finally found a place where I belonged in all the ways that mattered.

*Oh, Aunt Prudence, I never thought you would become so sentimental!*

Jemima, stop writing in my memoir. It is mine, not yours!

*But I feature in it, and you love me.*

Impertinent girl!

THE REST IS THE BEGINNING.

# NOTE FROM THE AUTHOR

This has been an incredibly difficult book to write to a deadline, particularly when I developed a full thickness hole in my macular that required surgery. It is also the most ambitious book structurally that I have tackled. Two historical time lines! What was I thinking? I have never written a memoir before and I'm not sure I will again.

I am grateful for my beta readers for reading what was a bit of a mess at the time. They laboured away while I recovered from surgery. Thank you to Louise Brogan, a big fan of the series who wanted first dibs on Prudence's story. Louise is also a champion supporter and cheerleader for who will guest star in the next instalment. Her suggestion of having a book featuring Milly has my brain running hot. Thanks is owed to my partner, Matthew Farrer, for his thoughtful feedback and editing comments. As we are both writers, sometimes it is hard to spare focus for the other's work. Please do not hate me for nagging. You are the best Dweeb on the planet. To Maxine McArthur who was familiar with the first three books —a big thank you for comments and support. Next up is Lucy Woolard, fellow writer, who did not know any of the books previously. She was able to give me a good sense readers new to the series might react and some very insightful comments, which I hope have been addressed.

To my editor, Brianne Collins, very sincere gratitude for really taking the book on and giving me a thorough no-holds-barred edit. My editing tunnel was dark and difficult to traverse but I got there in the end and I am really happy with the end result. Thanks are also due to Jason Nahrung for proofreading.

My daughter-in-law Ferdi helped me choose names and characters for the Singaporean characters in the book. With much patience, she took me to temples and museums and listened to me ramble on about my story ideas. To Taamati, my son, and Ferdi, thank you so much for hosting me for those four glorious weeks in your apartment, where I walked in the pool every morning then wrote. Thank you for the great food, the company and the support. It was a nice, long and heavenly writing retreat. The trip to China was amazing too. To Dev, writing buddy, in Singapore, thank you for being there to have tea with and to discuss stuff. I really enjoyed our time together and I wished we could have had more writing dates. Thanks to Joyce as well and for the gift of your sword fantasy books.

Lastly, thank you to Haruki for drawing the Chinese characters that appear in this book. I owe you a great dinner out somewhere.

Donna Maree Hanson
December, 2025

If you want to keep in touch, check out my newsletter
https://sendfox.com/donnamareehanson

# ACKNOWLEDGMENTS

The *Prudential Light* is probably the most research-intensive novel I have attempted. The bulk of the story was written in Singapore, where I was helped by things such as the weather. While in Singapore, I visited the Asian Civilisations Museum, which was fascinating and informative, and the National Museum of Singapore, which had a special exhibit on the origins of Singapore, including maps and paintings. I purchased and consulted *Singapore 1819: A Living Legacy* by Kennie Ting, Talisman Publishing, Singapore, 2019. This book provided a lot of context for Prudence's adventures and including some great commentary on Calcutta as well. As mentioned in the text, I consulted a resource of the era, *The East India Voyager: Or Ten Minutes Advice to the Outward Bound*, by Emma Roberts, published 1839.

There was also some great reference material on the internet including *A General History of the Chinese in Singapore*, edited by Kwa Chong Guan and Kua Bak Lim, World Scientific Publishing Co. Pte.Ltd. 2019. Also, the National Gallery of Singapore had scans of the original maps of Singapore as planned out by Sir Stamford Raffles.

# ABOUT THE AUTHOR

Donna Maree Hanson is a traditionally and independently published author of fantasy, science fiction and horror. She also writes paranormal romance under the pseudonym of Dani Kristoff. In April 2015, she was awarded the A. Bertram Chandler Award for 'Outstanding Achievement in Australian Science Fiction' for her work in running science fiction conventions, publishing and broader SF community contribution. Donna writes dark fantasy (the Dragon Wine series), epic fantasy (the Silverlands series), steampunk (the Cry Havoc series) and young adult science fiction (Space Pirate Adventures) as well as short stories across the speculative fiction genre. Her short story collection, Beneath the Floating City was shortlisted for an Aurealis Award in 2017. Awakening (2022), is science fiction with romance and the first in a proposed series. In April 2025, Amber Rose, the third book in the Cry Havoc series was released. The Prudential Light, the fourth book in the Cry Havoc series is up for pre-order and is due for release in December. The next instalment will be Edward Huntington Esquire: Gentleman Magician, The Lady and the Magician (Prequel) and Book Five will feature Milly and Jemima, among others.

In 2022, Donna completed her PhD candidature, researching Feminism in Popular Romance at the University of Canberra, Her degree was awarded on 30 March 2023. Donna lives in Canberra with her partner and fellow writer Matthew Farrer.

Awakening

**Short story collections**

Beneath the Floating City: Short science fiction stories

Through These Eyes: Tales of Magic Realism and Fantasy

Robots Hearts: Science Fiction Short Stories

*Under the name Dani Kristoff check out my paranormal romance books...*

**The Cursed Ones**

The Sorcerer's Spell

Changeling Curse

Destiny's Blood

**Spellbound in Sydney**

Spiritbound

Bespelled

Invoked

www.ingramcontent.com/pod-product-compliance
Lightning Source LLC
Chambersburg PA
CBHW050607190726
48283CB00007B/2322